BARR
DEMPS

TREAD
&
OTHER
STORIES

Tightrope Books
#207-2 College Street,
Toronto Ontario, Canada M5G 1K3
tightropebooks.com
bookinfo@tightropebooks.com

EDITOR: Alayna Munce
COPYEDITOR: Deanna Janovski
COVER DESIGN: David Jang
COVER PAINTING: *The Four Elements* by Candace O Bell
LAYOUT DESIGN: David Jang

Produced with the assistance of the Canada Council for the Arts and the Ontario Arts Council.

Library and Archives Canada Cataloguing in Publication

Dempster, Barry, 1952-, author
     Tread, and other stories / Barry Dempster.

Short stories.
ISBN 978-1-988040-42-4 (softcover)

I. Title.

PS8557.E4827T74 2018   C813'.54   C2018-902193-4

TREAD
&
OTHER
STORIES

CONTENTS

GREY
METAL DESK

The room is even shabbier than those temporary offices out-of-town companies rent for interviews. A couple of swivel chairs, a mostly empty bookshelf with magazines strewn across the second shelf, and a grey metal desk. A desk! Of all things, why a desk? Brice Mortson, standing with his back to the closed door, barely even in the room yet, doesn't have a clue how the desk is supposed to be used. Maybe the idea is to lie back in one of the swivel chairs and toss his legs up onto the shiny surface. Thank goodness he's alone in here. No matter that some women have told him he's better-than-average attractive (sultry eyes like Kevin Bacon's in *Diner*, though without the *Footloose* strut)—no doubt any attraction would fizzle if they could see what he was about to do.

His challenge is to jerk off into a plastic jar. After cleaning up with the aid of a complimentary box of Kleenex, the only item on the mysterious desk, he is required to screw the orange lid back on the jar, write his name on the label, and deliver the finished product to the receptionist's cubicle directly across from the main waiting room, handing it over to the young blond woman with a ponytail and a blank look as if her memory is erased in hourly clumps.

Why not a doctor's examining table with a disposable paper cover? Brice can picture hoisting himself up, making sure his shoes hang over the edge. But a desk? Years ago he had pictured himself falling onto a very similar desk with the tall and rumpled-looking woman who was teaching a night class in Italian at Eastern Commerce. That was before he was married, of course, before sex had revealed a purpose other than pleasure, before the whole world began to doubt he was equipped with adequate sperm.

He looks down at his groin, not at all surprised to find the terrain flat and smooth. He then turns to the small paper cup of lubricant handed to him when he first arrived and a blue sheet of paper with instructions on it, not instructions on how to jerk off exactly, but how to make sure the semen finds its way into the plastic jar. It reads like it was written by a technical writer.

❖

Once upon a time, he met a girl named Dorrie. He met her at the Soho Bistro, where she was working her way toward starting her own catering business. Although she seemed to be doing more waitressing than cooking, she made him one of the best cheese omelettes he'd ever tasted. It was so good it was named something French; *fromage* was there, and *nuage*, or so he remembers. He flirted while he ate, watching her prance from table to table, the backs of her calves a beguiling sheen. He came back two days later, this time ordering a baguette stuffed with ham and a new *fromage*, same letters, different taste. He didn't enjoy it as much as the omelette, but Dorrie's calves were still shining and an extra button on her blouse was undone. Every single time he looked up from his plate, he found her gazing back at him. He'd glance at the pearly shade of her wrist bone and instantly feel a heat rising from his own. She would lick her bottom lip, and without missing a beat the tip of his tongue would slip out in pursuit. None of this had anything to do with the mechanics of procreation or the space that materializes when one and one doesn't equal three.

They had sex the first time in the kitchen of her tiny apartment in the upper Beaches. They were on the cushy linoleum floor, with a scatter rug that kept scattering the more they slid around. He vaguely remembers wooden table legs, pine, which went really well with Dorrie's soft, pale nakedness, as did the cupboard doors, painted a low-lit yellow, with knobs that looked a lot like nipples, not Dorrie's nipples exactly, but the kind featured in old-fashioned porn magazines, the kind that look like they've been given several coats of varnish.

And now, hundreds and hundreds of fucks later, Brice is alone in a truly ugly room, unable or unwilling to even think of Dorrie who, right this minute, is probably working her way through the day's menu at Dorrie's Delights, her brand new café and catering company. She's most likely giving more attention to her empty womb than to the mushrooms sautéing on the stove or the croissants browning in the oven. Sex has been transformed into a function, a faulty function at that. It has nothing to do with arousal or mindlessness or even stress relief. A penis enters a vagina strictly for the fertilizing of an egg, an egg that will never be used to make a French cheese omelette.

He feels like he's in a time warp, thirteen years old again, about to attempt intercourse with a naked picture—the equivalent of returning to gibberish years after learning to talk.

Glancing at the blue sheet, he wishes it said *Pull your jeans down to your ankles. Do it now.* A video would make more sense than a magazine, a blond wearing nothing but a leer, purring *Touch yourself.*

He doesn't have to stay here, doesn't have to follow any of the unwritten steps leading up to the biggie: *Make sure the head of the penis is aimed for the centre of the jar.* And Dorrie? He could lie and say everything is fine, with him at least, or better yet, simply tell her what he's afraid might be the truth anyway, let a nagging fear blossom into a fake (though likely) diagnosis. Couldn't they just go on loving each other instead of adding one more life story to the planet?

Queen Street is doing its usual midday whoosh when Brice leaves the clinic, traffic breeze blowing up onto the sidewalk, lifting the ankles of his trousers an inch above his socks. Strangers correct their inner compasses, weaving around him as if he were a telephone pole. No one has a clue what he's just been through: the desk, the now crumpled paper cup of lubricant, and the glossy ad of the headless man and woman embracing one another in their underwear.

The truth is, he sifted through several centrefolds and a couple of sporty pictorials showing women getting naked on sailboats and soccer fields. But it was very clear that none of these women were interested in babies. They made him think of sex without agenda, sex for the sake of sex alone, which in turn made him feel like he was betraying Dorrie on some crucial level. He had given up when he flipped a page and found an ad for a workshop on *Sexual Intimacy*, with a bunch of jargon about communicating on all levels. The headless man was wearing tight white briefs and was leaning over an equally headless woman in bra and panties. Soon their underwear would disappear, that much was clear, but for the moment they were experiencing total *intimacy*, a level of sexuality their bodies alone would never be able to achieve. Dorrie might even feel flattered that faced with a choice between raw sex and relationship, he'd gone for the latter.

He ended up sitting bare-assed on the edge of the desk, coldness shooting up into his spine. Once he got going, he was able to take his eyes off the photo. He bounced up and down, making squelches he was sure could be heard out in the hall. He felt amazingly fertile, all his worries worn away in the delicious friction.

And now, odd as it might have seemed an hour ago, he can't help feeling sorry the act is over. He wants to tug someone's elbow as the crowds flow around him, announce he has just jerked off, a jar of wriggling sperm already in the hands of a technician who will soon be marking the contents with a big A-plus. This is the same kind of showmanship he felt at the beginning of his first solely sexual relationship. Her name was Cathy, a former gymnast who sold real estate. She would take him into clients' houses and screw him in their master bedroom suites while photos of beaming kids and grandparents smiled down from bureaus and wardrobes.

Feeling a bit dizzy, he decides to stop in at the little coffee house beside the clinic, get some caffeine into himself, try to put the day and its unexpected aura of fecundity into perspective. He orders an ice cap and a sticky-looking raspberry square and finds a table in the corner where he can watch people come and go. Slowly, his impulses start calming down. He's even able to make eye contact with a few strangers.

When he spots the blond ponytail, he's not sure at first why it looks so familiar. It's not until she walks right past his table, that blank look in her eyes, that he recognizes the receptionist from the fertility clinic. She doesn't appear to know him at all. It can't be an act; she chooses the table right next to him. He really didn't make any impression back there in the office. To her, he was one in a long line of sad men whose thirty-something crisis didn't come with a user's manual, whose genetic structures were on the verge of extinction, just like the dinosaurs. The only part of him she'd actually looked at was his right hand as it reached out to take the paper cup of lubricant.

He abandons his ice cap mid-slurp, three-quarters of a raspberry square still oozing on the antiseptic-white plate. Pushing his way between tables, he bumps several other customers, stirring up scowls. Back out on Queen Street, he blends in with the crowds, just another stranger.

Dorrie has been stroking his cock non-stop for the last ten minutes. It's not often he gets this kind of attention, in fact, if the circumstances were a bit different, he'd be whistling the *Rocky* theme under his breath, considering himself blessed. But tonight his entire groin is starting to feel sore, the way his arm did when he was a kid and someone gave him an Indian sunburn. And although he's not exactly soft, he's not exactly hard either. Dorrie is doing him a favour, trying to erase the memory of that sterile room, the grey metal desk that even now probably still holds a faint imprint of his ass on its cold surface.

"Maybe it would help if you closed your eyes," Dorrie suggests. She's facing him, kneeling by his hips, reminding him of a medic struggling to bring an accident victim back to life.

"Mmm," he mutters, obeying. But not seeing only makes him feel more distant. "I'd rather watch," he says, focusing once again on the sorry state of his lap.

"Do you want me to use my mouth?" This is major sympathy. Brice knows how much Dorrie hates oral sex. She'll shower his penis with kisses; she'll lick his balls, but don't ask her to put anything larger than the tip of a teaspoon in her mouth. She's been known to gag just thinking about it.

His intention is to gently push her away, say something like "Let's give it a rest, watch some TV," but he's surprised to discover that the push is much more like a shove. He just couldn't bear one more downstroke. "Sorry," he mumbles.

At first, he thinks Dorrie might be sulking; her neck is bent low, her coppery brown hair hanging into her eyes. But when she finally looks up, those eyes are full of childish hope. "It's not the end of the world, you know. I mean, if it's bad news. There's all sorts of other choices these days: artificial insemination, fertility drugs, adoption." She speaks in the kind of soft, low tones she uses when a customer at Dorrie's Delights complains about the food.

Tugging at the sheets with his right foot, Brice manages to cover himself, leaving just a fringe of pubic hair showing. Ever since quitting smoking three years ago, he has to fake relaxation after sex. It's even harder to relax when the sex didn't really happen. What he'd much prefer to do is get up, have a shower, make a snack, feel the blood pouring back into all his body's nooks and crannies.

"Are you listening?" Dorrie asks, flicking a finger at the sheet, pulling it a fraction of an inch lower. "We can even forget about having a baby," she says, "if that's what you want."

It doesn't take a genius to know she's lying, probably to herself, but certainly to him. Baby or no baby, their sex life has changed forever. He never realized it before, but the act of defying pregnancy was clearly partly responsible for their ongoing pleasure. Just as it had been with Cathy the real estate dynamo or Julia, his nice Italian girlfriend when he was twenty-two, or Marjorie, the accountant who did his books the first couple of years Mortson's Fine Custom-Made Furniture was open. The risk was a big part of the excitement, like they were abusing some major technology, mere children playing with real rockets.

"Are you with me on this?" she repeats, giving him the full glare of partnership.

He does his best to stare back, although what he really wants to do is blink and blink and blink until the entire planet begins to crumble. If the jar of his semen comes back negative, if it turns out to be just a gooey paste of nothingness, then the baby Dorrie so obviously wanted would torment them for the rest of their lives.

"Brice," she says, using her warning voice. "This is happening to the both of us. Don't disappear."

He tries to smile reassuringly, but this is exactly what he feels: he's already well on his way to invisible. Instead, he reaches out and touches her left breast, lays his palm there, discovers her heart is beating much faster than she's letting on.

It's barely ten after nine, and already he finds himself worrying that Steve and Marshall, the guys who work for him, might find out about his faulty sperm. Steve is a guy in his forties and ugly as cold pizza. In the close to a thousand days Brice has known him, he's only had one date, and she was a cousin of a cousin of a good friend, who turned out to be even uglier than Steve. And although Marshall is good looking enough for a twenty-three-year-old with some prospects for the future, he's interested only in having quick though exhaustively described sex with older men who might hypothetically be willing to buy him a car or set him up in his own Harbourfront condominium.

Brice can't remember having ever truly felt humiliated before. He owns his own furniture design business, still has the same head of hair he had in high school, and is happily married to a woman who has her own business. The great thing about reaching these milestones is Brice has found each and every new accomplishment to be completely what he wants. He could go on fucking Dorrie for the rest of their natural lives without even wondering what it might be like to try someone else. It occurs to him his good fortune could easily be mistaken for smugness.

But this Friday morning, everything feels changed, reduced. The shop on Jones Avenue suddenly seems cramped and dusty. And the Scrooge desk he'd started just yesterday looks stingy, the four small drawers on each side like the nubs of amputated limbs. The pine blanket box Steve is sanding reminds him of a baby's coffin. And the story Marshall is regaling them with about sex in the Park Plaza elevator comes across as pathetic rather than daring.

There've been times over the past couple of years when Brice might have gone so far as to say he loved these guys. Sure, they are jerks, maybe even losers, but they spend their days together sawing and staining, making beautiful things from dead trees. He thinks they love him too, his happiness somehow rubbing off on them. Steve is less ugly when the three of them are working together on a canopy bed, slowly shaping and carving beauty into a space where nothing had been before. And Marshall might be a screw-up, but he could often take a middle-aged bald man and transform him into a truly funny anecdote.

By two o' clock, with his roast beef sandwich from lunch churning in his stomach, Brice can't bear another moment of worry. Marshall is doing his best to be crude, "He put his fingers so far up my ass, I almost bit them off," Steve snorting with laughter, pretending to vomit. To stop himself from saying something he'll definitely regret, Brice slams his fist down on a piece of pine, causing it to split all the way up to a taffy-coloured knot. "That's it," he booms. "Let's call it a day."

Steve and Marshall are far too thrilled with the early quitting time to notice the fury on Brice's face.

When the shop is empty and the lights are shut down, Brice realizes he's left himself the chore of sweeping up, a job Marshall usually does, play-dancing with the wide, green broom, bringing the week to an end with a flourish. There is no pleasure in this for Brice, but it does relieve some of his panic. When the floors are clean and the tools back in their proper places, he stands by the door, the sounds of traffic leaking in, surveying the space the way Amundsen or Peary might once have gazed upon glaciers, wondering if this is as far as he is going to get. Has life finally shut him down? He never knew emptiness could hurt this bad. He pictures ghosts darting around his chest, dozens of them wielding small ghost hammers and saws, slowly turning his heart into a cell where he'll be trapped for the rest of his life.

The phone call comes the next Thursday. Ironically, Brice has just hung up from Dorrie, where the only mention of the whole situation was the suggestion that maybe they should think of taking a trip to Italy in the fall. *Now we might not have to save our money* was left unsaid. Since the phone is still in his right hand, the ringing startles him, and he drops it to the shop floor with a clatter.

He can't quite catch his breath enough to eke out an ordinary hello. The call seems beside the point; he's already spent a week grieving the outcome. He almost doesn't answer.

But then he does, shushing Steve and Marshall, who are kibitzing by the varnish table. He listens to every word, pausing only long enough to wonder if the female voice on the other end is the voice of the young woman with the ponytail, who he now realizes reminds him of one of those blond children from the movie *Village of the Damned.* This pause only lasts a second or two, but it's long enough for him to miss the crux of the call; he has to ask her to repeat herself.

What she seems to be saying is that the test is inconclusive. Maybe, maybe not. His sperm count is *seriously low,* but not low enough to call him sterile. She goes on to explain that the test is probably correct and he does indeed have a *fertility problem,* but another test, a superior one, has been ordered. She ends by saying there is always hope.

So he makes a new appointment, for the very next day. He even says thank you before hanging up. He feels like he's shrinking right there in the shop, his hands disappearing up the sleeves of his denim shirt. The experience is weird enough to make a narcissist like Marshall actually put himself aside long enough to ask, "Hey, Brice, you okay?"

Friday morning dawns the same as every other Friday morning Brice can remember, winter or summer, rain or shine: it's a tacked-on day, a mistake, like the last-minute discovery that you have one player too many for a soccer game. Nothing to do but go through the motions, make decisions, pretend to be engaged on a serious level, while inside every cell is on the verge of exploding: begging to sleep in, to walk in the park, to break habits and scatter them to the gulls.

He remembers his appointment at the fertility clinic the instant he kisses Dorrie good morning. There are several opportunities to tell her what he's up to today, but he has begun to appreciate the secret. If he doesn't say it out loud, then maybe it's not real. As far as Dorrie's concerned, they're both still waiting, patiently.

When he leaves the house, he walks to the same corner he does every morning, past the forsythia bushes that overnight seem to have burst into blossom. His usual pattern is to turn left at the first intersection, head toward Danforth Avenue, where he picks up a coffee and hoofs it the five or six blocks east to Jones Avenue. But today he needs to go south, down to Dundas, then Queen, where he can hop a streetcar west. Glancing back over his shoulder to make sure Dorrie isn't watching him from their front window, he swerves right, letting the wind blow him in the wrong direction.

Fifteen minutes later, ensconced in a single seat on a particularly jerky streetcar, he toys with the word *inconclusive*, trying to get a bead on it. His goal today is to be definitive, to somehow force his sperm to make up its mind. Is he or isn't he? He thinks about destiny as a lump of clay waiting to be manipulated in new ways.

He watches out the window as Friday morning unfolds in all sorts of variations, many of them complete with children. He counts four pregnant women in twice that many blocks. And strollers and baby carriages are everywhere; it's a veritable Indianapolis 500 of them. Miniature feet are pummelling the air wherever he looks, the colours pink and blue dominating all the faded reds and blacks of storefronts. In the midst of it all, hundreds and hundreds of reproductive systems. There's a hum of fecundity at the base of all the street noise, an electronic buzz that announces the world is working the way it's supposed to, every part of the human scheme fulfilling its own special mission.

Try as he might to think positively, Brice is sure the day will ultimately prove to be empty handed. A major system failure has somehow crept into his life. It's a marvel that one foot still goes in front of the other, a bloody miracle he's conscious enough of the outside world to register St. Michael's Hospital up ahead and to remember the clinic is just around the corner.

There's very little breeze on Queen Street, so even women's skirts look strangely stationary. He stands there on the sidewalk, smack dab in the middle of it all, and wonders how he might be seen if someone actually took the time to stop and look him over. He remembers reading an article about how women often choose their sexual partners by a kind of genetic intuition; they sense what different sperm can offer, searching for just the right combination of DNA to give their babies golden hair or noses that flip up perkily. No wonder he's invisible. Regardless of good looks or financial prospects, Brice Mortson has nothing to offer but the moment he's mired in.

The last thing on his mind when he walks into the clinic is masturbation. His first ejaculation in the plastic jar was an act of hope, however flawed. But the one he's expected to give today is a cruel joke, a tossing of emptiness at emptiness. It's something that will look good on his chart, a verification that will dig a deeper hole in his self-worth, a hole all the way through him, reaching some distant China of grief he hasn't even imagined yet.

The receptionist does her usual trick of ignoring everyone in the waiting room. Sitting beneath the Lawren Harris print of icebergs, there's a man and woman who seem to be happily engaged in small talk. Across from them, a man with a Jay Leno chin is flipping through an issue of *Time*. And three seats to his right, another man, blondish, much too young to be thinking about sperm counts, is sitting with his eyes closed, an iPod attaching him to some unheard bliss.

"Brice Mortson," Brice says, leaning against the reception window, stunned at how inadequately his name defines him.

The receptionist scans her computer screen, searching for his name. She still hasn't looked at him or changed the expression on her face one iota. "I can't find you," she finally says. "Are you sure you have an appointment with Dr. Sharmin?"

"Sharmin?" Brice repeats. He's never heard the name before.

"Are you sure you've got an appointment?"

"I'm supposed to ... " He can't think of how to finish the sentence without saying *jerk off* or *spank the monkey*, phrases that seem completely inappropriate in a room with a Lawren Harris print.

For a moment there's nothing between them but silence. Then the receptionist glances at him quickly. "Are you here for a sample?" Without waiting for him to answer, she reaches into her drawer of plastic jars and instruction sheets. "Sorry," she says quietly, the beginnings of a blush spreading across her neck.

Brice focuses on the jar as she lifts it in his direction. All he has to do is extend his own wrist a few inches and bend his fingers into a grasp. But it feels like he'd be accepting death to make even the smallest of motions. Once that empty jar is in his hand, the story is over.

"I can't," he says. "I need to talk to someone."

"Sorry," she repeats, a little louder this time. "You don't have an actual appointment, with a doctor, I mean."

He's aware his voice is rising, but feels volume might be necessary in a situation where the ideal outcome is for him to agreeably disappear. "I can't do this without talking to someone. Don't you have someone people like me can talk to?"

They go back and forth like this for another agonizing minute, Brice standing firm against his own muscles longing for the door. When he hears someone say, "Calm down," his first thought is that a part of himself has separated from his body and is about to take over. But when he turns around, he sees that the happy-looking man who had been making small talk with the happy-looking woman has stood up and is addressing him. "It's going to be okay," the man says, the woman nodding along with him, both of them making eye contact with Brice. The attention makes him feel a bit weak, and he stumbles. The man reaches out and grabs his elbow, steadying him.

Slowly, Brice allows himself to be led away from the receptionist. The Leno-like man is standing now, looking concerned. And the young blond guy has removed his earphones.

"I need to talk to someone," Brice says in a steadier voice, feeling like an entire week has gone by in which he's not said one single thing he really felt. Amazing, how quickly one can go from lucky to numb to totally turned inside out. It's a wonder the floor still resists his feet. It's incredible Dorrie didn't pack up and flee the very first time their GP suggested his sperm might be weak or worse.

"We'll make sure the doctor talks to you," someone says.

What can he say that won't sound inappropriate? Did each of these men have to jerk off into a jar, just like him? Is this the way family starts for someone who can't have a family? He allows himself to be led to one of the waiting room chairs, a softness that nonetheless supports him, holds his spine in place. Help is on the way, he can feel it. He smiles at everyone, trying to make his lips relax. "I'm afraid I can't have kids," he says, shrugging, the best he can do for an explanation.

THE
WORLD CUP

Marko doesn't feel that he's been dating Anna long enough to invite her to his place to watch the World Cup. It feels too early to share the kind of intensity that soccer instills in him, despite the fact that they both have family connections to the Netherlands, the team most likely to win. Marko's father was actually born in Rotterdam, while Anna's great-grandmother was raised in a small town called Egmond aan Zee on the west coast.

"You sleep with her, but you won't watch soccer on TV with her," his best buddy Will says, always trying to bring Marko down a notch or two.

"Sex isn't the same as soccer," Marko answers, careful not to say something totally stupid. "It's not as complicated."

Marko knows that a first step needs to be taken. On their three-week anniversary—dinner in the Beaches followed by a screening at The Fox of the chick flick *Please Give* starring Catherine Keener, who reminds him a little of Anna— he asks her to the baseball game at Rogers Centre the day before the World Cup. The Blue Jays are playing the Boston Red Sox, not a heck of a lot at stake, but a chance to see how she'll respond to the seriousness of competition. Will insists that he come along, to keep score, so to speak.

Curiously, Anna mentions the World Cup when she agrees to the baseball game. "That's not the same day, is it?" she asks.

Marko shakes his head, trying to stop a blush before it spreads over his entire face. He covers his awkwardness by bragging about the great seats his company generously provides from time to time: section one hundred thirty, ninth row, just off third base, a perfect place for sightlines and the occasional foul ball.

"A little perk for the nine-to-five grind," she says, smiling. When Marko first told her that he was an actuary for a reinsurance firm, she'd seemed sorry for him. He nearly cut her loose, but was intrigued by the fact that she could make him feel small without totally pissing him off.

They wake up together on Saturday morning, at her place. She breeds and boards poodles and isn't really able to spend the night at his house. She has a high school student named Jill who helps her when their erratic schedules coincide. Marko doesn't mind keeping his place off limits, at least at this point in the relationship; no traces of her in his little piece of the planet if things don't work out. But he's not sure how he feels about her two house dogs sleeping with them. They know enough to stay off the bed during sex, but once Marko and Anna disentangle, the chocolate poodle, Brandy, leaps onto the bed and flops down on Marko's legs, making it impossible for Marko to move without setting off a deep-throat growl, while Crème Caramel, the Pomeranian, prefers to be as close to Anna's pillow as she can get. The combination pretty much ruins any chance of another go.

"Check the weather channel," Anna says as she pads into the bathroom, Crème Caramel right behind her. One of her quirks is that she's unable to even open her closet until she knows what sorts of plans the skies have in store on a particular day. Unlike Marko, who, when he's not wearing a suit, relies on a collection of multicoloured T's and jeans, with five or six practically identical sweaters to see him through the winter.

Marko prefers channel twenty-four, the news update station. It just happens that they're doing a piece on tomorrow's historic soccer match, and Marko is so worried that Anna might overhear and mention the World Cup again that he instantly turns the TV off without even glancing at the weather box at the top of the screen. He tells her his first lie when she and Crème Caramel return from the bathroom. "Hot and sunny," he reports, knowing that in July the odds are most likely on his side.

It turns out the day is behind him one-hundred percent. Hot and sunny. They drive south to Marko's office at Bay and Adelaide, park the car, grab some Starbucks, then walk to the stadium. The game is only minutes from starting when they find their seats, Will already ensconced, his arm over the back of the chair beside him, his shirt off.

"Hey," Marko says, meaning sit up, look alive, put your shirt back on.

Will isn't into subtext this afternoon, but he does grin up at Anna as if they already share a private joke and moves over so that Marko and Anna can sit side by side. Marko chooses to be the monkey in the middle, but after about fifteen minutes of Will and Anna making small talk over his head, he trades places with her, savouring the extra inch or two the aisle seat gives him.

It crossed Marko's mind years ago that Will has a certain bad-boy charm, but the kind of women attracted to Marko always find Will dodgy, even insincere. While they giggle along with his flirty style and pretend to be flattered by his attention, they always confide in Marko afterwards that Will has *juvenile* written across his forehead.

Marko leaves them to their chitchat and concentrates on sending psychic messages to Blue Jays pitcher Brandon Morrow, #23. He's Marko's favourite on the mound, with his uncanny patience and the way he makes even the most planned release seem spontaneous. When Boston strikes out, he's delighted to see that their pitcher, Atchison, has a kink in his shoulder and keeps sending the ball straight into each batter's personal space.

During a lull when Boston is busy duking it out with an iffy umpire call, Will and Marko dash off to the concession stands to buy hot dogs and beer. Anna asked for a blue slushy at first, but Marko made such a face that she changed her order to a beer.

"What do you think?" Marko asks, not sure what he hopes will be the response.

"The usual," Will replies. "A little prettier than the last one. Great legs." He pauses for a moment, making Marko worry that his next comment will be the deal breaker. "She doesn't give a shit about baseball though. She hasn't even glanced out at the field."

"But you're hogging her. She's concentrating on getting to know you," Marko says, wondering why Will's comments hold any weight in the first place. After all, Marko doesn't need a woman to love baseball, as long as she's willing to let him love it.

Will shrugs, balancing a tray of beers without letting the cold plastic cups touch his naked chest. Marko follows a few steps behind, three hot dogs nestled in a row, heaped with a rainbow of condiments. When they get back to their row, there's a small blond woman perched on the arm of Marko's seat. Her hair is tied into a top-of-the-head ponytail, and she's wearing a too-tight pink halter top and showing a wide expanse of bare flesh above her hips.

"Kelly," Anna says, waving her arms with a flourish. They're old friends; in fact, Kelly sometimes works for Anna, helping her with dog walks and flea baths when she's not pursuing a career in fashion design.

Since there's an empty seat beside Will, they decide that Kelly will ditch her larger group of acquaintances and join them for the rest of the game. For a while, Will and the two women seem to all be talking at the same time. Marko goes back to the game, aiming a subliminal message at Fred Lewis, #15, that results in a homerun, and then lobbing the same message at the great Vernon Wells, #10, which ends up with a genius of a bunt that sends Alex Gonzalez all the way from second base to home, culminating in a grand dive into the dust.

"Happy?" Anna interrupts his reveries.

"Happy?"

"Whatever just happened seemed to make you happy," Anna explains.

Marko notices that Will and Kelly have carved out their own niche in the day and are now carrying on a private conversation. He reaches over and places his right hand on Anna's left leg. There's a mustard smear on his baby finger, but Anna doesn't seem to care. He spends the next hour or so keeping her in the loop, telling her players' names, their standings, explaining the difference between a ball and a strike.

It isn't until the game is over, 8–5 for the Jays, Marko and Will standing side by side at a wall of urinals, that Will opens his mouth and announces, "There's definitely a vibe between Kelly and me. I asked her to your place to watch soccer tomorrow."

Marko's stream of piss literally stops. One second, he's gushing, the next, nada. Someone turned the tap off. In the second or two it takes to download shock into rage, Will has zipped up and is already standing at one of the sinks, waving his hands beneath the automatic tap.

"What the hell?" Marko says, hurrying to join him. He doesn't bother with his own hands. "You can't just invite a woman to join us. I haven't even decided about Anna yet."

"So?" Will says, making two measly letters sound cartoonishly snide. "I can tell Kelly not to blab to Anna. She's cool."

First of all, Marko doesn't trust Will. He'd easily lie about swearing Kelly to silence just to save himself from having to fess up to a complete botch. But even if he's gung-ho on keeping it a secret, how can Marko trust Kelly? Don't women have some sort of code of honour? Years of friendship would definitely trump an afternoon at a ball game and the whiff of sex in the air.

"This is a serious betrayal," Marko says, hissing the words directly into Will's ear. "I'm fucked now. You've messed up everything."

Will squares off his shoulders and sheds all traces of friendship, his upper lip curling like a dog's. "If you think it's either soccer or Anna, then you are fucked." He gives Marko one last sneer, then turns around and strides out of the bathroom.

On the walk back to the parking lot, having left Will and Kelly to head off on their own, Anna seems oblivious to Marko's frustration. Will should have known better: the World Cup only comes around once every four years. Anna doesn't appear to be the kind of girl who wouldn't ultimately understand her boyfriend's obsessions. But Marko has a feeling deep inside that it's just too soon for such a test. His father always warned him that the worst mistakes in life are those things for which you're unprepared.

He finally struggles out of his thoughts and interrupts Anna, who's raving about the Henry Moore sculpture in the lobby of his office building. "I like Moore," she's saying. "I like how solidly he sees the world."

"Hey," he says. "Tomorrow's the World Cup. We can watch it at my place, with Mark and Kelly."

"Oh," she says. "I'm not sure I can leave the dogs. Jill doesn't come on Sundays."

Marko feels a flash of anger. Bloody dogs. He hates to be thwarted once he's made up his mind. "Full steam ahead" were his father's favourite words, meaning *control*, meaning *happiness*.

Anna is staring strangely at him. He's probably red in the face. "Why don't you bring them?" he hears himself saying. It feels like he's digging a bunker that will end up a grave.

"What a great idea," she says, clueless as to what could have happened. She leans into him and plants a dry little kiss on his right temple.

He hears what sounds like the thwack of a toe against a soccer ball somewhere in his cranium. But his head is so crowded there's nowhere for the ball to go.

Will and Kelly arrive together at Marko's tidy bungalow a couple of blocks north of Yonge and Lawrence. It's obvious that they've been together non-stop since yesterday afternoon; in fact Kelly is still wearing the pink halter top she wore to the baseball game. Marko spent the night at Anna's again, sex and dogs, but left after breakfast in order to pick up beer and snacks and make sure his rec room was ready for the big event.

Anna and the dogs show up ten minutes early, which makes Marko feel like disaster has been prearranged. Over the heads of the two dogs, she passes him a gift of a size four Puma soccer ball still in its cardboard box.

"Hope you don't already have one of these," she says, looking for some sort of gratitude. But Marko can barely hold the thing in his hands. It's like bringing take-out Chinese to a gourmet dinner. Of course he already owns a soccer ball, an Adidas one in checkered black and white, and it's made of superior polyurethane rather than the Puma's cheaper PVC.

He mumbles a tiny thank you, trying to shake the weight of what feels like a breach. Then he busies himself filling bowls with Cheezies and peeling back the foil on a sour cream and onion dip for the ruffled potato chips. He takes his camping cooler from the garage and puts it beside the TV in the rec room so that no one will have to leave the room to get another drink. He also tosses the throw pillows from the couch into the laundry room so that the dogs won't interrupt things with their love for chewing pillows.

Anna, who is wearing a sundress much too revealing for an afternoon soccer game, wanders around the house on her own, poking her head into his bedroom, his home office, and the guest room with the purple futon. The dogs stick close to her heels.

Will and Kelly are so into each other that Marko worries they'll become a distraction once the game starts, his detailed plans downgraded into a house tour and make-out session.

Once the pre-show starts, Marko plants himself in the brown leather rocking chair. He takes a gulp of beer and is soothed a bit by the cold bitterness flooding his mouth. Maybe this won't be so bad. The dogs have settled on either side of Anna's chair.

"What are those horns called again?" Kelly pipes up. She and Will have managed to untangle themselves from one another and are actually registering what's going on in faraway Johannesburg.

"Vuvuzelas," Anna answers, pronouncing it with a decidedly South African accent.

"Hey, I like how you say that," Will says. "Is that Afrikaans for vagina?"

Kelly giggles like a six-year-old. "It sounds like little pastries to me."

"It comes from a Zulu word," Anna explains, "that means making a *vuvu* sound."

What's next? Marko wonders. Will she be offering the history of soccer? Christ, she sounds like frigging Wikipedia. Once the game starts, he's going to tell everyone to shut up.

But when the time comes, he simply closes off all access to himself and transports his consciousness into the giant screen. He can hear murmurings around him, but the sounds don't translate into words. He's good at tuning out the world, having inherited this skill from his father. Marko loves to tell the story of how his father once went to a Harry Belafonte concert with a girl who was so out of it when it came to music that he managed to forget she was sitting beside him and was surprised to discover at the end of the show that she'd actually left mid-performance.

At the moment, Spain and the Netherlands are in a stalemate. There are a couple of close calls, but nothing gasp-worthy, nothing to make Marko sit up in his chair and yell "Fuck!" He begins to feel an ache of longing toward the Dutch. If they win, then he'll have to forgive Anna for her cheap soccer ball. Maybe the two of them will drive around the city with the dogs quiet in the back seat, blaring the horn and waving the Dutch flags he bought over a week ago out the window.

As 0–0 settles in with a kind of granite tension, Marko sneaks a glance at Will and Kelly first, then over at Anna, who has slid off her chair and is sitting on the rug with Brandy's head in her lap and Crème tucked against her hip. They all look slightly bored, although Will and Kelly seem to be doing something with their hands.

"What happens if no one scores?" Anna asks, obviously trying to connect with him.

Marko ignores the question, but Will jumps in with stories of other matches, games that went on for hours and hours.

"Maybe I should take the dogs out for a pee," she says, as if asking for permission.

Her words burn into Marko's ears. It's like an elevator door has suddenly snapped open on the thirteenth floor. It's the equivalent of leaving a conversation in the middle of a sentence. He's tempted to tell her to stay put.

She must realize by the look on Marko's face, which he guesses has come across as pure scowl, that she's somehow said the wrong thing. She stays stretched out on the rug.

"They can probably wait awhile," she finally says.

But damage has already been done: the ball glides down in the direction of the Netherlands' net, gets passed back and forth between two of the Spanish players. One of them, Andrés Iniesta, manages to clear himself a small space, and when the ball rolls over to him a third time, he kicks it so fluidly in the direction of the net that it resembles a wave tumbling toward the shore, an inevitability that pours past the Dutch goalie, entering the cave-like net with a whoosh.

The couch erupts with Will's whoops and Kelly's squeals, which instantly stir up both dogs, Créme yapping, Brandy booming. Kelly couldn't care less who scored, and Will is plain unreliable, an expert at changing his allegiance just to suit a whim. The game continues for another minute, then a further extension of two extra minutes. But the Dutch have been crushed. In Marko's addled nervous system, Anna's willingness to leave in the middle of the game has somehow finagled its way into the TV set and travelled all that distance to South Africa. There's no way he can recover from such disloyalty.

Will can see that Marko is furious and throws a Cheezie across the room that lands on Marko's lap. "Hey, there's a lot of Spanish guys going to get lucky tonight."

"Oh, Pedro," Kelly sighs, trailing off into a mock moan.

"Ooh, ooh," Will adds, trying to keep the humour going.

"I'm sorry," Anna interrupts. "Créme Caramel just piddled on your rug."

When Marco looks over at her, he sees a combination of frustration and bewilderment on her face. Sorry? The piss, the ball, spooking the Netherlands into losing the World Cup—all equally unforgiveable.

"Why don't you all leave before something even worse happens," Marko says. His jaw is so tight that it feels like a cramp.

"It was all that shouting," Anna responds, defending the dog.

"Excuses aren't going to change what happened." He can feel spit rising in his throat. He'll have to swallow before saying anything else.

"It's just a little pee," Anna says, looking angry now.

"We'll help her clean it up," Kelly says. For some strange reason, she looks afraid.

"I'll do it myself," Marko insists in a spray of saliva.

Anna stomps her right foot down near the puddle of dog piss. "What's wrong with you?" she asks.

"What's wrong?" he repeats. "We lost the fucking World Cup."

"So don't take it out on a harmless dog," she snaps.

Marko rocks himself to his feet. The Puma ball in its cardboard box sits beside the chair. He nudges it in front of him with the right toe of his sneaker. Then he swings his entire foot back as far as it can go, bringing it forward with an athlete's muscular flow. He kicks the boxed ball across the room where it hits Crème Caramel squarely in the face, changing the look of confusion on Anna's face to shock. This should be counted as a goal, he thinks. One–one, game on.

The dog's yelp is underscored by Will's loud "Hey." But inside his head, Marko can hear one of his father's favourite retorts, "Never apologize." As long as you're doing something for the right reason, it's the right thing to do.

There's a lost moment somewhere between yelp and *hey*. Marko doesn't realize that Anna has crossed the room until she's right there in front of him. She rears back her right arm and clips him on the chin, then tries again, this time glancing off his left cheekbone. "You're an asshole," she says.

His father had never hit a woman; it was a matter of pride to him, as if he walked around in a constant state of longing, but held back, never went that far. Anna stands her ground, visibly shivering from head to toe.

"I suppose you're going to tell me that it's just a game," he says, fingering the pain in his chin.

"It's so not a game that my head is spinning," she responds.

Marko feels exposed rather than understood. His father taught him well that language could just as easily conceal things as spell them out. "You got in the way," he tries to explain. "The dogs, I mean. The game had no choice but to self-destruct."

"It's just a fucking game," Will interrupts, causing the dogs to fly into a frenzy again. "Any moron knows this."

Marko doesn't feel the least bit angry at Will. He isn't angry at Anna anymore either. The real shame is how awful this lack of anger feels. He wants to ask Anna what's going to happen next, but he can see that she's not the kind of woman who really trusts second chances. His father made a point of telling Marko that women never truly forgive. There's a part of Marko that wishes he could reach out and pull Anna into an embrace, but there's another part that just wants her gone.

THE CHIHUAHUA WAR

Grandpa DeVries died when his grandson Abe was ten, but Abe remembers rainy afternoons when he was younger and the tales his grandfather would tell about the Wasikowska pig and the chasm-sized wedge it drove between the two neighbouring families. It seemed clear to Abe that his grandfather was every bit as culpable as crusty old Lech Wasikowska. It might not have been his choice in the very beginning, but he certainly embraced the madness of the feud, eventually passing it down to his own son.

The gist of it was that the Wasikowska pig had a penchant for both wandering and for chicken flesh. Besides the pigs, the Wasikowskas had a hundred-and-fifty acres in alfalfa and corn, while the DeVrieses specialized in Guernseys and chickens along with several fields of wheat. The first time Abe's grandfather discovered a couple of half-eaten dead chickens, he figured it was the work of a marauding coyote with more meanness than appetite. But then one dawn, he looked out his bedroom window, which had a perfect view of the chicken pen, and witnessed one of the Wasikowska pigs unlatching the gate with its filthy snout and then turning its energies toward snatching the first chicken it came across.

Grandpa DeVries chased the damn creature all the way home. Since the chicken death toll was only two, Grandpa didn't demand any payment, just a promise that Wasikowska would keep the pig locked up. But Wasikowska wanted proof. "Show me fingerprints," he bellowed, which made absolutely no sense, pigs having hooves, not hands. Over the next several weeks, the pig carried out at least three more raids, one of which resulted in another dead chicken, the best layer Grandpa had. Insults were hurled and threats were lobbed over the no-man's land between their properties. Grandpa even pledged he'd stop sleeping for a few nights, keep watch, but Wasikowska made it clear that the only way he'd believe Grandpa was to see it with his own eyes.

Bad feelings grew on a daily basis. Mrs. Wasikowska stopped speaking to Grandma DeVries when they encountered one another in town. Abe's father, John, was forbidden to play with the Wasikowska boys, who were soon being referred to as "sons of pigs." A deep chill settled in even though there were no new incidents. But then one midmorning, a grimy day in April, one of the Wasikowska pigs sauntered over when Grandma was out in the barnyard hanging bed sheets to dry. She laid down the basket of wet linen and watched as it poked its nose into various nooks and crannies. There wasn't any evidence of hunger or violence; in fact, Grandma wondered whether her husband's version of the one attack he'd witnessed had been compromised by his anger, whether the pig and the rumoured coyote might both exist. But then one of the barn cats, the orange and white tabby with only a stub for a tail, emerged from the barn, heading straight for the pig. She was the kind of cat that fearlessly investigated everything and was frequently putting herself in dangerous circumstances. She pranced up to the pig, sniffing out the situation. The pig stopped its ambling and stared her down. With decidedly un-pig-like speed, it suddenly lunged for her throat. Despite Grandma's screams, the poor cat didn't have a chance. The pig tore into it with a terrifying fury, blood splattering the soggy dirt.

Grandma DeVries repeated every detail of the attack to the local law. She and Grandpa wouldn't rest until that pig was strung up, its guts spilling onto the ground. But Lech Wasikowska called her a liar. What could the sheriff do? The pig had conveniently made it back home by the time he'd arrived, blending in with all the other pigs. Grandma couldn't make a positive identification. There wasn't to be any justice. The pig was never seen on the DeVrieses' property again, but war had been declared, and for the next thirty years, the DeVrieses and the Wasikowskas carried out all sorts of assaults on one another, from nails driven into tractor tires to a field fire that consumed an entire season's worth of Wasikowska corn. Grandpa was even beat up one winter night when he went out to check on the cows before bed. Three men wearing flour sacks over their heads punched and kicked him until he lost consciousness, an attack that resulted in a concussion and a broken left elbow that never properly healed.

At Grandpa's funeral, Abe remembers Mr. Wasikowska, so old and hunchbacked by this time that a barn cat could easily have knocked him over, showing up at the funeral parlour. Grandma had to be physically restrained, her black, shiny mourning dress straining at the hips and thighs as family members stopped her from throwing herself on Mr. Wasikowska's brittle bones. "Pig," she screamed. Abe had deep shivers running down the back of his neck. He wasn't sure what he was most spooked by: dead Grandpa or Grandma's living rage.

His own father, John, put the farm up for sale and refused to even think about the Wasikowska boys' offer to purchase some of the acreage, even though their lawyer presented a letter of apology along with a decent offer. John ended up selling to an agriculture conglomerate that was gobbling up family farms all over the province. He knew that the Wasikowskas wouldn't be able to compete and would slowly be driven beyond their financial capabilities. "Justice just takes time," John said over and over again. "And Dad will be watching from heaven."

Now that John was gone too—a slash of a stroke followed two days later by a major heart attack—Abe and his wife Susanne (whose family once owned a huge market garden a few miles from the DeVrieses' spread) rarely talked about their farming childhoods. They certainly didn't expect the Pig War to survive as anything more than a comical family story, told with a hint of derision. But then the Silverlanes next door sold, and the Grahams appeared, a seemingly innocent and charming childless couple whose only peccadillo was a sable Chihuahua named Nini who couldn't have weighed more than two-and-a-bit kilograms.

Wars can start over a measly sprig of crabgrass. Entire belief systems can come crashing down when anger bares its tiny gums. "How could one pig cause so much trouble?" his grandfather used to say, as close as he ever came to regret.

"Howdy" was the first thing Holmes Graham said, accompanied by a hearty wave. He stood six inches from his side of the fence, which Abe registered as a thoughtful thing to do. Friendly, but not the least bit pushy.

The day after Holmes and his somewhat younger wife Alice moved into forty-nine Mandolin Road, Susanne knocked on their front door to give them a rhubarb crisp still warm from the oven. She only stayed long enough to relay Abe's offer to lend Holmes any tools he might need in setting up the place. Back home, she did mention a yappy dog, one of those miniatures, but Holmes had scooped it up quickly and taken it into another room.

"At least it wasn't a pig," Abe said.

The first few weeks of their neighbourly relationship were pleasant and undemanding: a few chats over the fence, a request to borrow a socket wrench, a compliment on Susanne's yellow garden of coreopsis, brown-eyed Susans, and Denver daisies. Abe and Susanne learned that Holmes was a construction engineer and was often away on long-distance jobs, and that Alice did something with early childhood education, but was taking the summer off to concentrate on the new house.

One day, mid-August, the start of a cool spell after weeks of high humidity, Susanne was out in the garden, catching up on her weeding. She could see gangly clovers everywhere; they practically grew in front of her eyes. She was hand-trowelling under a gooseberry bush when she heard the Grahams' back patio door open and close. A second later, Nini was at the fence, yapping. Susanne glanced over from her kneeling position and saw that Nini was foaming at the mouth. She worried that the crazy dog might have a heart attack. If she remembered correctly, Alice had told her that Nini was eleven.

She stayed where she was and smacked her lips together and said, "Sweet Nini, be nice. Be nice."   But that only seemed to make matters worse. She finally climbed to her feet, brushed off her knees, and called out quietly, "What's the matter? I'm not going to hurt you."

The barking was pure frenzy by this point. Perhaps a treat might calm her down, show her that Susanne was a friend. Did dogs like gooseberries? She plucked one of the ripest ones and gently lobbed it over the fence. It bounced off Nini's nose and rolled into a thicket of uncut grass. The barking became even more enraged, so she tossed another berry which, this time, hit Nini square between the eyes. Two attempts were enough to convince Susanne that it was useless to try again, but she had one berry left in the palm of her hand. Oh well, she thought, just in case the third try was lucky. This one glanced off one of Nini's tiny ears.

Susanne's arm was still extended in a tossing position when Alice burst onto her back deck. Her mouth was wide open, but Susanne couldn't detect any sounds coming from it. A second later, mouth still agape, she shrieked. By the time she reached her side of the fence, the shriek had become words. "Stop that, stop that right now."

Susanne instantly tried to explain. "I was worried ... she'd hurt herself."

"How dare you throw stones at my Nini," Alice bellowed, scooping the dog up into her arms and clutching it to her breasts.

"They weren't stones," Susanne said, flabbergasted that Alice could think she'd be so cruel. "They were berries."

"Oh, so throwing berries is somehow less cruel than throwing stones. She's a goddamned Chihuahua. You could give her a concussion with a balled-up Kleenex."

Susanne could feel her face growing hot. Her eyes felt sore, overwhelmed by all the summer colours. "I was trying to win her over, give her a treat."

"Poison berries are a treat?"

"They're not poison," Susanne pleaded. "They're gooseberries." As she said this, Susanne realized that it was a stupid idea to think that a dog would eat a berry. But the incessant barking had frightened her, and she'd made a rash decision. "I'm sorry," she said. "I didn't know what else to do."

Alice didn't respond to the apology. She turned her back on Susanne, marched across the lawn, onto the deck, and disappeared into the house. The neighbourhood was completely quiet except for a splash from a pool several houses away. Susanne stood there for a few minutes, not knowing what to do. How could she go back to gardening? She had a sinking feeling that what had just happened was irreversible. She was on the verge of tears.

When Abe came home that evening, his head full of cobwebs from an all-day mortgage brokers' conference, he promised to talk to Holmes the next day, a Saturday. "I bet he's laughing about it right now," he said, chuckling himself. "Throwing gooseberries at a Chihuahua!"

Abe's apology didn't go well either. First of all, Holmes pretended not to hear him when Abe called over the fence. He was trimming a clump of cedars at the back of the yard. But Abe persisted and was shocked by the spiteful look on Holmes's face when he finally turned around.

They didn't really have a conversation. Abe mentioned the misunderstanding, trying to make it sound like next to nothing. But Holmes was fuming, still gripping the shears with both hands. "You come anywhere near my dog, and I'll call the police," was all that Abe remembered him saying.

Abe hated having to admit defeat. He promised Susanne that the hotheadedness would eventually simmer down, but Susanne was convinced that, without meaning to, she had started a new war.

"Worst case, we plant some lilacs along the fence line and learn to look the other way," Abe said. But inside, he was feeling sick to his stomach.

Abe and Susanne tried not to let themselves think about the incident for the rest of August, although both of them began having nightmares. Susanne was relieved when school started in early September; her grade-three classroom felt bunker-like. Soon the cold weather would come, and she wouldn't have any reason to go out into the backyard. Nini was still making daily appearances, but both Abe and Susanne knew not to poke a toe outside when the dog was loose.

The kids were also affected by the situation, Molly especially. She had a meltdown one Sunday morning and confessed that she felt like a prisoner in her own home. John, the most conciliatory member of the family, suggested that they send the Grahams a belated housewarming card and address it to Nini.

The third Saturday in September, a bright summery day that didn't have an ounce of aggression in it, John and three of his buddies were out in the yard playing catch, and one of them threw a high ball that sailed right over the white wire fence.

John thought about hopping the fence and retrieving the ball as quickly as possible, but before he could take the leap, Mr. Graham appeared on his deck, stomping to the spot where the baseball had landed. He picked it up and, turning toward the eight-foot wooden fence that ran across the back of his property, lofted the ball high and away without a thought to how it could have sailed out onto the road, hit a passing car, cracked a windshield, dented a hood.

Abe talked John into letting this pass. It was Holmes's prerogative to remove the ball from his own yard. And it would only stir up more anxiety if Susanne and Molly knew what had happened.

The next weekend, John, along with a bunch of other kids from the street, started a road hockey game. One of the goalies' nets was probably too close to the property line between the DeVrieses' and the Grahams', but no one noticed. Backyards were where the real boundaries were set.

Over the course of the game, the net was pushed a few feet farther into Graham territory by various attempts to score and defend. Finally, it was right in front of the Grahams' driveway, and John was the goalie. At one point, when the scramble for the puck was down at the other net and John was all alone at his end, Holmes suddenly showed up and without a word grabbed the net and dragged it up his driveway, tossing it into his garage and pressing the remote to close the door.

How could Abe ignore this one? It wasn't even John's net; it belonged to a friend from a couple of blocks away.

Susanne was convinced they should call the police and report the net as stolen, but Abe knew that going to extremes would only make the situation deteriorate even further. "We have to coexist here," he said. "I'm going to disarm him by not doing what's expected. I'm not letting this go to the next level."

And so he walked slowly and carefully down his own drive, along the street to the Grahams', and up to their front porch. The second he pressed the doorbell—an array of chimes—Nini started barking madly. He hadn't thought of this and was already well on his way to flustered when Holmes swung open the door.

"I've come to apologize," he said, his voice cracking. For one awful moment, he thought to himself that this was impossible, that he and Susanne would probably have to move. "That net shouldn't have been in front of your driveway." There, now he sounded penitent and firm just the way he'd planned. "The kids were obviously trespassing."

Holmes grunted and started to close the door.

"Wait, what are you doing?" Abe asked.

"Apology accepted," Holmes said flatly.

"Thank you," Abe said, swallowing what felt like a hockey puck. "I'm going to have to return the net now. It's not my net. It belongs to the Stuarts from the far side." He wasn't begging, just stating details. This was going to work; he was sure of it.

But Holmes obviously felt otherwise. "Then have Mr. Stuart drop by. I'll be glad to give him back his net." He closed the door so gently that all Abe could hear was a tiny gasp.

Abe stood on the front porch staring at the closed door for a few seconds. He was thinking about what he'd say to Mr. Stuart, how he would try to make light of the situation, something like, "A bit of a pickle, I know, but it takes all kinds." He felt astonished to be part of a feud. "Neanderthal," he muttered under his breath.

A couple of days later, Abe stopped at the community mailbox on his way to work. The postman was busy filling the slots. Abe said number forty-seven loud and clear, the postman stepping aside, letting Abe reach in and pull out his own sheaf of mail. Since the postman wasn't looking, he grabbed the mail for number forty-nine, then hurried back to the car, throwing both piles on the passenger seat and driving away.

When he pulled into the Coffee Time just west of the highway, he stopped at the gaping garbage bin to the right of the drive-through, gathered up all the Grahams' mail, and tossed it in with the crushed coffee cups, used napkins, and grease-stained bags. There were at least two bills, one from Enbridge, another from the town, and a couple of hand-addressed envelopes that were either personal letters or cards. No one would ever know what happened. He wouldn't even tell Susanne. This was his way of quietly letting go. The war was over now as far as he was concerned. Let that damn dog yap itself to death. Abe would smile whenever a Graham was in sight. If the hatred continued, it was their choice. Abe's resentment would be buried in some landfill before the week was out.

Consequently, Abe wasn't at all prepared when, a month later, John came home from what would probably be his last Halloween ramble (he was twelve and tall for his age) and slammed his bag of candy on the kitchen counter. He and his buddies had knocked on the Grahams' door, thinking that John's cowboy getup would be enough of a disguise in the dark. But Holmes had recognized him. He handed out individual bags of barbecue potato chips, putting one in each of John's friends' bags. Not only did he refuse to do the same for John, but he glared at him and said, "You ought to be ashamed."

Susanne was livid. Abe felt more queasiness than rage, but that was because he'd been living under the illusion that the worst was over since that September day at the Coffee Time trash bin. "What are you going to do?" Susanne asked. "This is turning into that pig thing."

Abe tried to explain that it was probably wise to just continue ignoring them as best they could. "It's not a pig this time, just a fifty-cent bag of potato chips." There was no way that the Grahams could have known about their stolen mail. Their refusal to give John a Halloween treat was more of a reminder of their ill will than a fresh taunt.

But Susanne refused to pretend that a new boundary hadn't been crossed. She sat down that same night and wrote a letter to the Grahams, shaming them for humiliating a twelve-year-old boy in front of his friends. She read the letter to Abe before posting it. It gave him heart palpitations, and he tried to talk her out of sending it. He even considered waiting for the postman and stealing the envelope the way he'd snatched the previous pile of Graham mail, but he felt that that would be a betrayal of his own family. Susanne was right. The Grahams had crossed another line and deserved every word that she had written.

Between the beginning of November and Christmas, a bunch of small skirmishes occurred. Holmes tilted his snow blower so high in the first snowfall of the season that it sprayed a carpet of slush onto the DeVrieses' family-room windows. Abe nicked the Grahams' full garbage can, knocking it over as he drove past on his way to work one morning. Alice Graham publicly shamed Susanne at Tony's Country Market one early evening, a week before the holidays, for having twelve items in the one-to-ten lineup. Abe countered a few days later by sneaking onto the Grahams' property after eleven and popping out a Christmas bulb dangling within reaching distance on the side of their garage, thereby darkening the entire string.

Still, the DeVrieses weren't ready for what they woke up to in the wee hours of Christmas morning. Everyone was asleep, so the sound of breaking glass was dream-like. Neither of the kids got up to investigate, but Susanne convinced Abe to slip on his bathrobe and make sure that everything was okay. He checked out the main floor, then padded down to the family room. An entire pane of glass had been reduced to shards, broken bits glimmering all over the tile floor, snow blowing into the room, covering the artificial tree in a white glaze. At the foot of the tree, wedged between two wrapped packages, was a large, smooth river rock.

Despite it being Christmas day, they called the police. A youngish, mostly bald officer showed up an hour later. By this time, Abe had picked the remaining shards of glass out of the frame, and the window was sealed with cellophane and cardboard. The officer was very apologetic in explaining that he couldn't just go and bang on the Grahams' door. There wasn't any evidence that the neighbours had been involved. "More likely teenagers," he said, although he took the river rock with him when he left, promising that it would be used as evidence should it ever come to that.

"First they ruined Halloween, now they've ruined Christmas," Susanne said, tearing up. "We've got to do something about this."

Abe realized it was up to him to safeguard his family, to put an end to such recklessness. He could feel his father nodding in agreement, saying, "You have to let the Wasikowskas of this world know who's boss."

Abe didn't sleep much for nearly a week. Susanne worried herself to the point of a constant migraine. Abe sat in the dark family room night after night with his video camera at his side, ready to film anything. But then he realized that as long as the DeVrieses didn't take the feud further, the Grahams wouldn't strike again, confident that they were the victors, that the war had been won.

But Abe wasn't able to concede. He considered kidnapping Nini, driving her to some remote location, and tossing her out of the car. He considered poison hamburger, slashed tires, water poured into the gas tank of Holmes's car, cut TV cable; the list went on and on.

Susanne and Abe began to bicker all the time. She wanted revenge, and she wanted it without a speck of mercy. Abe found himself uncomfortable with her extremes. It sometimes felt she wouldn't be happy until one of their houses went up in flames or someone got seriously hurt. Although he appreciated how hard it was for her to feel like a victim day in and day out, he didn't really like how tightly she clung to duress.

By mid-January, Abe's sleep deficit was seriously impacting his ability to reason. He'd lost the knack of measuring acts with consequences.

He imagined attacking Holmes with a wild swing of his snow shovel, decapitating him in one perfect sweep.

One day when they were both out shovelling after a snowfall too light to haul out the blowers, Abe had had enough. He threw his shovel aside and headed across the lawn, his legs sinking in snow up to his knees. It felt like mountain climbing. He came close to falling when he hoisted himself over the packed piles at the edge of Holmes's driveway.

"What the ..." Holmes sputtered as he saw Abe crashing toward him.

Abe landed on the drive with his legs spread wide enough apart to give him balance.

"This is my property," Holmes proclaimed, his voice a little shaky.

Abe pictured himself in the back seat of a police cruiser, his wrists handcuffed behind his back. "All this hatred is making me sick."

Holmes was taking small, effortful breaths. "I'll call the police," he said.

"But they won't be able to help," Abe said, absolutely sure of himself. His hands were shaking, so he held them out for Holmes to see. "We've made whatever point we were trying to make." He stopped and swallowed. "I can't hate you anymore. This pig is killing me."

"Are you calling me a pig?" Holmes asked.

"No," Abe swore. "That was a mistake."

"What are you talking about?"

Abe couldn't figure out what else to do but tell the truth. "Do you have any idea what kinds of things I've been plotting, how far I'm willing to go?"

"Don't threaten me," Holmes said, balling his gloved hands into fists.

"These aren't threats. They're confessions. I'm baring my fucking soul."

The look of alarm on Holmes's face seemed to grow more childlike. "So what am I supposed to do?" he asked, genuinely confused.

It had started snowing again, big, fat, movie flakes that seemed determined to soften the day.

"I want you to forgive me for everything I've done and am capable of doing," Abe said, realizing that he was asking for the impossible.

But Holmes seemed to have run out of words. He stared down at the driveway, which was already beginning to accumulate a layer of fresh white snow.

"Okay?" Abe asked, pushing a little.

Holmes lifted his head and stared at Abe. "I think you're possibly crazy."

Abe nodded. "Please," he pleaded.

"And that wife of yours isn't going to throw stones at Nini?"

Abe faltered for a moment. The word *berries* started rolling down his tongue, but he managed to suck it back. "Nini can bark to her heart's content."

Holmes nodded with just the top of his head.

The silence grew awkward. Forgiveness created a kind of intimacy that neither man could handle. Abe reached across the snowy distance, offering Holmes his hand. Holmes reached back, just a moment's pressure. They were not going to be friends. Susanne and Alice wouldn't be doing aerobics at Curves together. Molly and John were never going to feel totally comfortable living next door to people who were capable of throwing rocks through their family-room window on Christmas morning. Nini would probably never stop haranguing them with her incessant barking. But knowing all of this was actually a relief. It was what they were going to have to live with. Abe could hear that legendary pig, buried somewhere along the property line, just an inkling of a snort as it breathed its final breaths. He prayed all traces of it would be gone come spring.

WHO?
AM I?

Kevin's adoptive mother, a jolly jelly roll of a woman named Sher, had given him her permission to find his birth mother when he was eleven and had first been told that he was adopted. His adoptive father, Rolf, kept licking his lips like a cat that was about to toss a hairball, but Sher seemed satisfied that she'd done the right thing and could now continue with her very happy life, where Kevin was just one of her many blessings. She paused only long enough to tell him that she never knew anything about his birth mother, other than that she was nineteen and had hip-long black hair.

At first, all he could think of was *why*? Had his mother been shamed by a religious family, or was she living a post-sixties, no-strings-attached life where a baby would be a drag, or was it simply a case of not being ready: no money, no partner, no hope?

It felt sometimes that he was making her up like lyrics to a song he didn't know the words to. Wouldn't it be strange if it turned out that she'd been living around the corner from him all this time? Was she an eccentric with dozens of mewling cats or a Mary Kay saleswoman with a lipstick empire at her feet or a professor of semiotics who only thought about him in the abstract?

In his early twenties, he thought about her more in relationship to who he was. Did he get his talent as a dancer from her? Were her legs as long as his? Did she love the choreography of Mark Morris and Pina Bausch? Was she the source of his thin, bony toes or his double-jointedness, which allowed him to bend into flabbergasting shapes?

When he was twenty-five and was dancing with a small Toronto troupe called Head to Toe, Sher was suddenly diagnosed with pancreatic cancer and died, all within three weeks. Her jolliness fled at the mention of death, but she remained kind up until the end. "You might as well have been my own" was one of the last things she uttered. She had given up on opening her eyes, but her words were still clear.

Rolf reached over from the other side of Sher's deathbed and patted Kevin on the shoulder, which turned out to be a goodbye gesture. He took an overdose of sleeping pills two days later, leaving a note that said, "I'm nothing without her."

Kevin tried to carry on with his life, his dancing, but he started being seized by certainties that the next song he heard on the radio was going to be a message from his birth mother. He couldn't watch TV without experiencing the overwhelming sensation that his mother was going to show up on one of the commercials. Was she the woman with the squeaky Mr. Clean kitchen or the one stirring a skillet full of Hamburger Helper? The idea of providence about to fall on his head started to scare him. His best friend, Joel, suggested that he get away for a while, maybe backpack around Europe on his own, clear his head of the whole idea of family.

He felt more in control the first few weeks away. But in Amsterdam, he was inundated by the number of middle-aged prostitutes who besieged him with offers, calling him *sweet boy* or *liebling*. Any one of them could have been his birth mother. And then, in a Stockholm café one cold, dark night, he struck up a conversation with another woman, who told him that she'd given up a son for adoption: a boy named Per who she only recently discovered was a car salesman with absolutely no interest in her at all. After too many vodkas with wizened orange slices drowned at the bottom of the glass, Kevin almost offered to take his place.

He finally met up with a young Australian couple in Berlin who were both good talkers and listeners. After smoking a few joints one night, they sat up until dawn discussing family history. When it was his turn, Kevin told them about his dead adoptive parents and his recent delusional bouts with regard to his mother. Somehow, hearing himself stating the facts to relative strangers took away much of the weirdness and panic that he'd been experiencing. He cried telling them about Sher and Rolf and took their advice about trying to track down his real mother once he was back in Canada.

The second day he was home, he registered with Parent Finders, a group of fellow adoptees who helped newbies sort out the system. But he hit a dead end with the East General Hospital's records of his birth (a flood had wiped out several years' worth of names and dates back in the mid-eighties) and could only get a last name, Smith, from Children's Aid, with the understanding that this would be a maiden name and probably useless. He knew that he was giving up too easily, that she was out there somewhere, but he had to let her stay lost in order to get on with his own life. Along with his friend Joel, whom he'd met in a Danny Grossman master class, he started a new dance company that they called Jay Kay.

He first met Amy when she and a few other game designers made arrangements to attend some of Jay Kay's rehearsals. The idea was to wrap bands of electrodes around the dancers' arms and legs, which would then transfer the movements of their muscles onto a computer. They were developing a game where the good guys somehow out-danced the bad guys: secret superhero hip shakers. Kevin loved the distraction. Amy was the kind of woman who knew that if she had any hope of getting what she wanted, she had to be the most charming, in-charge person in the room. Something in Kevin appealed to her, most likely his ability to fling himself into any kind of rhythm, his willingness to try new things. And for him, Amy was the key to being in the moment. She wasn't interested in having children, which made Kevin realize that he felt the same. And she wasn't all that crazy about digging through the past either. Kevin told her that he was adopted, and her advice was that he find a way to translate the mystery into dance.

Every now and again, Kevin would wake up to the thought that he was missing something essential. His birth mother would be forty-five, still young enough to play a big role in the rest of his life. But then he'd think how much damage wishful thinking could wreak on the life he was building with Amy and Jay Kay. He'd jump out of bed on those shaky mornings and do his stretches until adrenalin pushed everything else aside.

He and Joel had been working on a choreography for nearly a year that would embody both of their attitudes towards biology and luck. Joel's mother had died when he was three, and he was raised by his father and paternal grandmother, neither of whom ever mentioned his mother's name again. The piece was called *Who? Am I?* and consisted of six female dancers stripping Kevin and Joel from bubble wrap cocoons, finally exposing them naked. The dance concluded with a twenty-minute *pas de deux* as they flung each other across the stage in search of their lost selves. Kevin had been naked on stage several times before, but this particular dance gave him the odd feeling that he was exposing some deeply private place beyond flesh. It was by far the best work he'd ever done.

After the first performance, he locked himself into a wheelchair access stall in one of the Fleck Dance Theatre bathrooms and shivered for ten minutes straight. By the time he felt steady enough to be seen, most everyone in the lobby's opening night reception had broken off into conversations. Amy had her head down in a small circle of strangers that resembled a football huddle. And Joel seemed to be standing on his tiptoes while listening to the dance critic for the *Post* talk non-stop.

He took the last glass of white wine from one of the waiters' trays and strolled the perimeter of the crowd. There was a woman who looked to be in her forties sitting on a bench near the front door. He studied her closely for a few seconds and was startled when she not only looked back, but waved. He moved forward and she rose to meet him halfway.

"I just wanted to tell you how wonderful that was," she said with the huskiness of a lingering chest cold. Her brown eyes had some amber in them, and her black hair was cut bluntly to just above her chin.

Kevin thanked her, but couldn't seem to find the manners to say anything else.

"Is the piece autobiographical?" she asked, obviously struggling for words.

"Everything I do is partly autobiographical, I guess. But some of it is pure discovery." He hoped that he sounded intriguing rather than narcissistic.

"It was so real that I found it hard to breathe," she continued. She cleared her throat and then gazed straight into Kevin's eyes. "It's possible that we're related."

Kevin froze. He opened his mouth to ask how, but nothing came out.

"I may have given birth to you," she said softly but decisively.

Surely giving birth would be a memorable experience, Kevin thought, but then quickly realized that it wasn't the birth she was unsure of, but his part in it. He couldn't help but giggle just a little.

The calmness of it all was unnerving. He was thinking that her chin was similar to his: slightly pointed, with just a hint of a dimple. Should he mention this? He would like time to stop the way it did in cheesy movies so he could examine her head to toe.

"I'm trying not to be presumptuous," she said, "but I've been checking into this for some time now, and if you're really Kevin Downe and were born at Toronto East General Hospital March 31, 1988, and raised by Rolf and Sher Downe, then you're probably my son." She reached out and touched the stem of his wine glass. "Do you mind?" she asked, taking the glass and drinking it down in one gulp.

Kevin was startled by her boldness, although the intimacy, the invasion of it, also felt familiar.

"Is it okay that I'm here?" she asked, using the empty wine glass to include the entire lobby. "This is probably bad timing. Your opening night and all. I was just afraid that I'd get cold feet if I waited another day." She smiled and her face looked a little frozen. "Last time I saw you naked, you were just a few days old."

Before Kevin could figure out how to respond to the flirtatiousness of what she'd just said, Joel came bounding over. He was a tall, big-boned man who quite clearly was used to asking for what he wanted. "I hope you're showering him with compliments," Joel announced. "Nothing less will do."

Joel went on for a few minutes about how exhausted he was. When he finally ran out of chatter, the woman looked down at her wristwatch and said that she'd better be on her way. "In decent weather, I'm only a forty-five minute drive from downtown, but you never know what winter has in store."

She headed for the elevator and Kevin followed, leaving Joel behind. He figured the forty-five minute drive was a clue, and it would be up to him to track her down next time.

"I should have introduced you," he said, hoping that this didn't sound too stupid, "but I don't know your name."

She made a *mmm* sound and then said, "I'm Liz." Her forehead was a little slick like she might have a fever. "Could I give you a call in the next day or two?" She reached into the side pocket of the red silk jacket she was wearing and pulled out her iPhone. "Okay, go ahead," she said.

Kevin wasn't sure what she meant until she added, "Your number." He said it once too quickly, then repeated it slowly. "I wish you could meet my wife," he said, trying to stall her.

"Married and everything," she said, handing him back his empty wine glass, their knuckles bumping.

He didn't say another word; he just watched the elevator doors coming together, saw that her head was bowed a little just before the doors closed completely.

"Was that woman a critic?" Joel asked when Kevin returned, but he didn't wait for an answer. He tucked his arm around one of Kevin's elbows and said, "Let's go find a few fans and bask in their praise."

Kevin let himself be led. His legs felt shaky. He'd managed to perform so wildly on stage and now could hardly shuffle across the lobby.

Amy was extra attentive the next few days; she gave him a blowjob one night, made a sweet potato shepherd's pie another. She'd seen the woman coming out of the theatre and had noticed something familiar about her. With Amy's help, Kevin was able to keep himself balanced.

"This is just the first step," Amy said, stroking his hair back from his forehead.

She found an old Ontario map in their antique hallway washstand

and together they drew lines in all directions. The woman could be living in Richmond Hill or Mississauga or Oshawa. Nothing else to go on but "Liz."

On the third night of a four-night engagement of *Who? Am I?*, he was leaving the theatre when he spotted Liz on the exact same bench as before. There was no one else in the lobby. She waved again, but this time stayed sitting. Kevin had to do the approaching.

"I thought you were going to phone," he said, surprised at how close his tone came to a scolding.

"It's complicated," she said.

Kevin suggested they go to a nearby bar, but she didn't want to leave the building. They ended up in the deserted food court on the floor below the theatre. Kevin was struck by how nimbly she folded herself into the small metal chair. He imagined dancing with her, lifting her up by the hips.

"Sorry," she said. Kevin couldn't tell whether it was the missing phone call she was apologizing for or giving him up for adoption in the first place.

"What's the rest of your name?" he asked. Facts were more important right now than feelings.

She scrutinized him across the table. There was that familiar chin again. And something in the shape of the eyes. "I'm not sure this should go anywhere."

Even though Kevin wasn't that tall, five foot nine in dress shoes, his legs were much too long for the food-court chairs with attached tables. They reminded him of grade-one desks. Of course, she wouldn't know anything about his childhood and may very well never have any interest in how often life had been challenging over the years. What did twenty-six-year-old men do with their mothers when they weren't able to reminisce?

"You won't even tell me your last name?" The scolding had evolved into a frustration bordering on annoyance.

She moved her right hand toward his side of the table, but stopped midway across to scratch a crumb that was stuck there and brush it away. "It's not that I don't trust you. And I understand how much you must want to know," she explained, keeping her gaze to the left of him as if she were talking to someone just over his shoulder. "But I don't think I'm ready yet. I'm doing it for her rather than myself. Or you," she tagged onto the end.

"Who is *her*?" Kevin asked.

She zeroed in on where his third eye would go if he had one. The pink seemed to drain from her face. "Can't we just talk without getting entangled in the past?" She flashed a small smile. "You could tell me what you love about dancing. How happy you are with your wife. Or just tell me about your day ..."

Kevin had no idea how to respond to this. He felt like he was about to go onstage naked again.

"I just want to know that you're okay, that I made the right decision."

"Don't we need to talk about the past in order to know that?" Kevin kept a part of his attention on the anger that was rising up his chest into his shoulders. He was determined not to lose control.

"I can't take on your past, not right now," she said so quietly that Kevin had to lean further into the table.

He could feel her beginning to fade into a sadness that had nothing really to do with him. How could he speak honestly to her? If he made one tiny mistake, she'd be gone, forty-five minutes into nowhere.

"Aren't you happy?" she asked. "Please tell me what makes you happy."

Perhaps all she needed was to hear the truth. Shouldn't a son be able to tell his mother about the good things in his life? Sher had always been fascinated by the details of his school day, who he'd hung out with at recess, what he'd seen on the four-block walk home. And so he told Liz about dancing, how much he loved figuring things out with his body. He continued by telling her about having lunch with Joel at the Sunset Grill and ordering, as he always did, a sprawling plateful of pancakes. He finished off with Amy making him a light supper of salad and hardboiled eggs before he headed for the theatre. "Like always, she kissed me goodbye at the door," he concluded.

Liz had her eyes closed. It felt to Kevin that she had taken in all those images of his day and was going to keep them. He hadn't realized that he'd been giving them away.

"Thank you," she said, a bit breathlessly. "I feel much better."

"Now it's your turn," he said.

She opened her eyes and gave him a mean look. "I tried to meditate when I woke up at four unable to get back to sleep. Then I watched the morning shows to make sure the world was still in one piece." She paused for a second, having trouble keeping what came next in the proper order. "I stood outside her door and didn't go in. I missed lunch, not to mention breakfast. I tried to eat an apple, sort laundry. I planned to visit Pine Hills, but couldn't bear it and so watched the afternoon shows instead. I really, really wanted the day to end." She folded her hands on the table, giving Kevin a glimpse of her grade-one self. "I don't have any happiness without her. But I had to make sure that you did."

They sat there in silence. Kevin couldn't help puzzling over who the other woman was, but was afraid his mother would disappear under the glare of any more questions. He wished that he'd had a more exciting day for her sake, more happy stories to give her hope or whatever it was she needed. When she stood up from the table in one fluid motion, she reached over and cupped Kevin's chin in her hand. "Please let me go," she said. "I'll find you when I'm really ready."

Kevin's anger surged for a moment. He tossed his head and took his chin back. "Can't you even tell me my medical history?"

"Don't you think I'd have told you if something was seriously wrong?" she asked. "I can tell you one thing. You're not going to die from not knowing."

He let her go because he was beginning to realize that everything she was saying was the wrong thing, because he couldn't stop his anger from overflowing much longer, because he was exhausted by it all and was desperate to get home and into the quiet tenderness of Amy's arms. She didn't look back once. Kevin waited until she was out of sight before freeing himself from the prison of that tiny food-court chair.

"So what's the plan?" Amy asked once he'd told her everything. She excelled at outthinking the unreasonable and coming up with irrefutable strategies.

They stayed awake until after three going over the evidence. It was Amy who came up with the idea of checking with the Fleck box office. Liz had probably ordered her ticket for the opening night performance and picked it up at the theatre. She would have had to give a last name in order for the transaction to go through. Then Kevin remembered that she'd said Pine Hills. They looked it up on the internet and discovered that it was a cemetery in Scarborough.

Kevin got so excited that his mind jumped forward to him showing up at Liz's door and her not having any choice but to congratulate him on putting all the clues together.

The box office didn't open until noon. Kevin wondered if his impatience was like his mother's. He managed to nap and then listened to some music. He also did a good hour of stretching exercises. At exactly the moment when the digital clock clicked to 12:00 p.m., he was on the phone with Tammy at the Fleck and, a short chat later, had the name Elizabeth Dixon.

He called the cemetery next, but only got a voice message. Not having a crumb of patience left, he gathered together his jacket, gloves, and car keys and headed east to Scarborough. He'd grown up at Victoria Park and Ellesmere. It had once been a land of strip malls and bungalows, but was beginning to look slightly more upscale with its big-box-store plazas and houses with second storeys added on. Pine Hills was southeast of his old neighbourhood, at Birchmount and St. Clair, just a short walk from the Warden subway station. He made the trip in just over twenty minutes, pulled up the long driveway to the cemetery office.

Before getting out of the car, he called Amy at work and left a message. "I'm at the bone yard," he said, trying to sound light and airy. "I'll call you when I've found something."

A woman in a dark blue sari was sitting at a large oak desk in the main office. Off to the side, there was a small room where a tall man sat scrunched behind a computer, his fingers painstakingly pressing the keyboard one letter at a time.

"I'm looking for Dixon," he said to the woman.

"Dixon who?" she asked, her voice rising on the last syllable.

"No, Dixon is the last name," he corrected.

She frowned. Kevin had to bite the inside of his lower lip or else he would have apologized. This was neither the time nor the place to be a nice guy.

"Are you family?" she asked.

"As a matter of fact, I am." He could feel his toes clenching inside his shoes.

She had to turn her chair sideways in order to reach her keyboard. Unlike the man in the other room, her fingers flew. Kevin could see the whiteness of the screen flashing as she scrolled through several pages. "Which Dixon are you looking for?" she asked, keeping her chair where it was but turning her upper body toward him. "There are many."

"How many?"

"Perhaps I mean several," she said.

"Several," Kevin repeated, mulling over the difference. Before she could respond, his cell vibrated in his jeans pocket. He mumbled a quick "sorry" and took the call. It was Amy checking in, wondering whether he'd like her to leave work early, meet him out in Scarborough. He felt too stuck in the past to figure out what he wanted in the present. "I'm okay alone with this for now," he said.

The woman was waiting for him to pick up the conversation. "So, Dixon," he said. "Elizabeth Dixon."

She turned back to the screen for a moment. "There is no Elizabeth Dixon here," she said, folding her hands on the wrist pad of her keyboard.

Of course not, Kevin realized. She thought he was looking for a dead Dixon. "It's not Elizabeth I'm looking for." He faltered just a little. "It's her family. My family."

"There are several," she repeated.

"Can't you just give me the several," he said, "and I can check them all out?"

Before she could respond, the scrape of a chair came from the smaller room, and an instant later the man, who turned out to be even taller than he'd appeared sitting down, entered the room and the conversation.

"We can only give you the names of the deceased," he said.

"That will be fine," Kevin said. "More than fine," he added, striving to sound appreciative.

"Are you with an insurance agency?" the man asked. "A trust company? A private investigation firm?"

Kevin didn't have a clue which might be the right answer. "I'm just me," he said.

The man asked the woman to mark the three Dixon gravesites on a map of the cemetery. "Are you adopted?" he asked.

Kevin almost choked out loud.

"We get a lot of that here," the man explained. He had small eyes, but they were brimming over with kindness. "If I were you," he continued, leaning backwards so that he could see the woman's screen, "I'd start with Chestnut Drive. Elizabeth Dixon."

"Elizabeth Dixon?" he asked. "I don't want a dead Elizabeth Dixon."

"Then head straight west, take a left turn on Oak, a right on Linden, then another sharp right on Chestnut. Three plots in."

Kevin thanked the man several times, then tried to get the attention of the woman to thank her. The minute he stepped back out into the parking lot, he called Amy, but had to leave another voice message. "I'm just on my way to Chestnut Drive," he announced. It sounded like he was going to a bungalow rather than a gravesite. He thought of lawn chairs and an unfamiliar family—grandparents, aunts and uncles, cousins, perhaps even brothers and sisters—sitting around a circle of tombstones, chatting with each other and the dead.

There were spring smells everywhere when he stepped out of the car. The temperature seemed to have risen as the afternoon unspooled. What a shame the dead can't smell. The first gaping detail was a fresh plot, a mound of dirt like an unplanted garden, dying flowers strewn on top. The March grass squished under his feet. The first tombstone had two names on it: Evan Dixon, death date 1996, and Marcia Vernon Dixon, 1997. Beside them, a smaller stone with the name Ross Dixon carved into it; he had died way back in 1958 at only three years old. Could he have been Liz's brother? Finally, the brand new grave: Carrie Dixon, born March 31, 1988, died March 12, 2014.

It took Kevin a couple of breaths before he recognized his own birthdate. Had there been a mistake? Maybe Liz Dixon wasn't his mother after all. But that made no sense. Carrie was probably the woman she had spoken about back in the food court after last night's performance. Trying to untangle all these thoughts made his head feel knotted. If he could just untie one, the pressure would make everything feel lighter.

Carrie must have been his sister. Had she been adopted? Had death reunited her with Liz? Or had Carrie been kept and Kevin given away?

Kevin glanced at the brand new tombstone again. There was a chipmunk sitting on top. It looked like every other chipmunk he'd seen in his lifetime—a chipmunk uniform. But for the first time, he noticed that its big black eyes were slightly slanted. This reminded him of Liz's eyes, and his own.

The hour or so that he had to himself went by quickly. He noticed all the different shapes, sizes, and colours of the surrounding gravestones. There were black ones that shone in the afternoon sunlight like panthers. And red ones that caught the sun and made it glow like blood. And so many shades of grey.

He struggled not to think the worst: that something had been so wrong about him that Liz couldn't bear to have him around, had gotten rid of him immediately.

He heard the slam of a car door nearby, and he stepped back a few steps closer to Carrie's grave. Liz appeared from around a grove of spruce trees and, judging by her determined gait, had most likely been tipped off by the cemetery office staff.

"What are you doing here?" she asked. She was wearing a long Russian-style grey coat buttoned from neck to ankle that made her look like a giantess.

"Did you keep Carrie and give me away? That's all I need to know."

She seemed to be afraid that Kevin was going to damage the gravestone in some way, her eyes darting from the stone to Kevin's hands and then back to the stone again.

"I couldn't handle both of you," she said. It sounded polished, rehearsed for years. "And who'd adopt a baby with brain damage?" Her long coat appeared to tremble. "You can't even begin to imagine the sleepless nights, the terrors, the feeling that you've brought a child into the world who will suffer and suffer. It isn't even a question of love, though I did love her."

"And me?" Kevin felt himself shrinking. He laid one hand on Carrie's gravestone. The rock was warm like a living thing.

"You were perfect," she said with a terrible flatness. "I knew you'd find a loving family."

"But that was twenty-six years ago," Kevin said more loudly than he'd meant to. He kept blinking until it felt more like a twitch. "Maybe I could have loved her too."

Liz grabbed at her throat and undid the top button, then her fingers scrambled lower and she undid another. "I was nineteen. I didn't even know who the father was. I couldn't handle the responsibility." She kept tugging at buttons until her entire coat was undone. "And then I couldn't handle the guilt."

And so he was shuffled aside, Kevin thought. He closed his eyes and tried to imagine sharing a womb with Carrie. Did he know in some preverbal way that something was wrong with her? Had he protected her for as long as he could? Had she cried when he was taken away?

"Who was first?" he asked.

Her brow furrowed. "First?"

"Who was born first?"

"She was," she answered. "You came about twenty minutes later, but by that time Carrie was having her first seizure. You slid out onto the table like a seal."

"Did I have a name?" Kevin asked. He could feel the last of winter crawling up his legs.

"I couldn't," his mother stated. "I was so completely lost."

"Did she know anything about me?" he asked.

"I'd tell her stories about an imaginary twin brother," she answered. For a second, it looked like she was going to sink to her knees, but she managed to straighten up again.

"I was imaginary," Kevin repeated. He wondered whether he should leap the way he did onstage, find a place for himself mid-air. He didn't belong here in the cemetery. "I'm real. I've always been real. How could you let her die not knowing that?"

He was so angry that his skin was burning. He felt like he might throw back his throat and yowl. His mother had not only given him away—she'd made him imaginary. There weren't words or even sounds to express this.

❖

He left the gravesite that day hating Elizabeth Dixon with a fury. He told Amy that he couldn't talk about it until after that night's performance. It was their best night yet. Kevin let Joel throw him across the stage with fresh abandon, and when their bodies would come together again, he would feel his very flesh melding with Joel's. The nakedness was sharper, less vulnerable than at previous performances, which made the audience respond more boldly, sometimes gasping, bursting into wild applause at the end. Kevin was dripping with sweat, his hair plastered to his skull like a newborn's. He gripped Joel's hand for the final bow, feeling part of a team. This was where he belonged.

Back home with Amy, he tried to express the transformation he'd just experienced, both at the cemetery and the theatre, but, before he could get much out, he broke down and literally cried for hours. He finally fell asleep with his head on Amy's lap.

Both the anger and the sorrow had diminished come morning. He even felt that he understood his birth mother's need to choose. How could she abandon the weaker of the two? But the fact that she didn't try to resolve this fracture while Carrie was still alive was unforgiveable. He couldn't stop thinking about his sister. She took over the space that he'd used to think of as daydreaming. He'd never imagined such a thing, and now he couldn't stop imagining. No matter how many times he reminded himself that she was real, no matter how many visits to Pine Hills, everything he wondered about her, every question he offered a possible answer to, rendered her more and more imaginary until he felt he knew her. After over a year of this, he contacted Elizabeth Dixon, and they agreed to meet at a Tim Horton's near the cemetery to talk about Carrie, but the Carrie that she mourned was so different from the Carrie he'd created in his head that he found himself faced with his own horrendous choice.

The fact that he chose his Carrie made him feel more compassion toward Liz. All she had of Carrie's twenty-six years was sadness and regret. He brought the conversation to a close, explaining that he was overloaded with information and needed to process what he already knew before he could take more in.

"Sounds familiar," Liz said, pushing her coffee cup away from where it had perched precariously the entire conversation.

"Excuse me?" Kevin said, although he knew what she meant. The brush-off that she gave him that second night at the theatre still gave him shudders when he let himself remember.

"Our relationship," she said, staring down at her coffee cup, "is nothing but information."

"Exactly," Kevin said.

"To be completely honest, I was the one who needed you to be imaginary," Liz confessed.

Even though he was sitting down, he felt like he was falling from a great height. The tables and chairs surrounding him were obstacles that he wasn't sure he was going to be able to dodge. He tried to focus on Liz, but she appeared to be moving in a wave-like way. He shut his eyes and pictured Sher's wide, smiling face. If she had still been alive, she would probably have gotten a kick out of Kevin being imaginary. "Like Winnie the Pooh," she might have said. "Or the Little Prince."

"Let it go," Amy advised when he got home. "You're as real as they come."

If this were a dance, they'd have to find a way of rendering the principle dancer almost invisible: darting in and out of shadow, popping up in one place, followed by a blackout, then showing up again—a *pas de deux* between ghost and flesh. And in the middle of it all, centre stage, there'd be a hunched woman who Kevin would stumble over numerous times. He wasn't sure yet whether she was Carrie or Liz. But he could already feel the pain of their collisions.

JEFFERS

When my nephew arrived at baggage claim, I was right there to greet him; I was allowed inside the frosted-glass doors since he was just a kid. He didn't know me from Adam since we'd never met, but I recognized him immediately: the only bald thirteen-year-old on the flight from Vancouver. He'd spent the last six months being treated for some rare, aggressive cancer of the blood. And then his mother, my sister, Sue, a single mom who had always just eked by on luck and love, died in a smash-up with a logging truck on a muddy highway somewhere near Kamloops. Since Leah and I were the only willing relatives the kid had (his birth father had disappeared before the stub of the umbilical cord fell off), we suddenly inherited a dying adolescent.

He couldn't have arrived at a worse time, Leah three months pregnant with our first child and suffering from vertigo so badly that some days she could hardly lift her head off the pillow; plus my father was sinking further into dementia every day, staying in our spare room until a bed became available anywhere they might take a seventy-seven-year-old ingrate who couldn't remember what a colossal shit he'd been his entire life. There was nowhere to put the kid other than the nursery, a billowy pink oasis from the otherwise overcrowded beige of our lives. What would unborn Tara feel about sharing her room with a boy who, according to the BC oncologist, had three months to a year at best?

Jeffrey was the last person on the flight to appear. I expected him to be shuffling his feet, but he had that pent-up teenage energy that made it impossible for him to stand still for more than ten seconds. Except for the fact that he was entirely hairless, not even a trace of eyebrows, he could have passed for a standard thirteen-year-old, down to his gloomy, hostile demeanor. He managed to express his disdain for me without uttering a single word. He looked at me with only the lower halves of his eyes and made a quiet snorting sound to practically everything I said. When I realized I was babbling, I shut up and we passed the time silently ignoring each other while watching the empty carousel go around and around.

He didn't make a move to help with his baggage. The big case was on wheels, the other a gym bag sort of thing that I was able to sling over my shoulder. I didn't check to see if he was following me; I just headed for the automatic doors, feeling a wave of sadness wash over me as if I were the one who'd just arrived with only a stranger there to greet me. The car was parked a good hike away. I felt like I was tramping through a bad dream, everything I passed tinted with the same bland fluorescence. It wasn't until I'd electronically popped the trunk of my Camry that I glanced behind me and saw that Jeffrey was still there, less than a foot away.

I drove faster than I would have with Leah in the car. When I'm in the car alone, I often push ten, twenty kilometres over the limit, but this night with Jeffrey slumped beside me like a shadow, I took the curves with an irresponsible arrogance. Maybe there wasn't anything I could talk about with Jeffrey that didn't contain death, but I could certainly rev the engine and squeal my tires.

"I'm going to puke," a small voice rose from the passenger seat. I couldn't tell whether he was huddled against the door or slipping toward the floor. *Puke* was a fairly common word these days. Leah often used it as a way of getting me to drive more smoothly.

I immediately eased my weight on the gas pedal and took the next turn onto the 400 North with hardly a swerve. "How's that?" I asked, but he didn't respond. "Any better?" I dropped my speed to a perfect ninety. "Why aren't you answering me?"

"I'm trying not to puke, for fuck's sake," he slurred.

It didn't seem right that I, a grown man, a good Samaritan, should have to suffer cursing, especially from a snotty thirteen-year-old. But in truth, I was fond of the word *fuck* and was rarely allowed to use it now that tiny unborn Tara was supposedly hanging off my every word.

Traffic began slowing down ahead until we were barely crawling. Construction was a serious problem in and around Newmarket, a bedroom community about an hour's drive from TO. I started in on my rant about bloody developers and the sorry state of public transport.

"I have to pee." That small voice again, interrupting.

I remembered that at his age, I'd sometimes claim that I had to pee in order to break the monotony of the long trips my father loved to take. Once we drove across the country, stopped for ten minutes to dip our feet into the Pacific Ocean, and then headed back east again. There was no way that I could maneuver into the slow lane, and even if there was, it wasn't much of a shoulder to pull off on. "Sorry, buddy," I said, "you're just going to have to hold on."

"I really have to pee." The voice was louder now.

"I can stop at the side of the road once we get to Highway 9," I promised. "That's the best I can do."

Traffic was at a complete standstill when he opened the passenger door and tried to scramble out of the car. He'd forgotten about his seatbelt though, and I was able to shift into park, grab him by the neck of his denim jacket, and yank him back inside. After leaning even further to slam the door shut, I was practically lying on top of him. By the time I'd managed to climb back to the steering wheel, the car behind was honking to let me know that the car in front was way ahead by now.

"What the hell were you trying to do?" I was steering with my left hand, keeping hold of Jeffrey's arm with my right.

"I have to pee," he repeated, coming close to a sob.

"Okay," I said, flipping through a bunch of possibilities. "There's an empty water bottle in the back seat," I explained, leaving the rest up to him.

"I'm not peeing in a bottle," Jeffrey stated. I could see the spray of his saliva in the glare of the car behind's headlights. I tried not to breathe in, thinking crazy thoughts about cancer being catching.

"Well, you're not peeing in my thermal coffee cup," I said. "What about your shoe?"

I could just imagine the killer looks he was sending in my direction. "I can't pee in front of you," he said.

"Then haul your ass into the back seat," I said, putting both hands on the steering wheel as traffic had started moving again. "And don't get any on the upholstery."

He fumed for a few seconds, then fumbled his seatbelt open. He twisted himself to his knees then threw himself over the back of the passenger seat. I reached over and gave him a little push. Next thing was the whirr of the window sliding down and the slosh of the water being tossed out, followed a few seconds later by a trickle then a gush as his bladder let loose. "It's going to overflow," he said, his voice booming with panic.

"So stop pissing," I shouted.

"I can't."

It turned out that he was worrying for nothing. The torrent ended with a trickle, then a matter of drops, just shy of the three-quarter mark. He had a bit of a problem screwing the top back on, but finally mastered it and climbed back into the front seat, his left leg kneeing me on the chin. I was surprised that he didn't claim the back seat as his, the easier to ignore me. Even more surprising was the mumbled "Thanks."

"Hope you zipped up. Your Aunt Leah's a stickler for everything put away in its proper place."

He turned toward me, and I could see a frown on his face, a form of engagement. "Am I supposed to call you Uncle?" he asked, goading me just a little. "I've had lots of uncles over the years. Dozens of them."

"Lucky you," I swatted back. "Maybe you'd just better call me Luke. I'd hate to get lost in that ocean of uncles. You might get confused."

Traffic was moving well now. Highway 9 was just around the bend. The car behind seemed to have his high beams on, so I deked into the right lane a little earlier than planned.

"You're swerving again," he said. "I'll puke into your coffee cup if you're not careful."

He tried on Luke the Puke for size while I went for the gold with Deaf Jeff the Limp Dick Treble Clef. He laughed out loud, a phlegmy hissing sound that reminded me of a camel. By the time we reached Newmarket, he seemed to have completely accepted me. Could it really be that simple? I realized that I'd remember this drive, the traffic jam, the peeing in a bottle, after Jeffrey was dead. Damn, hardly more than an hour together and I was already missing him. I hadn't planned on getting all amigos.

"This looks like anywhere," he said as we drove past the usual big-box stores toward the darkness of Holland Landing.

"It is," I agreed.

"How about I call you Duke?" He appeared to be asking seriously. "You'd be my one and only Duke. An original."

"And I'll call you Jeffers," I said, making it up right there on the spot. "One-of-a-kind Jeffers."

"I like it," he said quietly just as we turned down the snaky hill that led into the lowlands of Holland Landing.

By the time we pulled into our driveway, I was back to worrying that I'd taken on more than I could handle and that I was asking too much of the kid. Leah needed my complete devotion; she was already so weakened by the pregnancy that she didn't have the energy to take on a dying nephew. And what kind of death would it be for Jeffers, in an unfamiliar place with complete strangers? I was so full of fear there in the driveway that I wished I could tear time into tiny pieces, go back to being thirteen years old myself.

There are often transformations toward the end of an action movie that are believable in the compressed world of the screen, that would never happen in real life. But that doesn't mean our ordinariness isn't epic at times. For example, we discovered immediately that after three rounds of devastating chemo, Jeffers was an expert on vertigo and nausea. With the excitement and pride of a young doctor writing his first prescription, Jeffers recommended a glass of water an hour before eating, chewing on candied ginger between meals, and taking deep breaths while slowly walking back and forth across the living room. Two days later, Leah had her first rosy glow in a long time. By the end of the first week, she was calling Jeffers her hero and saying that Tara couldn't wait to meet him for real. Death was never mentioned, just the expectation that he would still be around in six months.

The weirdest thing was that Jeffers took to my dad like a burr to a sweater. I introduced the old man as Gramps just because he'd had a Gramps whom he'd hated way back in his own childhood. Anything to make him suffer.

"This is your grandson, Jeffers," I shouted. He had hearing aids, but lost them ten times a day.

He glared at me for a second as if I had snot rubbed all over my face, then he shouted back, "You think I'm a fool. I don't remember any grandson." He swatted the air and gave us a "that's that" kind of look.

"Sue's son," I said. I knew he'd already forgotten that Sue had recently died, but some part of him was aware that not all was well with her, that she'd been talked about a lot lately.

"Does Vic know about this?" he asked, referring to my mother, another dead one, six years ago. Her devoted dumb ass of a cat bit her finger and by the time she'd gone to see her GP, sepsis was rampant, all the way into her heart.

"Mom's dead," I snapped.

"Well, so is Sue." He leered, one-upping me.

"Now we're on the same page," I shouted, reaching out and slapping him lightly on his bony shoulder. "That's why Sue's son is living with us now. Your bloody grandson."

I left them to it, fully expecting to come home that night to a bubbling wreck of a nephew, begging me to lock up the old fart and throw away the key. But everything was cozy. I changed out of my grease monkey uniform and found Jeffers sprawled in the chair beside Dad's bed, Dad propped up on three pillows, the top one folded over to give his head even more height.

"He's been telling me family stories all day," Jeffers said, beaming.

"Sorry about that. His noggin's a sieve," I explained.

"I love it," Jeffers continued. "After the tenth time, it's like I finally get it. It makes me feel like I belong."

"Belong?" Dad piped in. "That reminds me of the trouble Luke had in the middle of grade seven or eight when we moved to a new house. He came home crying that the other kids were calling him Skin-and-Bones."

"Yeah?" Jeffers said. "So you've had nicknames before, eh, Duke?"

Dad then proceeded to tell us how I puked thirty-seven nights in a row when I had whooping cough. How I had a girlfriend in high school named Elsa who wore tight v-neck sweaters all the time. How I flunked my mechanic's licence three times before finally scraping by.

"It wasn't that I didn't know my stuff," I jumped in. "I just freeze when I'm being judged." What the hell? Why was I letting a demented shadow of a man and a dying kid get under my skin. "Don't believe half the things he says," I warned Jeffers. "Just because he says it a hundred times doesn't mean it's true."

My ability to shut out my father's constant jabber was a hard-won accomplishment, but sometimes a word or phrase of pure meanness would break through. Take "monkey boy" for example, how he referred to my adventure feeding the monkeys at the Peterborough Zoo back when I was around thirteen.

"He was wearing this garnet signet ring we'd given him as a grade-eight graduation present." Dad ruined the punch line with his laughter. "My blooming idiot of a son sticks his fingers between the bars, and one of those monkeys instantly turns into a jewel thief."

Jeffers was crazy for these stories. He'd howl with laughter and then howl all over again on the next go-around. Leah was so happy that the house was full of buoyancy that she convinced me to take it in one ear and out the other. She said I should think of it as a privilege that my escapades were helping an old man and a sick boy with the hard, slow job of dying.

I started writing down things that happened at the garage, fluffing them up a little, joining in the fun at night. After Jeffers had been with us for three weeks, I realized that we were hardly ever turning on the TV other than to check the weather. We were more entertaining than any sitcom family. Even Dad seemed to be in better control of his stories. He still repeated himself, but often improved on the details, making them more dramatic, more colourful.

And no matter how stupidly I came across in some of Dad's cruellest memories, Jeffers never judged me. He seemed proud of my ability to fuck up and keep going. He said I reminded him of a cartoon character who would get entirely flattened in one frame, then snap back to life in the next. Never give up was my motto. Anything was possible. Monkey boy was a legend. "You're the bestest," Jeffers said several times. I found myself waiting for him to repeat it.

He also managed to rein Dad in about Sue, frowning whenever he heard the word *slut* or *whore*. His mother was an original who brought temporary beauty into the lives of nameless men, and his vision of her seemed to infiltrate Dad's. "She was a goddamned pirate queen," he announced at the conclusion of a tale about her getting caught shoplifting.

Jeffers may have lost his mother in the flesh, but he'd found a way of celebrating her that he never would have were she still alive. I knew that Sue was as far from a saint as they come, but I liked seeing her with this new compassion.

He started hugging us goodnight and saying, "Love you" before heading off to his pink cocoon. It was the kind of nice that totally consumes you, where you forget for a while that everything will change.

I'd forgotten that bad things always seem to occur in bunches. And that there are times in which there are no reprieves. One busy Monday morning, just as I was heading out the door to the garage, our geriatric social worker telephoned with a bed for Dad at a facility called Providence Villa. If we refused, he'd be moved to the bottom of the list; it could be more than a year's wait, and it might not be as good a place as the Villa. We had less than an hour to make up our minds. And then he would have to actually move in by Tuesday before noon.

I'm not sure whether it was the shock of Dad's sudden departure that weakened him, but both Leah and I thought that Jeffers was looking pretty flimsy during Tuesday's bustle. For myself, I thought it was the sadness of losing his Gramps after just having found him, and I reassured him many times that we'd visit the Villa often.

On Wednesday morning, Leah had some spotting and cramps. I took her to the hospital, leaving Jeffers home alone. It turned out to be a false alarm, but we didn't get home until midnight and Jeffers was fast asleep. The next morning, I took a glass of orange juice into his bedroom and found him barely conscious, in fact he'd wet the bed and soiled himself.

I called an ambulance, not wanting to leave Leah without a car. She promised to rest today, recover from the long hours in emergency yesterday. She said that she had a good feeling about Jeffers and that we should tell ourselves that everything was going to be okay. How I was supposed to get the image of a thirteen-year-old lying in his own shit out of my head was a mystery, but I would do my best to ban all bad thoughts from my head.

"Your mom dated an ambulance driver once," I said on the drive to the hospital. I'd reached out at some point to pat his hand, and he'd held on. "She got him to turn on the siren while they made out." I wasn't sure he could even hear me.

He seemed to perk up a bit at all the attention he got from the nurses. He still hadn't let go of my hand. His fingers were trembling, but I knew it wouldn't be cool for anyone to point this out.

"Maybe they'll put me in Providence Villa," he said so softly I had to lean my ear just a few inches from his mouth. "Gramps and I could share a room."

"Don't be daft. You're not going into a nursing home," I scolded him. "We need you back home."

Need wasn't something I'd ever done well. Mom wasn't exactly the most attentive of mothers. She and Dad fought so much that he took any field work that came his way. She was always either simmering over something he'd said or missing him so intensely she shut the rest of the world out. And to Sue, four years older than me, I was more of a housefly than a brother.

I don't do future so well either, or the past for that matter. I spend most of my time somewhere between what I wish for and what I regret, that tiny space where anything is possible, the worst or the best, that instant where you don't have to nail down a choice yet, where you can touch the kitchen counter and feel the crumbs under your palm, where you can see the clock vibrating as it ticks, where you can roll over in bed, partially awake, and find the rest of you sound asleep.

After a week of doing all the heavy lifting at home, putting in my hours at the garage, checking in with Dad and then visiting Jeffers in the hospital, I slowly shed my panic and adjusted to the new routine. I need a routine, otherwise I end up trying to do four things at once and quietly imploding. I'm not like my father: I couldn't do to Leah what he did to my mother. And now he was my responsibility too, lucky bastard.

Jeffers was different; he was more of a gift than a duty. I needed him to be well. Sitting beside his hospital bed those first crucial seven days, I told him a million stories about my life. Now that Dad had gone away, I was the keeper of the memories. He believed everything I said; he ate it up. And then he'd retell some of it, changing a detail or two to make it better. It was my life the way it should have been, the way Jeffers saw it from the brink of death, where nothing else exists.

A middle-aged doctor with thick black sideburns suddenly appeared one evening and started ticking off good things; something about cancer cells in the blood no longer multiplying. When asked what they could do to prevent another such crisis, the doctor chuckled. "Develop superpowers," he suggested.

The next day, I walked into his room and found him sitting in a big, high-backed chair beside the bed. The following day, he was circling the fourth-floor halls. Two days later, he was back home. He still had a sickly yellow-green tinge to his skin like a rock bass and, according to Leah, he often puked while I was away at work. Life went back to a new semi-normal.

Some evenings we'd visit Dad at the Villa, though he'd deteriorated to the degree that he had trouble putting a sentence together. He didn't have the grammar anymore to frame his memories. Mostly we stayed at home and made Jeffers feel that he'd always been with us, that we'd loved him from the moment he was born.

I can't explain how I'd managed to never see my nephew until he was thirteen. Sure, BC was the other end of the country, but Leah and I had actually spent a weekend in Vancouver three years ago, just after we were married, and we didn't even attempt to make contact with Sue. Dad had started losing it around that time, and I was angry that he was completely my responsibility. She'd simply written him off without even asking me what I wanted. Our relationship consisted of maybe three phone calls a year that always ended in arguments. I never thought of Jeffers as real. I mean, I knew he existed, but I considered him like a character in a novel. There was nothing flesh and blood about him.

But now I touched him all the time. I could feel his fever burn into my palm. I'd stroke his smooth, bald skull when he had trouble falling asleep. One evening, well into her sixth month, Leah went to bed early, leaving Jeffers and me shooting the shit about sports, how neither of us were born with the jock gene, how we'd rather eat slugs than watch a football game.

"I went to a Raptors game with a buddy a few years ago," I said. "The whole place smelled like dirty socks and jockstraps. I had to leave mid-game."

"I'll never go to a Raptors game," he responded. I could see that he was feeling moody, though it wasn't self-pity. He was just stating a fact.

"You're not missing much, believe me." I screwed my face up and shrugged my shoulders.

"I made a bucket list the other day."

"Hey, cool," I said, not sure whether it was something he wanted to share. A bucket list seemed private to me, like the wish you make when you blow out birthday cake candles.

"I'd like to know what it feels like to be drunk," he said. "What do you think, is it worth the trouble?" His eyes were so blue in the lamplight that it looked like his pupils were swimming.

"It's getting really, really stupid, followed by a lot of puking and a kettle drum of a headache. If you're interested, just name your poison."

He laughed so hard, it came out as a snort. "Cross that one off the list."

"Okay, what's next?" I was already looking forward to an evening somewhere in the future when we would remember the night we ransacked his bucket list.

"I'd like to travel, but I don't feel much like Africa or the North Pole at the moment. But I've always wanted to see Niagara Falls."

"Do you have any plans for this coming weekend?"

"Is it that easy?" he asked, tucking his legs under him on the couch.

"Just think of me as your personal genie."

He gave me a crooked look like he was up to something dodgy. "I want to have sex."

I searched for something funny to say, but it was clear he was dead serious. Jeffers wanted way more than to feed garnets to the monkeys.

"Can you?"

"You mean, get it up?"

"I mean you're only thirteen years old. Have you had puberty yet?"

"Jesus, Duke," he said disdainfully. "That happened so long ago, I can hardly remember."

"You're sure?" I wanted to keep Jeffers a little boy. Puberty was the death of innocence. "I don't think it happened to me until I was at least sixteen."

Jeffers rolled his eyes. "It's all the growth hormones in our food," he said. "We get horny by eight or nine."

We were laughing again, which made it possible for me to redirect the conversation. He seemed to have forgotten the bucket list by bedtime. What the hell would I have done if he'd pressed the point? The only women I knew were Leah and Donna, the bookkeeper at the garage, who looked to be at least fifty and whose belly was bigger than her bust. And what did I know about prostitutes? I used to see them around Jarvis and Queen when I lived in Toronto. They looked painted up and desperate. Being with one of them would only technically be sex. Like eating a plateful of onions and calling it a meal.

The worry that he might broach the subject again made me a little wary the next day, but the day after that, I took him to see Dad, and the two of them talked gibberish until they were laughing like insane hyenas. The day after that, we went back for Dad and the three of us headed for Niagara Falls. On the two-hour drive, we sang old rock-and-roll songs, songs that had managed to cross three generations, like "Satisfaction" and "Heartbreak Hotel" and "You Keep Me Hanging On." The mood changed from song to song.

The car wove in and out of the lane as "House of the Rising Sun" poured out of me. Dad ended up singing "Great Balls of Fire" without forgetting a single lyric. Funny how the music remains.

Jeffers loved the Falls. Dad and I stayed back from the railing, but Jeffers leaned over as far as he could get without falling in, his bald head glistening with dampness. I couldn't persuade Dad to walk the tunnels under the Falls, so Jeffers had to go in alone. He reminded me of a rubber duck in the voluminous yellow raincoat. He could hardly walk in the big black boots. While he was gone, I tried to ask Dad's advice.

"He wants to have sex," I said, having to shout a little over the roar of water.

"Don't we all?" Dad said, smirking.

"Any ideas?" I asked, feeling strangely shy. I was sure Dad strayed plenty during his many separations from my mother.

"Fuck the biddy," is what I heard next.

"What?"

"What who with," he responded, his ears getting red. "It's all fucked."

By the time Jeffers joined us again, Dad was muttering non-stop like a dog shaking itself after a swim.

I couldn't let Jeffers go alone on the Maid of the Mist, but Dad was hell-bent on refusing to put on the disposable poncho. I ended up telling him that we were taking the boat home, that if he didn't come, he'd have to thumb a ride the whole way back to the Villa.

"I'll drive the car," he said, surprisingly lucid again.

"The car's on the ferry," I lied.

This seemed to confuse him enough that I was able to slip the neck hole of the poncho over his head. The poncho hung crookedly, but at least it would keep him partially dry.

Jeffers did a little puking on the boat, but he managed to stay vertical for most of the trip. His whole head was flushed, his eyes practically popping out of his head. The roar was too loud for conversation. I kept an arm around him the whole time. As for Dad, he was petrified. He sat on a bench and made a whinnying sound every time the boat hit a wave.

None of us had the energy for Madame Tussauds or the Ripley's Believe It or Not, but we really didn't need any manmade crap after being part of one of the world's seven wonders. "That was probably better than Africa," Jeffers said before falling asleep.

Dad had toppled over in the back seat and was snoring quite loudly. It was weird how happy I felt on the drive home. I wished that Leah had come with us, and that Tara was already born. It struck me that my relationship with my father was like being near the Falls, the crashing waters dominating everything. But when the Maid of the Mist sailed along the curtain of pounding water, it was almost quiet, just a crazy second of tenderness. Love had always been there, hidden out of sight.

The Niagara Falls adventure took its toll. After two days in bed, I had to take Jeffers back to the hospital. The next day, Dad came down with pneumonia. Dad in ICU and Jeffers in oncology. I rode the elevator fifty times running back and forth between both wards.

"If I don't die soon, you're going to lose your job," Jeffers said one day after Leah had gone upstairs to see Dad.

"Don't talk like that," I said, biting my tongue. "Schmuck."

There are worse things than death. Dad hooked up to a breathing machine was one, the damn thing blowing his jaw open, throttling him with one breath after another. It was like life was being forced on him.

Watching Jeffers have a spinal tap was another. Despite drugs, the pain was beyond description. I could feel it in my fingers as he crushed me with his fist. His skull beaded in sweat. He opened his mouth to scream or cry, but nothing came out.

Dad died on a Sunday at eleven in the morning. Leah was with me, in fact, I had a hand on her belly while they took him off the machine, and he gave a couple of terrible gasps before simply refusing to breathe in again. We sat there and watched his chin sag. A nurse pressed his eyelids down. Another nurse turned off the respirator, and we soaked in the silence for a while. I was too sad to speak, but was looking forward to telling Jeffers how easy it had been once the decision to let go had been made.

But something in Jeffers wasn't ready to follow in Dad's footsteps, not yet. His blood count was back up. Still, he was very weak and could only handle short conversations.

"I still haven't had sex," he said, pointing his finger at me. "And you call yourself the Duke."

"That's what you call me," I corrected, adding "little fucker" for dramatic effect.

He wasn't well enough to be at Dad's funeral, but I spent the next two days with him in the hospital, telling him about the Joan Baez version of "Amazing Grace" that we played at the beginning of the service and "Great

Balls of Fire" at the end, which seemed to shock some of the middle-aged people, though plenty of the old timers were tapping their toes and humming along.

Just over a week later, Jeffers was able to come home again. Leah had baked a red-velvet cake, which he'd only recently mentioned was on his bucket list. I hoped that sugar had superseded sex. I hadn't planned on mentioning this to anyone, but one of the cancer nurses, a tall woman in her late twenties with loads of orange hair piled on top of her head, asked to speak to me for a moment while another nurse was helping Jeffers get dressed. She just wanted to tell me that even though Jeffers was stable enough to come home, this wasn't a remission, in fact, it was probably just a brief interlude and that I shouldn't panic if he simply started to fade away.

"It would be nicer for him if he could die at home," she said, reaching out and patting me on the elbow.

"Can I ask you a question?" For the first time, I looked at her name tag. It read *Peggy Mitchum RN*. "Peggy," I said, "what can I do to help him lose his virginity?"

She looked startled, one half of her face paling, the other blushing. She swallowed before answering. "Is this a current issue?"

"It's on his bucket list," I explained. "Number one, I think."

"I sympathize with your concern and your wish to do whatever is necessary to make Jeffrey's last days as meaningful as possible, but I really don't have an answer to this particular dilemma." She reached out and held my elbow this time. "It's technically illegal for a boy his age to have sex."

"How do I tell him that?"

Peggy leaned a little closer. "I'm sorry; I know this is a difficult time. I wish I could help," she said.

I thanked her profusely. The word *illegal* hung in the air. I almost asked her to write it down on the medication list. It felt surreal, like flying a giraffe or swallowing a kaleidoscope.

"Good luck," she said.

I wished I could share this one with Jeffers. How we'd laugh our heads off. But Peggy was right about the fading away, although we still had what sometimes felt like endless time, especially in the evenings when I'd tell him tales about how Leah and I met or made-up stuff about Tara going to kindergarten, passing her pilot's test, and then going to live in Paris to become a famous fashion designer.

"Sex," he whispered one morning when the sun was blazing at the window. He stared up at me from his two white pillows. "You blew it," he said, followed by a grin.

"No way," I disagreed. But I couldn't keep just avoiding the subject. So I simply began a story about how the make-believe Jeffers, the one who will live forever, had a friend named Peggy with whom he had a real connection. They laughed so easily together. Her orange hair shone like a sunset. One day, she came into his room, closing the door behind her. She was wearing a soft white blouse with the two top buttons undone and a black skirt that was kind of lacey and would probably fly into a circle if she spun fast enough. She couldn't wait another minute to tell Jeffers that she was in love with him. Before he could admit that he loved her too, she had climbed up into the bed and curled herself against him. It felt like she had a fever, just like his. She took one of his hands, the one that wasn't black and blue from his IV line, and placed it on her breast. It was as round as a coconut, but made of marshmallow. There were no words to describe what happened next. It was the exact opposite to that bone marrow needle. It felt like he'd never have to puke again.

I didn't realize that Leah was in the room until she suddenly appeared at my side and slipped an arm through mine. "That's quite the story," she said.

"Scram," Jeffers said. "Leave me alone with my thoughts."

Leah led me out into the hall. "What was that all about?"

"Rite of passage," I said. "Secret man stuff."

Leah laughed. "You men!"

I went back to say goodnight to Jeffers while Leah was in the bathroom. His eyes were closed, but there was no sign of anything going on under his eyelids. He reminded me a little of E.T. with a touch of the Dalai Lama. I leaned over the bars on the bed and kissed him on the forehead, then the lips. I wanted these kisses for the days when memory would be all that was left.

"I'll never wash my lips again." He had one eye open and it sparkled. "Oh, Duke," he stage-sighed.

"Fuck you," I warned, "else I'll tell you a story about being buried alive."

"I just had a dream about going to Madame Tussauds in Niagara Falls. Gramps, Sue, Leah, and Tara, you were all made of wax. I hugged each of you until you began to melt. If I hadn't woken up when I did, you'd all have turned into puddles."

"Calling Dr. Phil, calling Dr. Phil," I said.

"What comes next?" he asked, the place where he should have had eyebrows rising higher on his forehead. "Who's going to know this puddle was my family, Duke? It's up to you from now on."

There's a story where Tara finally arrived by caesarian after eighteen hours of labour, while Jeffers died alone very early the next morning; by the time I got to him, he was cold. But that's not the story I'm going to remember. In my version, Tara entered the world at the exact same moment as Jeffers left it, and somehow I managed to be in two places at the same time. Both of them felt solid in my arms, yet made of air. I held them so long that when I let them go, my elbows could hardly straighten.

THE SNOWBALL FAIRY

The invitation was gaudy, even for Dixie, who loved to put as many colours into an outfit or a meal as she could scrounge. Their presence was requested at Hal's seventy-fifth birthday. It was to be a weekend event at Hal and Dixie's winterized cottage on Rice Lake in the Kawarthas.

David was the first of the Beamish brothers to say yes to the invitation—now neither Stephen nor Chris could pretend that their invitations had gotten lost in the mail. The three of them usually stuck together in their dealings with the old bastard. It gave them a sense of continuity and belonging to ignore him whenever a family function came up, a cousin's wedding or uncle's funeral. But this particular upcoming event had given David a creepy feeling that this might be their father's last birthday, and so he had gone ahead and said yes before giving his two brothers a chance to weigh in.

As children, the Beamish brothers craved Hal's attentions. They'd wasted the first ten years of their lives thinking that good behaviour might win him over. This, of course, made it impossible for the brothers to be close to one another, each knowing that the mysterious kingdom of their father's love and approval could only contain one of them at a time. Even though they each eventually came to see that Hal was a cold, cruel fish and banded together once they shared this common disillusionment, they couldn't quite forgive one another for the psychotic years of vying to be the favourite son.

It was hard to describe Hal's distance to anyone outside the family. He had never laid a finger on any of the three boys. No one could remember a scrap of criticism coming from his lips, nor the tiniest compliment. *Complacent* was Chris's word for him, but Stephen, the eldest, preferred *apathetic*. David would snort when they had these conversations, saying, "There's next to nothing. And then there's Dad."

Their mother, Jane, had always made excuses for her husband's indifference until that day in March, less than a month from their twenty-first anniversary, when he pushed his chair back from the breakfast table and announced that he'd fallen in love with someone else. An hour later, the back seat and trunk of his car were filled with suitcases and cardboard boxes of sci-fi classics that no one had ever actually seen him read. He didn't say a thing to his sons—Stephen was about to turn eighteen, Chris sixteen, and David well on his way to twelve. The three boys were lined up in the front hall when he left; surely their combined anger and confusion should have been powerful enough to burn a hole through the back of Hal's head.

Stephen's mouth tasted like someone else's bile. He thought he was going to cry, but he managed to swallow. So did Chris and David. Their Adam's apples rose in their throats and then dropped back down again. Hal quietly drove away, leaving Jane so deep in shock that the boys could hardly detect her breathing. She would have gone to bed and stayed there had her sons not taken turns making sure she got up every morning, setting modest but concrete expectations for various times of the day. She was a strong, proud woman and hated to reveal what a terrible blow this had been.

Hal wasn't a cad or a womanizer; in fact, he swore that meeting Dixie Caswell was like being hit by lightning, a freak accident that had changed his life. It wasn't the betrayal that the boys couldn't get their heads around, but the fact that their father was finally confessing to having feelings at all.

What they hated about Hal was the ability he had to make them dislike themselves. If one of the boys got in his way, he'd find a route around him. The energy it took for him to keep to himself was elaborate and creative. Sometimes Stephen would think he had his father cornered, like the time he stole the car keys and brought the vehicle back with a gash of peeled paint across the entire driver's door, but Hal just asked Jane to call the insurance broker and then got on with his day. Punishment would have meant that some hope had been breached, some damage done to his trust. But Hal truly didn't care about either his car or his sons. Nothing they could do would ever make a dent.

They tried a variety of ploys over the years, including alcohol abuse, vandalism, and academic disappointments. Chris brought a boyfriend home one night when he was in grade ten, just a few months before Hal left for Dixie-land, and proceeded to have what sounded like stage sex with the door wide open. It was Jane who slipped out of the master bedroom and closed the door with barely a click. Hal never said a thing about this or any other violation. And the boys never truly lost control because they couldn't bear to hurt their mother. They knew that she was as lonely as they were and needed them to give her a sense of well-being and accomplishment.

And now, twenty-five years later, Hal Beamish was possibly dying, at least according to the tone of Dixie's birthday invitation. Their mother had mentioned his failing health a couple of times over the last several months, but Stephen wasn't one to give in to regrets at the first sign of trouble. As CFO of a small town an hour north of Toronto, he esteemed every penny and was able to return home in the evenings with his small reservoir of carefulness and appreciation intact. His first marriage had been a shipwreck from start to finish; he'd married a woman who was very similar to his father, although he'd never actually said that out loud to anyone.

Chris mumbled something about narcissism over the phone to Stephen one night after they'd received the invitations, but the truth was their father had no need of the spotlight. He didn't crave attention so much as freedom. What could a man like Hal have to say about dying? He seemed as disinterested in himself as he was in his family, although he seemed to appreciate Dixie's ebullience and sometimes appeared to get pleasure from her capacity to be tickled by just about anything.

Stephen's second wife, Molly, a family-law attorney, was a great believer in facing the truth, especially when there might be money involved somewhere down the line. If he'd tried to wriggle out of this, Molly would have given him that what-a-disappointment look that made her upper lip wrinkle unpleasantly. She also invariably would have brought their son, Ryan, into the equation, saying how important it was for him to experience his family's dynamics. He didn't appear to be bothered by Hal's lack of involvement; in fact he sometimes referred to him as Grandpa Zombie. So the party was a go, all three brothers attending, as well as Jane and her second husband, Ed, another quiet man, but one capable at least of putting a sentence together, if given a chance.

Dixie emailed everyone to say that Hal was delighted. Dixie was a liar, but so sweet and invested in her lies that Stephen, for a fraction of a sentence, found himself imagining his father's whole face creased in a big smile.

Stephen claimed he was thinking about the new archival software at work when he almost hit a raccoon on Highway 7 just east of Port Perry, but he could tell by Molly's tone of voice that she didn't buy it, that she knew he was imagining the weekend frame by frame like one of those graphic novels drawn in India ink to create a deep, dark world where the unconscious kept popping to the surface.

"Pull over," she said. "I'm driving the rest of the way."

Ryan grumbled from the back seat, his face buried in a *Best of the Transformers* anthology. He hated any trip that lasted longer than the distance between home and his drum teacher's house. Changing drivers was adding at least sixty seconds to their journey, even though Stephen did his best to hurry.

The daze that almost killed the fat-bellied raccoon was caused by a rather simple dilemma: Dixie had asked him, as the eldest, to say a few words while Hal was cutting his birthday cake. Several years back, Stephen had taken a Toastmaster's course on how to dazzle a crowd with both content and delivery. But what could he say about Hal that didn't sound contentious? Would he refer to him as Hal? He certainly wouldn't call him Dad or Father.

"Did you see that?" Molly said. She was tapping him on the knee.

"See what?" he asked, scratching the spot she'd just touched.

"Another raccoon, but I braked so gently you didn't even realize I was doing it." She gave him a quick glance. Her face was beaming.

"Whoo-hoo," Ryan teased, not bothering to lift his nose from his book.

"Are you up for this?" she asked. Stephen thought she was responding to Ryan, challenging his sarcasm. Personally, he loved it when Ryan tried to make either of them feel foolish. It took a confident kid to be able to admit to himself that his parents were buffoons every now and then.

"So, are you?" Molly continued, jabbing the same spot on Stephen's knee. "This weekend. Are you going to be okay?" She dropped her speed by a few kilometres, enough for Ryan to sigh crankily. "It's hard enough to face a parent's death, but with so many unresolved issues ..." she trailed off, cupping his knee with her right palm.

Stephen felt strangely unsafe with Molly having only one hand on the steering wheel. He tried to shift his knee toward the driver's seat, but she only tightened the pressure. "I'm okay," he said. "I don't think he's going to literally die this weekend." For a split second, he imagined his father laid out on his bed, his skin waxy.

"Grandpa Zombie might die when we're there?" Ryan asked, sounding horrified and excited at the same time.

"God, no," Molly said, pinching Stephen's knee.

But then he saw him dead again: sprawled across the multicoloured living-room rag rug, his neck bent at an impossible angle. Then another flash, slumped over at the dining-room table, his face crushed into a purple and turquoise placemat.

"Ouch," Stephen said, a delayed reaction to the pinch.

The long driveway to Hal and Dixie's split-level log cabin was full of potholes, and the car tossed from side to side causing Stephen to bite his lower lip so hard that his mouth was soon flooded with the taste of blood. Ryan was already out of the back seat before the car had come to a full stop. Molly yelled at no one, then yelled again.

From the look of things—a sea-green Acura with three of its four doors open and a couple of suitcases sitting on the gravel—Chris had arrived only a few minutes earlier. In fact, he was standing beside the car, hands on hips, staring up at the house as if it were a mountain he was expected to climb. Just looking at Chris always calmed Stephen down. He and Chris could be twins: both pale yet rugged looking, hair the colour of muddy water, strong jaws, with dozens of crinkles around their eyes that gave them permanent squints. They took after their mother, right down to the span of her nostrils.

David was a different story. He was often described as looking single. He appeared at the front door, more than a little unkempt, taller than Chris and Stephen by a good six inches, and burly where they were sloped. He had Hal's darker, curlier hair and wide-spaced eyes.

There was another man standing between Chris and the car: Chris's new significant other. Stephen could kick himself for feeling the same jealousy he'd experienced over all of Chris's partners, father figures who were so smitten with Chris that they treated him like an adored only son.

"Chris," he called out. Chris turned toward him, threw his arms open, and then walked the several yards between them, folding those arms into a hug. He felt thinner to Stephen, and just a tad taller. Chris had always been a bit of a shape shifter.

"Dude," he said into Stephen's ear, "what the hell are we doing here?" They both laughed, and Chris clung to the hug. It was David who finally separated them, throwing one of his rambling arms around each and squeezing them hard. "Shoot me dead," he said. "If it isn't the Beamish brothers come to comfort their dying father."

"How is he?" Stephen asked, squirming to not feel quite so small in David's grip.

"When you hold a mirror up to his nose, he seems to still be breathing," David quipped.

"Does he look sick?"

"He looks like it wouldn't matter if he was sick. Same as always."

Another car came rocking up the driveway, pulling in behind Stephen, blocking him in. Their mother filled the passenger seat quite nicely, though Ed could hardly see over the steering wheel. What must it be like to feel yourself shrinking? Stephen wondered. He kissed his mother on both cheeks, then pumped Ed's hand gently.

"Looks like we're all here," Jane announced after collecting more kisses. She'd grown handsomer over the years with her thick white hair fiercely swept back and a new ruddiness to her cheeks.

Chris introduced Michael to Stephen and Molly, and then pointed in the direction of Ryan, who was already down at the shore, leaping alongside Dixie's black French poodle. Apparently, David had bumped into Chris and Michael walking the boardwalk a few Sundays ago, and Jane and Ed had already had them over for lunch sometime last month. Stephen couldn't help feeling a little left out.

Michael was closer to Chris's age than the men Chris usually got involved with, although both his hair and moustache were gunmetal grey, and there were fine lines on his neck.

The screen door clapped behind them. Dixie had likely been holding back until the Beamish family had had time to pull themselves together into a supportive whole. "Yoo hoo," she warbled. She was wearing something in several shades of orange. Turning back toward the closed door, she repeated herself. "Yoo hoo, Hal, they're here."

Stephen felt that everyone around him was holding their breath. Chris was resting his hand on the small of Michael's back. Even David, the great galoot, was completely still.

The door opened with a painful creak, and then both Hal and his shadow emerged from the house at the same time. He looked over everyone's heads, a connoisseur of empty space. No one jumped into the air to get his attention. No one checked the sky above them.

Jane was the first to break the silence. "Hello, Hal." Her voice reminded Stephen of a hammer coming down on a crooked nail.

"Hello, Jane," he responded, bird-like.

Stephen suddenly found himself in need of a deep breath. He opened his mouth and took a big one that was so shockingly loud that everyone came to life around him, retrieving their luggage, slamming car doors, moving slowly in the direction of the house.

The Beamish way of dealing with social awkwardness was to pay more attention to the things in a room rather than the people. Stephen found himself looking at the postcards and clippings stuck to the fridge door with magnets: a possible new cure for arthritis, a picture of Tuscany at dawn, a Modigliani reproduction of a woman lying bum-up on a cranberry-coloured settee. When he was finished browsing, he opened his gaze to the whole kitchen and saw Chris eyeing glass canisters on the counter filled with various kinds of pastas and beans. David was on the other side of the counter, rifling through a pink wicker basket of teas. Even his mother was participating, studying a row of purple glassware on the windowsill above the sink.

Dixie had planted herself in the centre of the room and was talking non-stop to Molly, who just looked stunned. Stephen tuned in and out; none of it seemed to be about his father. She was mentioning hair a lot, which made Stephen notice how black it was: an artificial black with an undertone of indigo. It was also the stillest head of hair Stephen had ever seen. No matter what she was doing with her head, her hair didn't move a bit.

He could also hear voices coming from the dining room. The entire first floor of the log cabin was open concept, but carved into different spaces by various pieces of furniture. He left his post at the fridge and took a few steps over to a chopping block that had built-in drawers underneath it. Michael was leaning against one of the cherry wood dining-room chairs, telling Hal a story about a bullying crisis at the East York high school where he taught grade-ten chemistry. Hadn't Chris told him that their father wasn't a listener?

Only Hal's profile was visible, but Stephen could see Michael straight on. He was a pretty man, both boyish and girlish at the same time. But he was no match for Hal's infamous lack of curiosity or empathy. The more Stephen heard, the more it became clear that Michael was rather full of himself. He was like Dixie without the purple. Blah, blah, blah.

Michael went so far as to ask a personal question: "Were you ever bullied as a kid?" It wasn't unheard of for Hal to respond to an objective question, but it always fell short of an opinion, just a statement of fact. He never responded to a question with a question of his own. His expertise was in ending conversations.

"Once," he answered Michael. Exactly what Stephen expected: the suggestion of more, but on the slammed side of the door, over and out. But this time, he continued. "A girl threw a snowball at me. Grade seven. Quite the shiner."

"Was she the bully?" Michael asked.

"No." Another door slammed. Stephen felt relieved. He was already overwhelmed by the snowball and the shiner. But then Hal went on. "I cried. Couldn't help myself. I just blubbered. No more than a second or two." He leaned a little closer to Michael who, in turn, leaned a little closer to him. "A guy named Chuck Ingram. He called me 'The Snowball Fairy' for the next three months."

"What did you do?"

It was probably Michael's ignorance of Hal's infamous detachment that had disarmed the old man to such a degree. Michael was treating him like any ordinary Joe. And Hal, a dying man, was lapping it up.

"I finally socked him in the face," he said, his voice slowing down. "and then *he* started crying.

The conversation ended there. Michael said something about the cycle being broken, but Hal had already turned away, his gaze just missing Stephen by a fraction of an inch. He then physically moved away, around the far end of the dining-room table, the long way back to the kitchen, where he stopped at the fridge door and, after staring at it for close to a minute, straightened a few of the postcards and clippings, most likely the ones that Stephen had touched.

Stephen's heart was beating so fast, he couldn't synchronize it with his breathing. The Snowball Fairy. He longed to walk over to the old man, bend down, and repeat those words until Hal's whole face blossomed into a bruise. But then he couldn't stop himself from imagining throwing his arms around his humiliated father. He came close to bursting into tears himself, right there in the kitchen by the chopping block, with everyone around. He had to tense every muscle in his body in order to regain control, the way he had when he'd almost hit the raccoon that morning. The muscles in his legs were especially sore. It took as much strength to stop an errant teardrop as it did to stop a killer car.

As the light from the south-facing bank of windows in the living room began to sweeten and thin, Stephen felt a restlessness that started in his toes; he made balls of them inside his sneakers. Molly had gone for a "freshen up," and Ryan was sequestered at the dining-room table, attached to his usual pair of earphones, the poodle spread out at his feet. David and Dixie were both in the laundry room on the other side of the kitchen, fiddling with the fluorescent lights; according to Dixie, they flashed so relentlessly that she got a migraine every time she tried to do a wash. Chris and Michael had pushed each other down the hall and into their bedroom, giggling like pre-pubescent boys. And Ed and Hal were in separate corners of the family room, watching a golf tournament from Atlanta. That left only his mother, who he at first figured had gone for a nap.

Stephen had forgotten the intensity brought on by being in his father's presence. Someone had to internalize all the emotions Hal discarded. After ten minutes in his vicinity, Stephen's quibbles started turning into sorrows, his frustrations, failures.

He was at the point of fantasizing about his fist shattering one of the glass patio windows, when he noticed something stirring down at the dock. At first, he thought it was a heron, but then he made out the shape of his mother. In the time it took for him to slip into his denim jacket, sneak through the back door opposite the family room, and stride down the hill to the lake, Jane had positioned herself crouched into a ball at the end of the dock, arms around her legs, peering down into the slate grey water.

When she felt him step down onto the dock, she turned her torso around. She hadn't been staring after all, but crying. Her pale face had rivulets running between her eyes and upper lip. One foot slipped and dropped into the water, but she managed to finagle herself into a full standing position. She was a little out of breath when she finally spoke.

"I didn't know it was you," she said.

Stephen shrugged. He couldn't stop staring at the tears. He wanted to wipe them away, but was afraid he'd be too rough, the way he used to be when rubbing peanut-butter-and-jam stains from Ryan's mouth.

"I was afraid you were him," she continued, patting the pockets of her blue-checked slacks for Kleenex.

"What's to be afraid of?" Stephen asked.

"I'm not *afraid* afraid," his mother corrected. "I just wanted to be alone."

"But you said the word *afraid*," Stephen persisted. He could feel his gaze slightly off kilter. He wasn't really making eye contact with her.

"It was a mistake," his mother said, frowning.

"What?" Stephen pestered. "The word or the emotion?"

Jane held her hand up in the air. "Stop," she said. "I was afraid Ed would catch me crying and think I was crying over Hal." She frowned even deeper than before. "Are you happy now?"

"So you're not afraid of Hal seeing you cry?"

She sniffed magnificently, holding her head high before continuing. "I couldn't care less about Hal."

Stephen didn't know what to say. He longed to echo her that he didn't care either, but he knew this wasn't true. "Don't you care that he might be dying?"

"Of course I care," she said, eyes bulging just a little. "But not because he's Hal."

"I don't think that even makes sense," Stephen said.

But she'd had enough. Her tears were gone, just faint trickle marks on both sides of her nose. She patted him on the bum as she squeezed past, starting back on the path up to the cottage. "It isn't always a case of one thing over another," she said. "You're still thinking like a child."

Stephen felt a flash of anger so powerful that he stomped both feet. "Okay, *Mommy*," he exclaimed. Jane didn't turn around, but he knew that she was definitely frowning.

By the time Stephen had joined everyone at the full dining-room table, he had decided that the bully story his father had shared with Michael had been a ruse. Michael had cornered him, and so he'd told a tall tale to get away. There was no such person as The Snowball Fairy. There was barely someone named Hal.

They all dug into the meal with what appeared to be real appetites, leaving the conversation up to Dixie and Michael, with the occasional sideline courtesy of Ed. Ed had a habit of clearing his throat quite loudly and then escalating until it sounded like he was choking. When everyone would turn to him, he'd open his mouth, lick his bottom lip, lizard-like, and spout an opinion or share an anecdote. Although Ed was the perfect husband for Jane, attentive and reliable, Stephen couldn't say that he actually liked him. There was something slithery about him, something weedy.

Stephen didn't have a clue what they were talking about. He heard words like "health care," "cracks in the marble," and "the new Clooney girl," but couldn't put them together into anything resembling a narrative. He wished he could cross-examine Hal's suspicious confession about being bullied as a child. He pictured his father's cheeks glowing like the fake coals in Jane and Ed's rec-room electric fireplace. Embarrassment might not have been top of Stephen's wish list, but it would be a step in the right direction, a bona-fide emotion.

But dinner passed without Stephen joining in, the royal-blue tablecloth a field of crumbs and stains. Dixie, Jane, and Michael were busy chatting amongst themselves. David appeared to be trying to join in, but missing his cue every time. Chris rolled his eyes at him, which Stephen didn't know how to interpret. And Molly seemed totally unavailable, intent on Ryan's manners more than anything else.

Suddenly, those closest to the kitchen were belting out an unrehearsed "Happy Birthday." The cake, wedding white with a ring of plump crimson strawberries around it, looked like it could easily become a third-degree blaze. Michael was carrying it, holding it out from his body. Ryan's and Molly's voices joined in on the second line of the song. Knowing that his noncooperation would stand out, Stephen clambered onboard with *Happy Birthday dear* ..., unable to call his father anything, jumping back in on the last line, his voice as hollow as singing into an empty can.

The cake sat in front of Hal, the candle flames growing wider and taller at the same time. There was a wall of smoke between Stephen and his father that Stephen stared into, thinking of the gas jets in a crematorium, how hot it would have to get to burn through bone. Hal blew every single candle out. Stephen felt a bit overwhelmed by the smell of wax and strawberries. The smoke hung on until Ryan and Molly were both coughing. Dixie was leaning over Hal's shoulder, helping him to slice the cake into equal portions. Everyone deserved their share of icing. A strawberry each. The piece that arrived in front of Stephen still had a charred candle stuck in it.

He couldn't concentrate on the speech that followed. Dixie did all the talking, so once again Stephen veered in and out of attention, registering words like "stage two," "gamma rays," and "the odds are." He could tell by the elevation of various voices and then the lower rumble in response that questions and answers were in full swing. Grinding his teeth and clenching his fingers into fists didn't help much in bringing him back to the present moment. He tried looking at his father again, but Hal was wearing his usual mask.

Molly asked him something about a coworker's wife who worked out of the Odette Cancer Centre at Sunnybrook. But Stephen couldn't respond any more than he could swallow a forkful of cake. One of the strawberries had bled into the icing; it looked ugly and lethal. He tried to inhale more deeply, but couldn't get his lungs to work at all. Several people were staring at him by this time.

"Stephen, would you be willing?" Dixie asked.

Willing to do what? He didn't know what she was talking about. He couldn't admit that he hadn't been listening. That was such a Hal thing to do. He cleared his throat, said sorry, and pushed his chair back from the table.

"Stephen," he heard Molly call.

"Stephen." Either David or Chris.

"Stephen," Dixie sang.

How foreign his name sounded, two impenetrable syllables.

Molly was so livid that she picked up a pillow in one hand and then slapped it hard three times until it flew out of her grasp and landed with a *ffftt* in the space between Stephen's side of the bed and the wall.

"Whoa," Stephen said, ducking although the pillow had already landed.

He often noticed how striking she was when she was angry. He had admitted this once, which only made her angrier. He was reducing her to physical assets and dismissing her emotional validity, according to her. But it wasn't her vulnerability that drew him in at times like these, or her dusky eyes or the curve of her naturally coral lips, but the freckles that fanned out from her nostrils toward her cheeks; they darkened when she was mad. Tiny imperfections that made the perfect parts more precious somehow.

Tonight the freckles were hives, the colour of the strawberries on Hal's cake.

"Did you expect me to make a decision for you?" She shook a finger in the air, not necessarily at him, but to call attention to the fact that there was more to come. And sure enough, "I can't answer for you. No one cares what I have to say."

"How can you think that?" Stephen asked, feeling confident that he was wearing his infamous dumb face, that Molly would point it out at any second. It would make more sense to simply ask her what answer she was referring to, but if she knew how thoroughly he'd absented himself from the dinner-table conversation, she'd be even more furious than she already was.

"Don't look at me like that," she said, right on cue.

"Like what?" Stephen played his part without missing a beat.

Despite Molly's easy access to fury, she wasn't a very good fighter. Stephen could throw her off by sticking to the script. Repetition untangled her anger, left it dangling there.

"You shouldn't have just walked out of the room," she said. "Or if you had to, you should have at least taken Ryan and me with you."

"I just wasn't thinking straight."

"David had tears in his eyes," she continued.

"David hasn't separated himself as well as I have." He remembered that it was David who okayed this weekend in the first place. It seemed only fair that he be in the most discomfort.

"Chris just looked lost," she said. She always softened in Chris's presence.

"Chris and I exchanged looks before I left."

This was the wrong thing to say. How could he relay unspoken messages to his brother and then turn around and ignore his wife?

"I was thoughtless," Stephen said.

"You were," Molly agreed. She was running out of words. "You should go find David and Chris and apologize."

"I will," Stephen promised. He wanted to ask her what exactly his father was dying of and how long he had left. But she'd get angry all over again if she knew that he hadn't even been listening.

He kissed her on the cheek. Her freckles tasted like salt and frosting.

"You should look in on Ryan," she said. Neither of them had a clue what to say to a thirteen-year-old, but agreed that being available was important.

Stephen tipped an imaginary hat, which made Molly smile. It crossed his mind that it would take some of the pressure off if he just stayed in their room with her and watched her unbutton her tailored green blouse. Just to watch would have been enough, but then he wouldn't have completed his brotherly duties. The Beamish boys had to stick together.

The log cabin was mostly dark, with an island of light in a corner of the kitchen emanating from a multicoloured Tiffany lamp and another in the family room from Ryan's laptop lying face up on the couch, the glow a pale grey like a sky that the rain has rinsed away. Ryan himself was curled up around the screen fast asleep. Stephen wasn't sure whether Ryan's breathing was the cause of a slight whirr in the room or if that was the sound of the computer. He leaned over the grey screen, careful not to fall into it, and kissed Ryan on the forehead. He tasted much less salty than his mother. Stephen hadn't kissed his son since he'd entered the adolescent years. There was a tacit agreement between the two of them: love didn't have to be demonstrated in order to exist. But tonight felt different, the grey light and all.

Should he knock on Chris's door, or should he stop by David's room first? But if David had really been crying, he might be dealing with a heap of embarrassment and not be in the mood to talk. He should leave David for the morning.

There was a crack of light at the bottom of Chris's bedroom door. Stephen tried not to stand too close in case he might cast a shadow through the crack. He leaned his torso toward the surface of the door and then laid his ear against it. He couldn't hear a sound and so tapped very lightly on the solid wood. It sounded much louder than he'd expected, creating an echo in the hallway.

He could hear a shuffling within, followed by a few seconds of re-ignited quiet, then the door opened about a quarter of its width. Chris was standing there in white pajama bottoms, his muscled chest bare and shadowy. Across the room, Michael appeared to be fast asleep, one ankle stretched clear of the sheet, its black hairs making it look extraordinarily naked.

Chris opened the door another quarter and slipped through it to join Stephen in the hall. He stood so close that Stephen could smell his breath: red wine, for sure, and maybe Michael's cologne. Or was it Dixie's perfume?

"What's up?" Chris whispered.

"Just wanted to apologize," Stephen whispered back.

"Not to worry," Chris assured him. "I didn't hang around much longer."

"What a night."

"You can say that again," Chris said, his arm brushing against Stephen's. "It came from out of nowhere."

Stephen didn't know what else to say, but hoped "Poor old bastard" might suffice.

"I'm beat," Chris said. "We'll talk options in the morning." He had long been in the habit of having the last word, so Stephen instantly backed away, reached out, and patted him on what happened to be his elbow.

"Sleep tight," he said, watching the door swing open again and Chris in his white pajama bottoms and bare chest disappear into the low-lit room like a tall, lean ghost.

Stephen stayed put until his eyes recovered from the light and could navigate the darkness again. He then tiptoed back to his room. Not a peep coming from Molly's side of the bed. He tripped across the pillow that she'd thrown when they were arguing and landed on the bed with a thud. He wondered whether Hal would have derived any pleasure from watching his oldest son take a tumble. No, neither pleasure nor sympathy. Who would make him feel small when Hal was dead?

The last thought, and now the first. Stephen woke up the only person in the cabin not knowing Hal's diagnosis. How much time did he have? Would it be painful? What was it they'd asked of him? Was Stephen expected to be one of the caregivers? Could dying really supersede everything else, cleanse the muddied windows, bury the tarnished silverware?

Opening his eyes to a sunlight too bright to let any bad feelings take root, he turned to what he hoped would be Molly, fresh and honey-like. But there was only an imprint of her body in the sheets like a snow angel. She had probably already left for a run. She ran nearly every day on Concession 2, not far from their home. There must be all sorts of possible routes here in cottage country.

Stephen rolled to the edge of the bed and dropped his feet to the cool pine floor. He stood and stretched his belly away. Pulling on a pair of soft black jeans and a mint-green t-shirt, he glanced at himself in the mirror. Forty-three wasn't nearly as old as he'd expected it to be. Seventy-five probably had its surprises. What did Hal think when he saw his own reflection?

He remembered being about eleven or twelve and becoming obsessed with razors. His mother gave him a big stainless steel one with the blade removed and his own can of shaving foam. Eventually, a hair or two actually sprouted, and she bought him a smaller, but intact model. He got good at the sweep of it, and one Sunday morning took it into the bathroom where his father was shaving with his electric Gillette and started lathering up. He then turned the hot water on full blast and began to wield his wrist. His father ducked the splashes and didn't complain. Stephen did an excellent job, dipping his chin all the way down his neck into the full sink to wash away the suds.

"Pretty good, eh?" he'd said, lowering his voice to an approximation of Hal's baritone.

Hal unplugged his razor, then blew the hairs into the pink tin garbage can. "Pretty good, eh?" he said when he'd straightened up.

Stephen had laughed at the time, but on the way to school, started wondering whether his father had been making fun of him. Or maybe he was acknowledging in his quiet way that Stephen was a man now and would finally understand the subtle tones and signals that men used to communicate with one another and save their energies for more important things.

Without shaving this morning, Stephen headed off to the kitchen in his bare feet. Hal and Jane were sitting facing each other, their knees touching, while David leaned back against the counter with a rainbow-coloured mug in one hand, the other hand stuffed in his pocket. He looked beefy, but in a babyish way; there was something unmolded about David, even at thirty-seven.

"Morning," Stephen said, wondering whether he should head straight for the glossy Keurig or stop and acknowledge his parents first. He decided on the latter, coming up behind his mother and bending over to kiss her on the scalp. He then nodded in his father's direction and was surprised by Hal's eye contact.

He was ready to move on to the counter and pour himself a coffee when

David stuck his arm out and said, "What do you think you're doing?"

Stephen halted, trying to look surprised. He was, in fact, momentarily taken aback, but instantly realized that he should have knocked on David's door last night.

"Hey," Stephen said, keeping his voice steady and calm. "How about we take a walk down to the dock?"

David shifted himself so that he was just skimming the kitchen counter. His weight was back on his feet. "I'm not going anywhere with you," he muttered.

"I'm sorry." Stephen jumped right in. He sounded apologetic, but if David had made a move to hit him, Stephen would have met his fist more than halfway. "I'm really, really sorry."

David's chin was trembling. Stephen knew that there'd be tears. He could handle that. He considered throwing his arms around his brother, not waiting for David to actually break down. But there was the sudden sound of a chair being pushed too far beneath the table. When Stephen turned, he saw his father standing, gripping the back of the chair he'd been sitting on, his knuckles white.

"You traitor," he sputtered. "Your own flesh and blood can't even count on you."

"Count on me?" Stephen asked. "I didn't think you knew I was on the planet."

"You'll be safe and sound here on the planet long after I'm dead and gone."

Stephen glanced at David and could see that an out-and-out argument would only widen the gap between him and his brother. David was his only responsibility. "I'm sorry," he said.

Hal shook his head and made a tsking sound with his tongue. "You couldn't spare me five measly minutes last night, let alone a kidney."

"Whose kidney?" Stephen asked.

"I know we've had our problems, but Dad's right, this is flesh and blood," David said.

"You've made it clear that it won't be yours," Hal said. Stephen wouldn't have been shocked if Hal had spit after this, but he just eased himself back onto his chair, his temper worn out.

David was crying now. "One of us will probably be a match."

"You need a kidney?" Stephen asked.

"Not from you," Hal said.

"So you're not dying?"

"I'm sure that's what you want."

"When did what we want ever figure into the equation?" Stephen asked. Someone in his head was blathering.

"This isn't the time to be fighting," David said.

Stephen felt his head clear. He was a possible donor. This information made him feel incredibly powerful. He had something that his father wanted.

"I'd rather die than have a piece of you inside me." Hal spoke up again in sulking tones. For a moment, he looked like a man who might be nicknamed The Snowball Fairy.

No one seemed to remember that Jane was still in the room. Stephen was shocked to hear her voice. "Shut up, the both of you," she said. "You're like two peas in a pod. You don't see anyone but yourselves."

Stephen felt that all his anger and resentment was in danger of caving in, being crushed. How could his mother even think that? "I'm not at all like him," Stephen shouted back.

He tried not to make leaving in a hurry look like running away, but from Molly's panting and Ryan's dishevelment, it was clear they were being rushed. Hal was nowhere in sight, but Dixie had made a valiant attempt to be hospitable right up to the last second in a floor-length, mauve satin dressing gown, her hair held in place by several tortoiseshell clips. She fiddled with things close at hand, working hard to keep her smile pliable.

Chris and Michael had just woken up. Stephen had knocked loudly at their door and shouted through the wood, "We're heading out." Minutes later, they appeared in the front hall, Chris rubbing his eyes, Michael in mid-yawn. David stood near them, his neck bent into some sort of medieval shame or grief. Stephen couldn't bear looking at him. None of this was David's fault; David would always be the baby.

Jane did her best to apologize without actually saying anything. She kissed both Molly and Ryan and then blew one in Stephen's direction.

"Let me know the doctor's name, and I'll arrange to have myself tested," Stephen said. "*Mi casa, su casa*," he added, surprising himself at how flip this sounded. "If I'm a match, then the kidney is his."

"Me too," David said, lifting his chin.

"Yeah," Chris said, stifling a yawn.

Molly headed for the driver's side, but Stephen gently shoulder-bunted her and slid in behind the wheel. He pressed down on the gas pedal a bit too hard and bits and pieces of gravel flew out from beneath all four tires. Dixie stepped clear of the driveway, Jane just behind her, guiding her toward the porch. Everyone safe and sound.

Stephen didn't realize how fast he was driving until he heard the squeal of rubber as he turned from the dirt road to pavement. Molly was sitting thin-lipped beside him, refusing to say a word. Stephen knew that he was being reckless. He could feel an empty pit inside him where they'd lift out his kidney kicking and screaming.

The speed wasn't helping; he was growing more anxious with every kilometre. What he needed to do was talk, not about the human sacrifice he might soon become and certainly not about the conversation he'd had with his mother and father less than an hour ago. The Snowball Fairy story was perfect. "Listen to this, guys," he said, pressing on the gas even harder. "You'll never believe it."

He wasn't sure whether the sound coming from the back seat was a guffaw or a gasp. He turned his neck around to look and by the time he'd managed to turn forward again, Molly was definitely sucking a huge amount of air into her lungs. He didn't have the time to even touch the brake. The racoon, or at least he thought it was a coon, thumped against metal, flew up into the air with all four feet looking perfectly balanced like an acrobat's, then landed on the side of the road with another, louder thump. Stephen could see blood when he looked through the rearview mirror.

"Stop, stop, stop!" Molly was yelling with her eyes closed.

"I'm sorry," he said, picking up the rhythm of responsibility again. He'd repeat it like a mantra if that was what it took to make it real. But he wouldn't stop. He couldn't do anything for a dead raccoon. He couldn't save anyone's life today. All he could manage at the moment was to accumulate distance; any direction would do, as long as it took him far, far away.

BAD
BOYS

Before Frances was born, before she could tell her own story, her father was caught robbing a bank in a small Ontario town called Hastings, famous for its bridge spanning a tiny waterfall, part of the Trent River system. He was sentenced to twelve years because he had brandished a weapon, even though it turned out to be just a starter pistol. Her mother said that he had also embezzled funds from several charities and community programs. Apparently, he could smooth talk his way into anything.

"Your father was a classic bad boy," her mother said in a voice low enough that her new husband, Frances's stepfather, wouldn't hear and feel insufficient. "Charismatic as all get out. He could have been a game-show host or a Rolls-Royce salesman." Her eyes got overcast at this point, and she added, "God, he looked handsome in his mug shot."

The worst, or best, part of the story, depending on your preferences, was that he died in prison when Frances was still a toddler. The official story was an embolism, but there was also talk of a foiled escape with a knife made from a margarine container, a rusty paperclip, and some butcher's string. She would lie awake nights, imagining her father scaling the prison walls, his baby-blue eyes lit with a wicked glow.

Her mother remarried when Frances was five, and the family moved from Etobicoke to the mostly rural community of Sydenham. Once Frances finished high school, she worked as a security guard at Kingston's Canada's Penitentiary Museum. Her dream had been to be a prison guard at the infamous Kingston Pen where her father had been incarcerated. The sound of metal doors sliding closed with a clang made her heart gallop. But the prison had shut down when she was barely an adolescent. To her, the death of the prison was nearly as sad as the death of her father.

Her favourite exhibit was the one devoted to prison escapes, of which there were twenty-six attempts between 1835 and when it closed in 2013. Two of them stood out from the others for their sheer bravado. In 1923, inmate Norman "Red" Ryan, dubbed the Jesse James of Canada, set fire to a shed, then when everyone was busy tending to the flames, used a ladder to scale the wall, impaling a pursuing guard with a pitchfork and then stealing a car. He managed to lay low for nearly a year, though his luck finally ran out in a Minneapolis post office.

Then in 1999, Tyrone Williams "Ty" Conn, a bank robber, also used a ladder along with a homemade grappling hook and a scattering of cayenne pepper to prevent dogs from following his scent. He was found in a Toronto apartment two weeks later and committed suicide while on the phone with a CBC producer.

Sometimes Frances daydreamed about being one of the guards whose job it was to stop these legendary criminals from escaping. At other times, she pretended to be the radio producer, Theresa Burke, urging Ty to surrender, promising to visit him and do all she could to help him reform. Mostly though, she'd think about her father. "I'll be waiting for you outside the main gates," she'd say out loud the way other girls swore oaths to Justin Bieber or One Direction. Bad boys shining in the dark, desperately in need of transformation.

Frances had moved to Toronto, found a basement apartment a few blocks north of the Scarborough Bluffs, and started a one-year diploma course in law enforcement at Herzing College. She was interning at the Toronto East Detention Centre, often referred to as simply The East, a maximum security remand facility at Eglinton and Birchmount. Wednesdays through Fridays, she job shadowed two different correctional officers, one of whom, Dennis, was a bit of a flash fire, while the other, Hugo, was a dull fellow who tried hard to pass himself off as mysterious. She spent most of her time listening to Dennis blab about his plans to apply for a desk job one of these days and to Hugo, who purposely mispronounced the inmates' names in a juvenile attempt at humiliation. She much preferred cafeteria duty, where she was assigned a corner all by herself and could get an overview of the prisoners and, at the same time, study some of the small, intoxicating details that made one bad boy stand out from another, like how low down on the handle one man's fingers would grip a spoon or the way another guy sipped his tea, holding it in his mouth for ten seconds or so before swallowing. She recognized herself in some of these quirks, which made her feel a shiver of her father's presence.

There weren't many female guards, status quo for a male facility, but the few that Frances came across seemed more competent than either Dennis or Hugo. Frances was bigger than most. She had always had a stocky build, again a genetic gift from her father, and at five foot ten appeared to loom. But she saw the female guards using their minds much more than their brawn. The boundaries were more clearly set than with the male officers. The East wasn't quite Kingston Pen, but it might eventually create its own lore, and Frances was determined to be a part of that.

Her duty of choice was Friday afternoons in the visiting centre, one until three thirty. Frances could easily tell the girlfriends apart from the wives. The girlfriends dressed provocatively, yet held themselves at a distance. The wives were all over their men, taking as much territory as they could get. Male visitors were rare, mainly fathers with crushed-in faces or sons who looked stunned that The East was a prison rather than a gas station or billiard hall.

Her first week there, Frances noticed a tall, lanky guy with long black hair, probably in his late thirties, visiting a short, muscle-bound fellow around the same age. The visitor was visibly nervous, chewing on his thumb nail, hunching in close every time he spoke to the prisoner. Frances never expected to see him again. She felt a little sorry about this. There was something sorrowful about his blue eyes.

She tracked down the identity of the muscle man, last name Zimmer, and saw that he was charged with impaired driving and involuntary manslaughter, with a record of two other arrests for drunk driving. Zimmer was clearly more stupid than bad.

Next week the tall, nervous guy was back, his hair slicked like sealskin. Zimmer was trying to make an important point, pounding lightly on the table. The visitor seemed even more nervous than the first time, eyes darting around the room. His gaze included Frances, but with no more interest in her than he showed in the soft drink and snack machines. She wasn't the least bit insulted. It wasn't her looks that could snag a man like him, but her knowledge that he was fragile beneath the swagger.

She'd met a man at the museum just a few weeks before she moved to Toronto. He was there alone, but kept regaling other patrons with stories about being related to Ty Conn. Finally, a father with two boys who might have been twins complained to her.

Frances waited until the fellow was peering into the glass case housing the grappling hook, and then she glided in beside him, a quiet tête-à-tête, suggesting that he keep his excitement to himself. He snorted and stepped back from the case.

"My uncle made mincemeat of the rules," he bragged.

It just came to her a second before she said it, but she felt sure that the word would please Conn's nephew: "He was a maverick, all right."

"You can say that again," he responded, a tad less sure of himself.

"Legendary," she whispered, leaning in toward him with both shoulders.

By the time she got around to repeating her request for his cooperation, it was like they shared a secret. He left quietly after this, but Frances noticed that he was standing out on the street when she locked the front doors. Perhaps if he'd pulled the collar of his jacket up, some stance that indicated he might follow her rather than engage her right there and then, she might have tried to make something happen. But he'd been far too easy to control. She fancied a man like Conn who would put up more of a fight.

She planned to set her sights on one of the prisoners in The East, someone she could share stolen looks with, brush against in a hallway, watch as he ate, all those seductive preliminaries. Even though she only worked the day shift, she contrived staying on for a three thirty to eleven and waiting outside the showers for him to float by smelling of clean, hot skin. But The East was too busy a place for her to focus. Even the chaos of cafeteria duty soon got to be too much. A crowd of bad boys somehow depleted their individual appeal. It was hard sometimes to tell them apart.

The tall, lanky visitor stood out though. On the third Friday, he walked into the visiting room with his hair pulled back and tied with a red rubber band, and she felt something in her chest wriggle. In the few pictures she had of her father, his hair was similarly slicked back. She stared at him the entire visit. It was clear that he felt the intensity of her attention; he kept glancing at her, his cheeks flushed. She hardly blinked. By the end of visiting hours, she had burned his image into her retinas.

As her placement at The East drew to an end, Zimmer's visitor had become the high point of her week. That Friday afternoon, she was so relieved to see him that her mouth automatically spread into a wide grin. He couldn't help noticing and grinned a little in return.

His hair looked fluffy this time, as if he'd recently used conditioner. She wished that Zimmer would act up in some way so that she could intervene. She imagined that the air around the visitor smelled slightly of vanilla. Bad boys were often just a tiny bit girlish. They weren't afraid of something as simple as smelling good.

This last visit went by with a dreamlike intensity. She realized that she was gaping at times. The visitor was surrounded by a kind of energy field that reminded her of barbed wire. On her tour of the room, she actually grazed his upper arm with her elbow, and her breath cut short.

This was her last day at The East, but she already had plans for furthering the relationship. She simply showed up at the visitor's entrance the following Friday and waited for him to come out. He didn't seem to recognize her in her street clothes and walked right past her.

"Stop," she called after him. "You with the long black hair."

He halted and then slowly turned around. At first he looked worried, but that quickly changed to confused.

"Sorry," she said, apologizing for her boldness. "You might not recognize me."

"No, I know you." The muscles of his face relaxed. He looked pleased with himself for having figured her out so quickly. "What do you want?"

"I've been watching you," she said.

He stepped back a bit, a crease rippling across his forehead.

"Nothing bad," Frances explained. "I just like your hair. What's your name?"

He cocked his head to one side and licked his bottom lip before announcing, "Curtis."

"I'm Frances," she replied. "Curtis and Frances sitting in a tree, k-i-s-s-i-n-g."

For a second, she saw rage pass across his face, but then he seemed to settle for a scowl.

"I get silly when I'm nervous," she said. "How about we hunt down a Tim Horton's and get to know each other better?" She had a powerful urge to throw her arms out and hug the shit out of him, but she resisted.

He didn't say anything, but when she headed in the direction of the main road, he followed, eventually taking over the lead. They walked in silence until The East had receded. Frances kept one eye on him without twisting her neck. She liked the small circle between his bowlegs, how he rocked a bit from side to side. This space gave plenty of room for his thighs to move without swishing, a sound that Frances despised.

A few more blocks of small talk, all of it Frances's, until they came to the neighbourhood Tim's. The air smelled of cinnamon. The elderly woman behind the counter looked butch in her brown shirt and pants combo with matching baseball cap.

"The chili is good here," Frances stated. "Not specifically here, I guess, but in general."

Curtis gave her a crooked look and said, "I'm not here to eat. I don't eat with strangers."

They both ordered coffees, and Frances added two sugary donuts, one chocolate, one honey, just in case. She pulled a wad of serviettes from the dispenser and followed Curtis to a table by the window. His ass stuck out with a *boing*, what a high-school friend, referring to Billy Joel, called a shelf. Her own buttocks were long and coltish and would have to be stroked rather than grasped.

When they were both seated and he was caught up in dividing the small pile of serviettes into two, Frances took the opportunity to stare at the tanned backs of his hands, slightly darker at the knuckles and furred with fine black hairs. No matter what he did to her, how many ways he might break her heart, she would always close her eyes and remember those hands.

"You're beautiful," she said out loud.

His whole face changed colour. For a moment, he looked like he might be sick. "I've already got a girlfriend," he sputtered.

"That doesn't really matter," Frances said. She was disappointed, but knew that bad boys slept around. Unfaithfulness was one of their distinguishing features. "You're here with me now. That's what counts."

"Why me?" he asked. "Why were you watching me at The East? You're a guard, not a cop, right?"

She could see that he had secrets. "I like that you're afraid of me," she said. "You remind me a little of my dad. He was killed in a prison break."

"Your dad was a con?" he asked, crushing an empty creamer in one fist. "And now you're a guard. How weird is that?"

"What's so weird about it?" Frances bristled. "It's kind of like the family business."

Curtis snickered. "What the hell would your father have said about you being a screw?"

"It's not which side of the bars you're on that counts, but what kind of presence you leave behind." She brought out her biggest smile, hoping it might dazzle him.

He reached across the table to the plate of donuts and tore a chunk off the honeyed one. "You want to fuck me?"

"I'd like that," she said, dropping her voice to a level she hoped wasn't too mannish. "I'd also like you to steal something off this table, the coffee spoon or the mug."

His eyes popped open. "Who told you I was a thief?" he said. "I'm not a fucking thief."

Frances pushed the plate of donuts across the table with a clatter. She could see that he was on the verge of fleeing. "It was just an idea."

He took a deep breath and seemed to feel better. "Is this what you do on your day off?"

"I don't work there anymore," she replied.

He took a swig of his coffee and tried that thing with his eyes again, but this time they just looked like slits.

Frances realized that she was having fun. She could tell that Curtis was a genuine bad boy. The other guys had dropped their paranoia and meanness the minute she'd let them touch her. Before her shirt was even unbuttoned, they'd be moaning and squirming like little kids begging for attention. She reached under the table and put her hand on his knee. "What can I do for you that no one else has ever done?"

"I can tell you one thing," he said, slapping her hand away. "It's not a hand job in a fucking Tim Horton's."

"So you're a man who knows what he doesn't want," she said.

He glared at the donuts in front of him. He put the remaining three-quarters of the honey donut into his mouth. He didn't actually stuff it in; it was more that his mouth seemed to grow to make room for all that sweetness. "You're one of those girls who's got a hard-on for cons," he said, bits of donut squished against his gums. "Daddy's girl," he teased. "Sorry for bursting your bubble, darlin'. But I've never been inside."

"You just haven't got caught," she said, trying to sound wise and sexy.

"Whoa," he replied, stretching out one of his hands as if he was pushing the air away between them, creating a greater distance. "I'm not saying another word without my lawyer."

Frances couldn't help herself, she burst into laughter. Bad boys always clammed up. It was one of their attributes. They preferred to do something rather than talk about it.

"With your lawyer, that would make a threesome," she said between giggles. "Are you sure you're up to that?"

"You're sick," he said, scraping his chair back and standing up.

Frances tried to do the same, but ended up knocking over her chair, which banged into an old man's chair, causing him to spill his coffee. Curtis was the perfect good Samaritan. He helped the old man to his feet and handed him the bunch of napkins that Frances had grabbed from the dispenser. He apologized to the Tim Horton's staff who appeared with a mop.

"Can we start from scratch?" she asked while he was struggling back into his jacket. "I really like your hair. Isn't that worth a second chance?"

"Jesus," he said, sighing. "My hair, my fucking hair."

It turned out that he was up for the job of sexton at a church in the Beaches and had a meeting with the wardens in less than an hour. She almost doubled over. A sexton! She loved it, a bad boy living in a church.

"You're not going to disappear into thin air, are you?" she asked. She touched his cheek with two of her fingers. His skin felt stubbly and cold.

"I have a feeling you'd just track me down," he said.

"Can I meet you afterwards?" She could be relentless when it came to holding on to something that she wanted.

"If you're there, and I'm there," he said, dropping the rest of the sentence and walking away.

Frances stayed in the Tim Horton's for a while after Curtis left, picking at the chocolate glazed donut and sipping cold coffee. She imagined that everyone around could see that she was the daughter of a dangerous man. Let them wonder what a good-looking guy like Curtis would want with a marked girl like her.

A guy in his forties with hair the colour of a red squirrel interrupted her reverie by pretending to stumble over her feet. She grimaced, then quickly left when he tried to initiate a conversation. She could bag herself a hundred middle-aged nerds just by snapping her fingers.

She took a bus and then walked west on Queen Street East until she came to the church where Curtis was being interviewed for the sexton job. She decided to wait on the front lawn of the church, where she couldn't be missed. It was an impressive building, though a bit old and tacky: clearly, God hadn't done an upgrade in ages.

Dropping her purse into the thick spring lawn, she stretched her length out and closed her eyes, feeling the last of the evening light unclenching. She was thinking about Curtis's hands, wondering whether he would touch her as gently as her father had when she was a baby. Suddenly, she sensed a shadow and heard a throat being cleared.

It was a really old guy, not the usual masher, seventy at least. "Are you okay?" he asked.

"Why?" Frances shot back. "Am I doing something wrong?" She wished she could just hop to her feet and brush off her knees, but she was a clumsy girl.

"Not really," he said, offering a quick little smile. "I just don't find that many young women lying in my grass."

"Your grass?" she repeated.

"I like to think so," he said, his face lighting up.

It was clear to Frances that the guy liked her, but he didn't creep her out like the forty-something nerds.

"If you want the truth, I'm just borrowing it. I'm the priest here," he explained. "But I guess that everything we have in this life is on loan."

Frances thought about Curtis and her desire to have him to herself. How much easier a task it would be if she winnowed down her ambitions to just borrowing him for a while. Who knew at what point a bad boy became a sad man. Dreams aren't made to last forever.

"I appreciate you lending me your lawn," she said. "Would you care to join me?"

The old guy seemed delighted by the invitation. "You'd need a miracle to get me back on my feet."

"Don't you believe in miracles?"

"Good question," he said, running one wrinkled hand through his short-cropped white hair. "I think of them as last-chance sorts of things, after every other solution has been exhausted."

Frances thought that she'd better be ready with a miracle in case nothing else worked with Curtis, though she felt that the story of their relationship had gotten off to a good start.

"Do you think you might offer a girl like me a tiny miracle? I could do with a boost."

She was careful not to give him all of her weight; she pushed up with her right hand at the same time as he was pulling at her left. She rose like a statue, her skin white in the dusk. Just as she was about to thank him, Curtis came loping around the corner of the church. He stopped in his tracks and frowned in their direction.

"Do you know this fellow?" the priest asked.

"He's on loan to me at the moment," Frances said, realizing that the old priest was still holding her hand. She slowly disengaged their fingers. "He's almost my boyfriend."

This was, Frances tried to explain to Curtis once they were seated in the Chinese restaurant, exactly the right thing to say. Father Bryant had dropped in to meet Curtis mid-interview with the church wardens, and Curtis had gotten the feeling that the priest's first impression wasn't a positive one. But when Father Bryant discovered that Frances believed in Curtis, he seemed to cast aside his initial concerns, even going so far as to pat Curtis on the back.

"You're a shoe-in," she said.

Curtis still seemed a little spooked by Frances. She could tell that he was afraid that her power would somehow diminish his.

"We'd make a good team," she said over steaming plates of chop suey, lemon chicken, and white-on-white rice.

They walked all the way up to Kingston Road after dinner. Then they caught a bus east to Birchmount, just a block from Frances's basement apartment.

"I feel married to you," Frances said when he was undressing her like a big Christmas present. "The priest and all."

He paused mid-button and glared.

"Nothing to worry about. You're just my borrowed husband. We can get divorced later tonight, if you'd like.

Naked, he took her breath away. His ass dominated, though he had surprisingly nice biceps, and his skin tasted like salted popcorn. His cock, an average length, reminded her of a sepia portrait, someone grandfatherly. And once he got over the fact that her legs were a bit thick, like elephants' legs, he seemed to enjoy the cushiness of her belly and the giant flop of her breasts. Lucky for both of them, he was an ass man, and when he rolled her over he moaned and mumbled, "Fucking A." It was wide-awake, nothing-sentimental-about-it sex. They consumed each other the way they'd dug into the Chinese food. Nothing gourmet here. Bad boys liked big servings of ordinary things.

She wasn't the least bit surprised or disappointed when he refused to spend the night. Bad boys need to get away. They also need their routines in order not to lose sight of themselves. She lay uncovered on the bed while he dressed and then blew him an old-fashioned kiss.

"Are you going to give me your number or what?" he asked just before leaving.

She rolled off the bed and walked heavily across the room to her computer desk. She wrote down her number in tall, blocky digits on a pad of lined yellow paper. "There," she said, "you'll be able to make this out even if you go blind."

"See you soon," he said, reaching out and tugging a handful of her pubic hair. Bad boys were still primarily kids: full of beans.

Frances didn't waste a minute on expectations. Bad boys never call when you want them to. The next day was a Saturday, her day to hang around 41 Division, up at Eglinton, watching the cops come and go. There were some badass policemen. The sight of a holster made Frances giddy. On Sunday, she got up really early and took a bus and a streetcar to the Salvation Army's Gateway men's shelter on Jarvis. The men were let loose on the streets at nine on Sunday mornings.

A lot were old, mostly alcoholics or drug addicts, but there were bound to be some genuine bad boys amidst the lifelong losers. She preferred them to have their own lodgings, but sometimes a bad boy who was down on his luck was a kind of ground zero.

She arrived home on Sunday around dinnertime after a day of walking the streets following a young Native man whose hair reminded Frances of Curtis's, thick and straight. Several times she nearly announced herself. But she knew that she wouldn't be able to resist reaching up and touching his hair. A part of her was already committed to Curtis, even though she knew that commitment was the last thing Curtis wanted.

On Tuesday, she woke up and couldn't remember Curtis's name. It took her a shower and a bowl of All Bran before it came to her. This used to happen with her father's face: sometimes he would just disappear in a yawn. Before she went to sleep that night, she swore she wouldn't so much as entertain a single thought about either her father or Curtis the entire next day, a vow that she honoured. On Thursday she got a call from The East offering her a contract position, three months to cover a mat leave. She'd be back inside by Monday.

The day after she got the news from The East, she finally heard from Curtis, wanting her to meet him after visiting hours were over at The East. He was moving into the small sexton's apartment at the church in the Beaches and would appreciate her help. Frances struggled a bit to keep her voice steady, but managed to eke out a definite "Sure."

He strode right up to her in the parking lot and kissed her on the lips. "Thanks for this," he said. "I thought my place could do with a woman's touch."

He seemed pleased that she was impressed he'd borrowed a buddy's car, an old, white Ford Escort. The trunk was tied down, with the bottom section of a bike sticking out, and the back seat was packed high with cardboard boxes. He chatted about how he'd spent every spare minute over the last week sorting through his stuff. He was proud that everything he owned in the world could fit in a Ford Escort. Bad boys weren't fond of being weighed down by possessions.

There were a couple of sets of stairs off the side entrance of the church that led to the sexton's apartment. The linoleum in the kitchen was scarred and bumpy, and the bedroom was a big barn-shaped space without a single window, panelled in dark wood. It was like a side-by-side, five-person coffin. But there was a small study off the narrow living room with a door that led out to a spacious roof terrace. You could see Lake Ontario from there.

By the time they'd lugged everything from the car to the apartment, Frances was sweaty and panting a little. But Curtis tackled her on the bare queen mattress in the dark bedroom, and before she knew it, he was down between her legs, the combination of his tongue and her cunt making squishy, quicksand sounds. A few minutes later, he slid up over top of her, and she reached down and grasped two handfuls of his ass. Bad boys are hard to resist when they're at their baddest. She sighed deeply, knowing that she was beyond help from this point on.

Lying in the darkness with their legs entangled, she launched into some fairly intrusive post-fuck talk, but Curtis didn't seem to mind. She asked him how he knew Zimmer and why he was so devoted to him, visiting every Friday.

"He's my foster brother," he said, tightening one of his thigh muscles, sending a shiver up both of Frances's thighs. "He came from a hellhole. We met up in a group home out near the airport. For some reason, the head of the place had it in for little Zimmy from the start. I've been watching out for him ever since."

"You took your eyes off him the day he was drinking and driving and killed some poor sucker." Frances was just trying to get the facts out, but Curtis's warm breath on her face stopped for a few seconds. "I mean, you were bound to blink every now and then."

"He was an alcoholic by the time he was eleven. His social worker actually preferred it; kept him quiet and all."

"And you?"

"I'm like a skunk. Mess with me, you'll never get the stink out."

In the windowless darkness, Frances couldn't gauge how serious Curtis was being. Was he smiling or glowering? She wondered how the blind read a person's face with their fingers without disturbing the actual expression.

"You're a real man," she said, another expression that her mother used to employ when she'd reminisce about Frances's father.

"Zimmy's my brother," he said in a case-closed tone of voice.

"And that girlfriend of yours?" she teased, pinching the first thing that came to hand.

Curtis squirmed and chortled. "She was just a casual thing. And then I met this prison guard. How could I get any safer than that?"

She stayed over that night. She always carried clean panties in her purse. Bad boys appreciate an organized woman. She washed her Friday pair on Saturday morning and borrowed one of Curtis's sweatshirts. They didn't do much more than unpack boxes and have sex. On Sunday, with the sound of hymns coming from the church beneath them, she didn't even bother getting dressed until the evening, when she had to go home and get ready for her first shift at The East.

Curtis's duties as sexton started on Monday. Most of what he'd be doing was cleaning and repairing, stopping the place from falling apart. Bad boys are often good with their hands. Her stepfather had inherited a whole whack of tools that used to belong to her father.

In her first two weeks back at the job, she only spent one night in her own apartment. On the first Wednesday, she packed a suitcase full of clothes and took a cab down to the Beaches. Curtis didn't seem to mind, although she knew better than to say anything out loud.

During her shifts, she often saw Zimmer. She did what she could to make him more comfortable, topping up his canteen funds with her own money, slipping him a chocolate bar or an extra piece of fruit, giving him more shower time, and letting him use the phone when he'd already reached the limit on his phone card. Curtis was grateful for her kindness.

But by the end of a month back at The East, Frances was beginning to worry that their daily schedule might be smothering Curtis. She remembered her mother confessing that she'd failed to keep Frances's father suitably inspired. "I just wasn't up to him," she'd say. "I was too ordinary." Her father had robbed that bank in order to explore the unpredictable, to escape the routines of making dinner, watching TV, moaning and groaning in the same bed every night.

She managed to convince Curtis to take her downstairs into the church and fuck her, once in a front-row pew and another time up against the organ. These little breakthroughs seemed to really please him. But she knew that soon enough, everything became rote. She was anxious for more, something with real risk. Bad boys could vanish if they weren't regularly challenged.

"Let's do something freaky," she said one night as they were checking out the eleven o'clock news.

"Like ...?" Curtis spread the word out, leaving the ingenuity up to her.

"Like finding out where the wardens live and breaking into one of their houses on a Sunday morning."

"I'm no thief," Curtis said, sounding disgusted.

"We could jam a bank machine or break a window or trash one of those fancy flowerbeds at Kew Gardens."

"Who the hell do you think I am, some kind of punk?" He glared at Frances.

Bad boys often like to think of themselves as Robin Hood. They only break corrupt rules. Frances had to come up with something ennobling, a gesture against a system that would be a correction rather than a crime.

"How about we break Zimmy out of The East?" she asked. "Give him a brand new start."

Curtis stared at her as if there were angels circling her head.

"Ty Conn lasted two weeks before going down in a blaze of glory. And Red Ryan was free for an entire year," she explained, thinking that any amount of freedom was preferable to spending what could be, according to Zimmer's lawyer, up to seven years. "If we could get him to Mexico, he could spend the rest of his days on one postcard beach after another."

"Are you serious?" Curtis asked. From the tone of his voice, being serious was something he wanted her to be.

She searched through her memory for a better word. "I'm just trying to keep the adrenaline flowing."

Curtis finally brushed her off with a lackadaisical "You're bonkers," but Frances began to do research. Bad boys were notoriously undisciplined and needed a partner to put things into focus. The simpler a plan the better. Taking a page from the book of a convict named Omid Tahvili, who'd escaped from a BC jail in 2007 and was never found, a guard would have to be an accomplice. If Frances took on the responsibility herself, she'd end up behind bars. But if it could be made to look like another guard was the guilty party, then both Zimmy and Frances would be free.

Either of the guards she used to job shadow might do: Dennis with his swelled-head talk about the future or Hugo, for whom dullness was an art. Dennis would be harder to fool, although his ego would be easier to manipulate. Hugo wasn't exactly dumb, but it took more energy than he usually had to think things through.

She decided on Hugo after flirting with Dennis at the lockers after an evening shift. Dennis was a braggart and wouldn't be able to keep his mouth shut about anything that happened between them. But Hugo was more cloud than man and rarely spoke above a whisper.

A couple of weeks into planning the best route and time, she realized that she needed Curtis on board to help out with a few matters, including driving the getaway car. She waited for a Monday night after he'd washed and waxed the entire church floor and was too exhausted to chew his dinner properly.

"This is going to happen with or without you," she swore.

"How are they not going to know that you're involved?" he asked.

Her plan was to pretend that a phone call had come in as she was writing reports in the office. It would be an emergency, Zimmy's dying father calling to say goodbye, and Frances would then page Hugo and ask him to bring the inmate down to the phone bay. She would meet them there and then would claim that another call just came in, saying that Zimmy's father was being brought to the visiting centre. Sure, that might sound a little strange, a dying man coming to The East to die in his son's arms, but it was just strange enough to possibly be true. There was only one guard on duty at the visitor's entrance on an evening shift. All she had to do was get Hugo between the soft drink and snack machines, out of camera range, for ten seconds, in which Zimmy would sneak up and smash him on the head with one of the chairs. With Hugo unconscious, she would pretend to be Zimmy's human shield and would let him drag her to the visitor's entrance, appear to stumble while Zimmy grabbed her riot club, clobbered the guard who didn't have a clue what was happening, then opened the main lock with that night's code. Frances would admit to giving him the code in a moment of pure terror and would indeed sound the alarm after being dumped at the end of the driveway and making her way back to the prison door.

Curtis listened quietly. "And then they run the videos of the last couple of months and ID me as Zimmy's buddy who visits every Friday. How long after that before they connect you to me?"

"But you'll be in Mexico with Zimmy, and I'll come join you as soon as I can," Frances said. She loved outsmarting the law. If she'd been male, she'd definitely have been a bad boy.

"Even if all this worked, where would we get the money to survive in Mexico?" he asked.

"No worries there," Frances boasted. "I'm the daughter of a fucking bank robber."

She could see in Curtis's eyes that she'd said the wrong thing. She knew that bad boys looked out for one another. Maybe she had violated some secret code. "I just want you to know that I'll do anything you want. Anything," she repeated.

Curtis was flexing the fingers of his right hand, making a fist. Maybe he was getting ready to hit her. Bad boys were known to go to extremes when pushed.

"A fucking bank robber," he said, throwing his hands into the air and shaking his head. "Who knew?"

Frances didn't have a suitable response. She just knew that Curtis was a cream-of-the-crop bad boy. Alpha one. Perfect specimen. She couldn't bear to lose him. She remembered being sixteen before it struck her that her father was really gone, that she hadn't made a bit of difference in his decision, that love wasn't even in the equation. She cried a lot after that, wondering whether her father could hear her from somewhere deep inside the afterlife. If only he'd had the sense to take her with him, she might have been the secret ingredient to a successful bank heist.

"You'll never be bored as long as you have me around," she said to Curtis. Just let him try and dump her, see how far he'd get. She'd been trained in firearm etiquette, how to wield a riot-control club, put someone in handcuffs in seconds flat.

He leaned forward for a kiss, and she nipped his bottom lip. "Shit," he said, grabbing her by the ear and pulling.

"You're either alive or you're dead," she announced, going for his neck this time, biting hard. She wished she could tell him that she loved him, but bad girls, like bad boys, never tell the truth.

TWO-MAN TENT

Something gave way inside me the night I watched Uncle Jules drop down to his knees on our porch-lit back lawn and crawl through the flap of the two-man tent that was my older brother Keir's current pride and joy. At the time, I thought of it as an acknowledgement that no matter how long I lived or how much I accomplished, I would never best Keir at anything.

That summer I was twelve; my voice began to rasp, a few reddish hairs cropping up around my nipples and a shock of slightly thicker hair under my arms. Suddenly I didn't like myself, which was a jolt since I'd never anticipated having feelings toward myself more difficult than variations of happy or sad. For example, I'd never imagined the complexities of jealousy before: the myriad number of ways I could feel left out.

When Uncle Jules came to spend the night on his way to a gig in Buffalo, he agreed to share the two-man tent with one of us. Uncle Jules gave off a cool glow, and anything he touched took on that glow. I thought I had a chance of being chosen. Sure, the tent was technically Keir's, but he'd already had sleepovers with at least three of his basketball buddies, plus my birthday was less than a week away.

We were sitting out on the patio—Mom and Dad, Keir and I, my sister Marnie, and Uncle Jules—swatting at the dusk mosquitoes that were beginning to gather around our ankles. Uncle Jules was using his knife and fork on the edge of the picnic table to drum a new song he'd just written. We were all trying to hum along in our various inharmonious ways. We'd never done the family thing very well, unless Uncle Jules was visiting. He had a gift for bringing us together. If jazz drummer, world traveller, and ladies' man Jules Taylor liked us then we were probably better than we thought.

Despite his drinking problem, Dad always stopped one whiskey short of sloppy when Uncle Jules was around, and Mom seemed so relieved that she relaxed her constant scowl and could easily be described as pretty. Marnie stopped pretending that she'd been kidnapped and would one day find her real family and leave us behind without so much as a goodbye. Keir became less competitive, more brotherly.

That night was especially memorable; our combined energies creating an alchemical connection. Uncle Jules caught a firefly that was flitting around the table and then gave us all close-up peeks between his fingers. I begged him to write a tune on the spot about the firefly. We both tried to hit the same high notes: what dissonance! Still, Uncle Jules praised me, saying that I was avant-garde. It was a perfect night, but like so much perfection, made of fragile, easily shattered stuff.

The bugs finally drove us indoors. It was close to ten, and Uncle Jules wanted to get an early start in the morning. Mom suggested that Keir and I take the tent, and then Uncle Jules could have the room that we shared all to himself. But Uncle Jules swore that he was looking forward to sleeping outside, that he hadn't fallen asleep to the chattering of crickets for years.

"So who's it going to be?" Dad said without slurring. "Maybe you and me," he said. "Old times. We could talk until the sun comes up."

"No," I cried out, sounding closer to eleven than thirteen. I'd blown it; I sounded so desperate.

I looked at Keir, who was leaning one hip against the kitchen table. He was golden beneath the pot lights. It was clear that he'd never had an instant of not liking himself. I looked at Uncle Jules looking at him and knew that it would take a miracle for me to be the chosen one.

What good would it do me to hear the clear, flute-like sound of Keir's name being announced? No one ever said Kenny without raising their head the way a dog does just before it barks. Hoping that I could stop myself from tumbling into failure, I spoke up: "I'd rather sleep inside," I said, a pure lie that I ached for someone to strip bare. I wanted to hear Uncle Jules groan in that jazz-hero tone of his, insisting that I reconsider. But no one said a word. Keir disappeared into the bedroom and came back in a jiffy having changed into his black soccer shorts and billowy white t-shirt, his version of pajamas. Everyone either believed me, or they weren't interested in why I'd given up the prize so easily that night.

I watched Uncle Jules crawl into the tent. Keir was already inside, a beast of a shadow in the flashlight's glare. At one point, they made a two-headed monster. I saw their reflections merge as if they were kissing. When they finally turned off the flashlight, my sense of hearing sharpened, and I could make out murmuring. I felt so left out that I had to shut the bedroom window. I didn't like the self that could only listen, the self without a silhouette. Lying in bed, stranded in sleeplessness, I made the decision not to love Keir or Uncle Jules anymore, not to want to be loved by them either. But I couldn't help yearning for the soft notes of their breathing out there in cricket land.

I stayed in bed the next morning until after I heard Dad saying goodbye to Uncle Jules. I even added an extra ten minutes, giving Dad the chance to head back to bed. When I finally arrived in the kitchen barefoot, accompanied only by quiet squelches from the damp bottoms of my feet, Keir was sitting at his usual spot at the table. I registered him enough to see that he was perusing a motorcycle magazine.

Ignoring him wasn't easy. It took focus and strength. When I'd slept in the tent with Keir, I'd been so busy trying to prove to him that I wasn't scared by the occasional huffing of animal breath or snapping of twigs that I'd ended up not being able to sleep at all. Keir drifted off the way a gull lands without once flapping its wings, leaving me all alone to face everything. It took a superhuman effort not to be just a younger brother.

I didn't discover the note that Uncle Jules left for me until later. "Sorry I missed you, buddy. All my love," scrawled on a paper towel in bright blue ink. It reminded me of being four or five and Uncle Jules telling me that I came from the sky, which was why my eyes were so blue. Keir's eyes were copper brown, with bits of glitter in them. It was obvious that he came from the dirt, shiny dirt, but dirt nonetheless.

Once Mom entered the room, I had to work harder to stay disengaged. But I was determined to make them all pay for not noticing that my surrender was really a rebuke. When Mom messed my hair with the flat of her palm, I didn't try to smooth it down again; I left myself mussed. When Dad tickled my ribs, I squirmed, but silently. "Get a load of this," he said in a sleepy drawl. "Mr. Personality."

Later in the day, when I had grown tired of the loneliness it took to sustain distance, Mom asked if we were going to sleep outside again tonight. Keir's "No!" made me gasp a little. I was the one mad at him. Why would he so adamantly deny me? In the end, Marnie stole all the attention, asking if she and a girlfriend could sleep in the tent and then stomping her feet when both Dad and Mom shared an even louder "No!"

"Just what the devil ordered," Mom said, snickering, "two fourteen-year-old girls in baby-dolls. The neighbourhood toms lined up for miles."

I could understand Marnie's frustration. We were all born so close together—just ten months between Marnie and Keir, fifteen months between Marnie and me—that it seemed unfair that Marnie couldn't do what Keir and I did. But the differences were often huge: boys and girls were worlds apart, older and younger often felt like polar bears and penguins.

"Would you let me sleep in the tent with Kenny?" she asked.

"I don't want to sleep in the tent with you," I said without even thinking.

"Get this through your head, young lady," Dad interrupted, spelling it out. "You're tentless until you're at least twenty-one."

Keir and I couldn't help enjoying it when Marnie was given a dressing down. She was so imperious the rest of the time that watching her jewelled crown slip down around her neck like a dog collar was a real treat. She actually called us *commoners* once. Forgetting last night for a second, I sought out eye contact with Keir, hoping that he'd respond with a wink, sending Marnie even deeper into la-la land.

He looked right at me. I saw a Keir that I'd never encountered before, a dark, unruly version of himself. It was a dumb animal kind of look, inescapable, full of anger. It wasn't a look that had anything to do with me, other than to suss out whether I might make a convenient target.

I blinked a couple of times, hard, muscular blinks, and went back to ignoring him. That night, he slept on top of the sheets in his clothes, but I pretended not to notice.

Uncle Jules didn't visit again that summer. He played The Rex in October, but he insisted on sleeping on the couch. I noticed a couple of secret-code messages going back and forth between him and Keir, but, having just officially become a teenager, I'd accepted the fact that Uncle Jules had his own relationship with each of us. He and Marnie would often disappear into her bedroom for hours. Who knew a girl with one facial expression would have that much to talk about with a grown man.

I was too busy trying to puzzle out my relationship with Uncle Jules to pay much attention to his intimacies with my sister and brother. My parents too, for that matter. He had the knack of making Mom giggle and Dad slow down just a bit. Me, I was his buddy, which had previously meant playing card games, tossing Frisbees, watching dumb comedies on TV. But I wanted to have something more meaningful than that.

He slept over a couple of times in November. Once he took the couch, but the second time, I ended up on it. I remember Keir leaning sideways at the breakfast table and resting his head on Uncle Jules's shoulder. It was something I could never do. It had always been clear that Uncle Jules wasn't the kind of relative that a kid could climb all over. He wasn't a demonstrative man, though every now and again he'd make a tiny gesture: a kiss on Marnie's forehead before she went to sleep, a slap on the backside when he'd ask Keir or me to fetch his lighter, a pat on Mom's hand to let her know he cared. But these were rare occurrences. I'd never seen one of us initiate a touch before. It was weirdly exciting to me. It suggested a change that I didn't want to be left out of. I decided to return to emulating Keir, to figure out a way of becoming more than myself.

The day after the last November visit, I walked my friend Stanley home from school in order to pick up a DVD of a Mexican western called *El Topo* that he was lending me. On the walk back, I cut through the high-school parking lot and noticed Keir at the other end with a small group of friends crowded around a blue mountain bike. Sauntering over, I felt some tension in the air, but since I'd already been seen, I kept on approaching. Keir's best friend, Cat, was there, plus another guy, Michael Seristino, who had slept in the tent a couple of times last summer. I didn't recognize any of the other three: one tall, one Asian, one beefy.

"Whose bike?" I asked, adding "Cool" to make it clear that I was impressed with it and would be impressed with whoever owned it.

No one answered, the tension getting thicker. Finally, Cat gave me a divided look and responded, "It doesn't belong to any of us."

"So what's it doing here?" I asked.

"It's none of your business," Keir interrupted.

I must have looked sad because Cat told my brother to lay off, and my brother said it was none of his business either, and then the beefy guy said that it was my brother who needed to lay off and stop doing stupid things like stealing bikes.

The story seemed clear enough: Keir had skipped the last class of the day, which was band, without giving a heads-up to any of his friends, then showed up again just after the last bell with this blue bike, left unlocked in the bike rack outside the nearby Variety Village sports centre. Apparently he'd done a few other similar things over the last month.

"What the fuck's the matter with you?" Michael Seristino asked for all of us.

It's rare for change to be easily traceable. Usually, it happens in small increments, and we never really know when that first step was taken. But that afternoon, listening to my brother's friends scold him and make him promise to shape up, was the last time Keir actually spoke to me. It's not that he went out of his way to ignore me the way I'd ignored him, in fact he kept up with every "Excuse me" or "Want some?" that was necessary. He just wasn't the same brother anymore.

His last words came as we walked home that afternoon, after Cat and the others had left us. We were still a few blocks from Phoenix Drive. I tried to think of something that would be supportive, that wouldn't make him feel like a juvenile delinquent, and ended up saying, "You can talk to me, you know," in a high-pitched voice; for the moment, I'd somehow lost the crackle of puberty that at least suggested manhood. It was a sorry offer; I knew it immediately, but I couldn't think of anything else that wasn't mushy.

"It means a lot to me that you believe that," he said in the softest of tones. And then he smiled, a true-blue smile that spread over his entire face. "You're the best," he continued, snaking an arm around me and squeezing me hard.

With words like these, he covered his trail. He left me behind with the mystery of the blue bike. These words were the abracadabra of change. Nothing was ever the same from that moment on.

Christmas that year oddly felt like a re-enactment rather than a celebration. Dad drank like he did every Christmas, but try as he might, he just couldn't get drunk. Mom's dinner was probably her best yet, but it lacked that special something that made everyone burst into applause on other years. Even Uncle Jules's polish was a bit thin. He told stories that I swear I'd heard before word for word. Dad and Uncle Jules's third sibling, an older brother, Chad, came with his wife, Marilyn, and their nineteen-year-old daughter, Shelly, but they seemed like fake family, rented guests; nothing they did or said made any difference. I tried to share this with Keir, but he just said, "Pardon me?" and walked away.

We were all so exhausted by the time Chad and his family left that we didn't even try to tackle the dishes. For Mom to leave a mess was a sign that something was terribly wrong. Dad finally passed out on the couch, which meant that I had to share my parents' bed with Mom, who treated me like she always had and snuggled into me. But I was so worried that I'd wake up with what had become a ritual morning boner that I couldn't fall asleep at all and at three in the morning crept out of bed and tiptoed into the bedroom that Keir and I shared. I'm not sure what I was thinking. I wondered whether there might be some space for me in Keir's bed, or whether I could possibly slip in beside Uncle Jules in mine. This was definitely regressive behaviour—something about being the only one awake in the house made me feel like I was eleven again.

I turned toward my bed first and saw the sheets pulled back, with no one inside them. When I shifted my focus to Keir's side of the room, I could only see Uncle Jules. He seemed unusually small, the way a porcupine looks smaller with its quills calmed down. He was moving gently back and forth. I couldn't really see Keir other than his toes sticking out at the end of the mattress.

It wasn't exactly jealousy that overcame me, though I definitely felt left out. And the notion that sex was involved didn't even cross my mind. I just wanted my brother to rescue me from my sleeplessness. I wanted them to make room for me in the double bed.

"Keir" was all I said. Or maybe I said it twice. It wasn't a demand or an accusation. It was just a plea.

Suddenly, Keir erupted, kicking out both his arms and legs, shoving Uncle Jules aside. Then he was out of the bed, naked from the waist down, hitting me across my chest. I heard myself yelling. Uncle Jules was up on his feet by now, pulling up his pajama bottoms, wrenching at Keir's shoulders, trying to peel him off of me. We ended up in a pile of heavy breathing. Then Keir started sobbing.

I finally slithered free and got back on my feet. Uncle Jules had risen to his knees and was bent over Keir, cradling him and saying, "It's okay; it's okay," over and over. I stood there staring, shivering like crazy, wanting to cry, but my eyes were so dry I couldn't even blink.

"Go back to bed, Kenny," Uncle Jules said in an I'm-in-control voice.

"I have nowhere to sleep," I tried to explain.

"Now," Uncle Jules snapped.

And so I backed out of my own room, mad, confused. Uncle Jules must have managed to subdue Keir because someone shut the door with a click. I didn't know what to do. Returning to Mom's bed was impossible. Dad's snores were filling the living room with rumbles. He was spread-eagled all over the living-room couch. Without thinking, I picked up a throw pillow and dropped it on Dad's face, then pressed it hard against him. I kept it there until the snores stopped and Dad thrashed around a bit, nowhere near as wild as Keir though, just enough to toss off the pillow and regain the rhythm of his snores.

I didn't think of what Keir and Uncle Jules had been doing in the bed together. I didn't even remember that Keir was half-naked until after Uncle Jules was on his way home. I had no idea how Boxing Day was going to unfold; it was entirely possible that Dad would just stay passed out on the couch. And the state of the kitchen was horrendous enough for Mom to consider slipping out her bedroom window and finding a new home where everything was spic and span.

But we all worked hard at assuming the normal stances—except for Keir, who was apparently "sleeping it off." The story was that he'd had too much to drink over the span of Christmas day. It seemed made-up to me, since there was one thing that Keir and I had always sworn we wouldn't be: drunks like Dad. Regardless of the truth, attempts were made to get us back on track. Uncle Jules started in on the dishes. Even Dad was inspired to clean up the area around the living-room couch. He found a braided silver ring in between the cushions that no one had ever seen before. He said he'd check with Chad later in the day, but it fit so perfectly on his middle finger that I remember thinking I wouldn't be surprised if he kept it for himself.

Uncle Jules stood up from our brunch of leftovers and announced that he was going to head back to Montreal now rather than wait until tomorrow, when flurries were expected to turn into white-outs in various places, especially near Lake Ontario. He disappeared into Keir's and my bedroom to pack his gym bag, and we could hear the low notes of a brief conversation.

He hugged Mom and whispered something in her ear, then he moved on to Dad, who just sort of bumped chests with him, then Marnie the spider monkey, who tossed her long, skinny arms around Uncle Jules's neck, clinging for several seconds. When he came to me, he just sort of leaned closer, squeezing my right shoulder. He didn't make any eye contact, staring right over my head.

I felt a strange rush of panic, as if this might be the last time I'd see him. "Are you back for New Year's?" I asked, knowing that he had a New Year's Eve gig booked at some swanky spot in Yorkville.

"I'll let you know," he answered Mom, not me.

"But you already said you would," I pestered.

Mom shushed me, and Uncle Jules dashed out the screen door, down the porch steps, and into his 1982 Mustang GT before I could say another word. Once, over a year ago, he'd taken Keir and me for a spin around the neighbourhood. I remember Keir shouting whee! from the passenger seat. I would have been happy if we'd just kept on driving.

Uncle Jules belonged to us, but like a luxury we really couldn't afford on a regular basis. He was a special occasion. None of us had ever been to visit him in Montreal, although Keir used to say that he was going to spend a summer with him one of these years, hinting that he might even move there when he finished high school. I would pop in with "Me too," but no one took me seriously.

Now that Uncle Jules was gone, I wanted my brother back. The only way that was going to happen was to start telling the truth. "I'm too old to sleep with you," I said to Mom later that day. "I tried to suffocate you," I continued, addressing Dad. "Keir and Uncle Jules were sleeping in the same bed," I said to both of them. Despite the heat of the moment, I had shivers running from neck to tail bone. At that moment, with no chance of taking the words back, time lurched forward. I saw it all clearly and knew what it was called.

I also knew that I'd lost Keir in the process. He was the chosen one, the object of Uncle Jules's desires. And I was the snitch. Of course, Keir was also a victim, but with that came a guilt that I had no idea how to acknowledge, let alone quell. If he managed to look me in the eyes, he'd see his own nakedness.

Uncle Jules didn't return for New Year's. Dad stayed drunk. Keir got to move out of our bedroom and was given a makeshift space behind the furnace in the unfinished basement, where he pitched his tent and slept alone.

Those were the days when a grown man diddling a kid was privately shunned, but there were no public consequences. Mom cried a lot for the first few days, but then never spoke of it again. We all dropped the high expectations that we'd had for Keir and watched him wither instead, become something so much less than what we'd once imagined. He ended up in and out of commercial real estate, with a drinking problem, just like Dad. It was like he'd been marked down in some awful way. It was many years before I attempted a conversation. And even then, grown men, we couldn't get much further than me saying, "It wasn't your fault."

When I was nineteen, I showed up at one of Uncle Jules's gigs in Old Montreal. It was a grungy place that smelled like onion rings and spit. When he realized it was me, he looked like he wanted to bolt, but the years hadn't been kind—he suffered from a bad hip, rocking side to side as he walked. I'd gone to the club with plans to publically shame him, but the loss of his cool was shame enough. He had the look of someone who secretly whipped himself raw every night before going to bed.

We chatted a bit. Neither one of us mentioned Keir. When we'd run out of small talk, I screwed up my courage. "I would have given anything to sleep out in the tent with you that night when I was thirteen."

His eyes darted, he swallowed hard.

"I would have given anything," I repeated, wanting him at least to understand that at one time I'd have laid my loneliness in his arms without a single hesitation.

THE HIRED HAND

We were sitting around the scraps of lunch, me with my *1,001 Crossword Puzzles* propped open at page 306, she stirring a by-now-cold cup of tea with a blackened silver spoon as if she were ringing a bell to announce the endless end of the world. Suddenly, the tinkling stopped. Still thinking of myself as the perfect caregiver, I immediately lifted my eyes from a clue reading *hot-air balloon gas* to make sure she was okay. She was staring at me across the table with a look of utter distaste.

"Who do you think you are?" she asked, keeping her teeth tightly together.

"I'm Tate," I said. "As always."

"Tate?"

"Your husband," I added. It sounded funny for me to be saying it to her, although, in the early days of our marriage, I used to often refer to myself as *your husband*. It gave me a new identity, a way of defining myself as part of something bigger than I'd ever been on my own.

She grunted high in her throat and made a girl-trying-to-throw-overhand motion with her right arm. "I don't have a husband," she said. "I'm hardly more than a child."

I blamed the neurologist, Dr. Auster, entirely for this most recent barrage of memory loss. Sure, she was leaving the iron on high overnight and trying to boil an empty kettle and forgetting numbers she'd long known by heart, but she never forgot who I was until Dr. Auster not only said the word *Alzheimer's*, but spelled it out for her, pronouncing the zed as *zee* and including an apostrophe. She went pale and looked a little like she might vomit. I tried to talk about it on the subway back to Scarborough, but she waved me away with her green woolen mitts, and by the time we arrived home, she had misplaced the entire experience. But something about that day had shaken her confidence in me; she realized, down deep, I was just another helpless person in the face of so much ruthlessness.

Grace was a born worrier even though she'd lived a lucky life up until this; her fears were always worse than what actually happened. Despite what I knew about the horrors of the disease, I tried to think optimistically for a while. There were worse ways to die than drifting into a second childhood.

But that mask-like face she wore as she announced that she was just a child made me feel sick with despair. There was an awful coldness in her eyes, miles of frozen corridors. She didn't care a whit about my feelings. The part of her reasoning that loved me had simply gone dark.

"Oops. I forgot to make lunch," she announced, having already forgotten the self of a few seconds ago.

I didn't stop her from getting up and bustling around the kitchen, preparing new sandwiches. I was overwhelmed with the vastness of being forgotten. After over thirty years of marriage, all I could do was sit there and watch myself being expunged like a bunch of chemical equations reduced to a blackboard smudge. We had always agreed that we would choose each other into eternity: if heaven existed, the one who went first would be waiting at the gates; if reincarnated, we'd arrange to meet one summer night and within seconds feel like we'd known one another in a previous life; we even agreed to face nothingness side by side, if that was all there was.

But it had been Grace who'd made these deals with me, not this impostor who was slowly but surely eating her way through Grace's cerebellum. The disease was not only erasing our life together, but our chance of an afterlife as well.

Nicholas hadn't stopped crying since the moment Grace mistook him for her dead brother. Having rarely seen him show anything more than smugness since he was fifteen, I was shocked by the bottomless pool of grief he discovered within himself at twenty-nine. As a boy, he'd been intensely attached to Grace much longer than I thought was healthy, but she'd insisted that clinging was just a roundabout way of arriving at independence. And she was right, I guess. He invented new computer languages, made piles of money, and went through a string of beautiful, devoted women who always seemed to continue liking him after he stopped loving them. But facing the great black void of his mother's confusion was simply too much.

Sylvie, twenty-six, a dead ringer for a young Grace, was one year shy of her chiropractic degree when Grace first fell ill. She threw herself into her studies with renewed vigour and rarely mentioned the situation, even when Grace forgot who Sylvie was. I could understand the temptation to just avoid the pain, but it made me respect her a little less.

There were other things to worry about besides how our children were coping. For instance, Grace seemed to have recently lost my name entirely, calling out "Yoo hoo" whenever she wanted my attention. And one night, as I slid into bed beside her, she started screaming and wouldn't stop until I hustled myself out of the room.

We still had some lovely moments though. Grace would often hold my hand while we sat on the couch watching television. She'd occasionally lift it to her lips and kiss each of my fingers one by one. There were still some nights when she'd let me into the bed we'd shared all these years, and we'd both forget everything else for twenty minutes or so.

"I love you, whoever you are," she whispered one night, a strange, warm glow washing through me.

"I know you," she announced one afternoon. She was sitting on the bed in the spare room, Nicholas's old room, pouring over our savings account reconciliation book while I sat at the small desk paying bills on the internet. "You're the hired hand." She was beaming as if she'd just given the correct final answer on *Jeopardy!*

"Hired by who?" I asked, wondering which one of her dead relatives had popped back to life that particular day.

"By my husband," she said, straightening her spine a little, tiny spots of pinkness appearing on both cheeks.

"Is your husband good to you?" I couldn't help myself. Feeling small wasn't enough; I was aiming for infinitesimal.

"Not particularly," she answered, the pink spots spreading up to her cheekbones. "That's why he hired you."

Grace had often seduced me over the years, but it was one thing to fall together in our dark bedroom, quite another to join her on Nicholas's childhood bed as someone other than myself, both lover and cuckold. I resisted, staying put on my chair.

"You're no help at all," she finally said, dropping the bank book and sliding herself full out on the bedspread. She then pushed her hand down the waistband of her skirt and quickly found the right spot. For the next two minutes, she stared right at me. Her concealed hand moved faster, and she opened her mouth just wide enough I could have inserted a spoon. She came with a shudder, then crossed her ankles and pressed her thighs together. Her eyes never once left me. Something she'd never done in front of me in over three decades of marriage, she'd now shared with a hired hand.

One midspring night when I was sleeping on the couch, I heard floorboards creak, but I was too far into a dream for just one noise to rouse me. So what if she set fire to the house? Why hadn't I thought of that, a murder-suicide? When I finally woke up, it was still dark outside, but a small glee club of various birds was performing loudly. I instantly remembered the creak of the floorboards and began to worry.

She wasn't in bed. The covers had been neatly folded back, and her slippers were missing from the rug in front of the dresser. I checked the bathroom and kitchen, then, slowly, thoroughly, all the other rooms, the closets, the crawl space behind the furnace. It was a good ten minutes before I thought to check the front door. It was shut tight, but unlocked.

Grace hadn't left the house on her own since that day she was diagnosed. I'd read about Alzheimer's patients wandering streets that were no longer familiar, getting lost a block from home, panicking, walking into traffic, accosting strangers. Before opening the door, an image flashed into my head of Grace making her way in the dark to Valhalla Park on the edge of the bluffs overlooking Lake Ontario; I imagined rushing up behind her just before she threw herself out into the black air.

But what I found instead was Grace hunched over on the small front stoop in her lime-green shorty nightgown, her shoulders shivering from the April cold. I reached out and laid a palm on the top of her head.

She turned and looked up at me. "I've been waiting for you to come home," she said.

"I never left." The moon was still in the sky, but its lines were beginning to fray. Soon enough, the sun would start its plucky opening act.

"Don't you lie," she said.

"I swear."

"It's okay, Tate," she said. My name in her mouth melted what little moonlight was left. "Boo hoo, what's up with you?" she added in a singsong voice.

I helped her to her feet, put my arm around her, and promised that I'd never leave again. I vowed to sleep on the floor by the bedroom door on the nights when she kicked me out of bed. Perhaps I would stop sleeping altogether, give her my full attention twenty-four hours a day.

The list of things I didn't tell Nicholas and Sylvie grew longer. Nicholas was still Grace's favourite; she seemed delighted by him even though his role of son was no longer a part of her store of knowledge. But it was clear that neither of the kids wanted to know that their mother had stopped bathing on her own, that I had to drag her kicking and screaming into the tub each evening like it was some sort of torture device. They didn't know that she had developed a fear of the TV set, mistaking characters for real people, many of whom were dangerous, carried guns, and committed acts of violence.

She became fixated with her own father. "He's home all alone," she'd say, referring to the three-storey semi near Parliament and Wellesley where she was born. "Why won't you do what you're told and take me there?"

"He's been dead for thirty years," I'd repeat, watching the grief and shock hit her again and again. I'd tried lying, saying that he was visiting his brother in North Bay, but I found the yearning harder to bear than the sorrow.

She ate jalapeno peppers straight from the jar and gave me such a look of betrayal. She tried to put both arms into one sleeve and created her own straightjacket. One morning, she fell down the basement stairs, claiming they hadn't been there a moment ago. The last time Sylvie dropped by, Grace accused her of having stolen her face.

In early June, I had to rush her to the hospital when she bit down on one of her favourite blue Mexican glasses and cut both her lips and tongue.

"What hurricane did you ride in on?" she asked the doctor, a youngish man with thick, shoulder-length, fly-away hair.

"Aren't you the witty one," he said, reaching out and taking hold of her chin so he could raise and lower her head for a better look at the damage.

She somehow managed to slide out of his grip and sunk her teeth into the fleshy area between his thumb and pointer finger. "This is me, and it's still mine," she explained, sounding like a Zen koan.

It got worse from there. She struck a nurse who was trying to wipe the blood off of her neck. Her screams echoed throughout the emergency department. When I tried to console her, she hissed, "You've been gone so long, you're all that's left."

The doctor had to sedate her in order to repair the damage from the broken glass. When she came to, and her blood pressure was back to normal, they handed her back to me, happy to be rid of us.

It was the shit I found wrapped up in a pair of her nylon panties and shoved to the back of her underwear drawer that pushed me over the edge. It just happened to be on a night when she wouldn't stop obsessing over her father.

"You win," I shouted. "I'll take you home," meaning Laurier Avenue, where she was positive her father was pacing the floors, praying for her safe return.

I suggested she pack a suitcase, telling her that I wasn't bringing her back to Scarborough no matter what, but she stared at the rows of skirts and blouses hanging in her closet and said, "Yuck. I wouldn't be caught dead wearing any of these."

We drove west through evening rush hour, plenty of time for her to forget where we were going or for me to soften and take her out for dinner instead, plying her with coffee, which always seemed to lessen the crazy thoughts and generally calm her down. But the constant stop and go seemed to cast a spell over the both of us. The radio volume was dialed low so that the music sounded like the car taking deep, rhythmic breaths.

We were just about to pass over the Bloor Viaduct when Grace spoke up. "The day I was diagnosed, I thought of coming here on my own and jumping." Her voice had a flat, hypnotized tone to it. "I'd forgotten that they'd put up all these suicide barriers." She put the palm of her hand against the glass of the passenger-side window as if she were waving goodbye to something that was no longer possible. "Wouldn't Daddy have been mad?" she continued. "Pop goes the weasel."

The transitions between clarity and confusion were down to mere seconds. I couldn't keep up anymore. It was all I could do not to gun the gas pedal and smash through both bridge and barriers, fly out over the Don Valley Parkway, land in a wreck of flames.

Instead, I made a left at Parliament. We crawled the last few blocks to Laurier. Just before the final turn, I saw a slender young woman, with her blond hair in sexy disarray, who reminded me of Grace on our wedding night and the twenty-three bobby pins she had to remove before her hair was free to sweep across my face.

I could hardly swallow when I stopped the car in front of her childhood house. My plan was to leave her there, to pull away the moment she climbed from the car, before she walked up the front steps and knocked. I would be crossing the bridge again by the time someone opened the front door. It was essential that I not be there for Grace to be able to travel back in time. If I was about to commit a crime, it was a crime of wishful thinking.

"I forgot to bring my key," she said, feeling on the floor by her feet for a non-existent purse.

"There is no key," I said, feeling cruel to the point of evil.

She looked at me, then nodded. "Of course not. Daddy always waits up, no matter how late I am."

There was a tear in one of my eyes, not quite formed, but enough to make me think of Nicholas and to wonder whether he'd start crying again when he learned that I'd abandoned her. Sylvie would disown me and be surprised that it didn't make her feel any better.

"Thanks for all your help," Grace said as she opened the passenger door carefully so as not to scrape the curb. "Your cheque is in the mail," she said, giggling.

She hopped out onto the sidewalk with a bounce that used to be her trademark enthusiasm for life and its wild array of challenges and delights. God, how I'd loved her when she'd try to explain that she was different from me, that I was the foundation and she was the thirteenth floor.

I meant to pull away immediately, put some traffic between the horror and me, see if finishing off Grace's story was really that simple. But my foot was dead weight on the brake.

She tripped up the steps and rapped her knuckles against the front door. She reminded me of those perky Avon ladies that used to arrive with a suitcase full of tester creams and potions. But what did she have that a stranger living in downtown Toronto would want? She wouldn't be able to explain herself. A few sentences in, she'd forget who she was.

From my sightline in the driver's seat, I could only see the lower half of Grace: her black skirt with tiny orange crowns in neat little rows and a pair of black Chinese slippers. The man who swung the front door open, the daddy of all strangers, was wearing beige slacks and grey Birkenstocks. I couldn't hear a word, but could concoct the chill of his response as Grace stuttered. It crushed my heart to imagine her confusion.

The two pairs of legs seemed to press together. Perhaps it was an illusion of light and vantage point, but it looked a little like Grace and the stranger were embracing. Then the stranger's legs turned and disappeared into the house, followed by Grace's black and orange skirt. The door closed behind them.

I felt the need to clear my throat, which turned into a cough, which finally twisted itself into a sob. The wail of it was unlike anything I'd ever heard coming from my own mouth before. How could I think straight with all that noise? I bit my tongue twice before I managed to regain a little self-control.

This wasn't supposed to have happened. Grace should have stumbled back to the car after the stranger shut the front door on her hopes. I would have to repeat for the billionth time that I was her family now. She would have cried for a block or two before she caught her breath and said something totally inane like "The doves have names."

It was sheer desperation to think I could leave her. No matter how little was left of the real Grace, she belonged to me. She was my mad responsibility, my ravaged joy. The emptiness of the passenger seat felt shattered.

My logic told me that the man who answered the door was probably calling the police this very minute, having settled Grace into a soft chair and given her a glass of water. But a touch of paranoia suggested that Grace had been stolen, that the man had need for a woman like Grace to mistake him for her father.

I coughed again, three, four times and then wrestled the car door open and tumbled out onto the street. My legs were old-man wobbly, but I made my way up to the door and knocked the whole back of my hand against the wood with an awful clatter. Then I saw a doorbell and stubbed it with my thumb. I could hear chimes coming from deep inside the house.

What was I going to say when the man appeared? I wondered whether I'd have to tackle him and whether I could do that without breaking an arm or wrist. But when the door flew open and a Mediterranean-dark man somewhere in his forties appeared in front of me, the words just popped out.

"She's mine," I said in a voice resembling a stage whisper.

I held his gaze for a few seconds and then let my eyes sweep over his shoulder to where Grace was perched on the edge of a huge olive-coloured leather chair. There was a smallish angora cat sitting at her ankles, its head cocked back, looking up at her face.

"I don't understand," the man said with what sounded like a thick Spanish accent. "Who is this woman? She says she knows my father."

I let my eyes wander a bit more, but couldn't detect the presence of anyone else in the room. Nothing was as it had been back when Grace and I were dating. Walls had been knocked down; the combined kitchen, dining room, and living room was so big that the man's voice echoed. The walls were painted a shade of cherry that gave the entire place a twilight feel.

"I believe it's her father she's looking for," I explained.

"*Her* father?"

It struck me how little it takes to plunge someone into confusion. "She used to live here." I struggled to be as succinct as possible. "This was her father's house."

I could hear Grace muttering to herself, but I raised my voice a few tones and tried to outtalk her. "She has Alzheimer's," I added.

"My father is dead," he said softly.

"So is her father," I clarified.

He didn't exactly look less confused, just more comfortable with the confusion. We were all exhausted by the lack of clarity. Even Grace seemed to have given up on finding her father. I helped her out of the leather chair and, cupping her elbow in the palm of my right hand, steered her out the door.

"Sorry for the bother," I said.

The man followed us out onto the porch. "I'm sorry her father is dead," he called after us.

On the drive home, she only spoke twice. The first time, she made a *mmm* sound followed by "Well, that was a delicious dinner." The second was preceded by a giggle. "If Daddy only knew."

I smiled along with her—maybe she was having one of her lucid moments (it was true; her father was the kind of man who had enjoyed things like irony and mistaken identities)—though I knew that she'd be gone again by the time the smile faded.

TREAD

Gary wished that he'd known his father back in the days when the man was still earning his nickname. He'd had a penchant for walking trips, tracking down some serpentine river or mountain pass. Ted became Tread: one foot in front of the other, the miles adding up. His mother, Gary's Grammie June, always said that from the time he was seven or eight, Tread lived more comfortably in distance than he did close up, the future enticing him to turn the next corner regardless of timeliness. He rarely talked about these expeditions and everyone—his parents, sister Jill, and Uncle Eddie—seemed to think that his silences meant that there had been hardships along the way that he simply chose not to relive. He was the perfect traveller: adaptable, obsessive, remote.

By the time Tread came to live with Gary, his wife Ella, and their two snuggle-soft spaniels named Ballad and Muse, it was clear this small Ontario town would be his final destination. He was just the bones of the man who had once walked his way across the entire continent of Africa. Queensville, an hour north of Toronto, might as well have been the end of the world.

Gary was surprised at how disappointed he was with his father. He would rather imagine old man Tread taking one stumble too many in the Gobi Desert or losing his bearings amid all the African countries with their ever-changing names and disappearing into legend. It had been two years since his mother's death, Tread's beloved Rachel, and Gary still couldn't accept the fact that his father had basically been sitting in the Scarborough condominium where they'd moved after Gary had grown up, watching television, not even bothering to renew his subscription to *National Geographic*.

When Gary was born, Tread was ripening toward forty-two, most of the major solo journeys in his past. But Gary cherished the idea that the reason his father was so much older than all his friends' dads was because he'd been too busy combing the jungles of Brazil or following Aboriginal songlines in the unbreathable heat of the Australian outback to father a child. In Gary's mind, the spark of his own being spent years in the void, patiently waiting for Tread to give the go-ahead. The penultimate destination was Gary himself. What a lot of pressure to put on a child, he supposed, but he felt more than up for it and was quite happy to make sure to never stand in his father's way.

It wasn't easy to get his father talking. His mother was much more forthcoming (they'd met under the Brandenburg gates on a hot June afternoon; Rachel on a Eurorail pass, Tread on a tramp through Germany), but her travel stories were much more limited: just that one trip to Europe and then the holidays they took together, first as a couple, then the drives across the States with Gary in the back seat imagining that the long, endless highways might one day arrive in the Congo or on the teeming streets of Calcutta. Gary used to beg for his father's memories when he was still young enough to think that he'd eventually uncover the secret to Tread's silences. He'd wheedle and dig, never giving up hope that something would trigger a story, occasionally gathering enough facts together to take the basic plotline and fill it in with his own fantasies.

No wonder Gary never became much of a traveller. He made the excuse of education—a master's in Canadian history, followed by an eventually abandoned doctorate on the Riel uprising; he turned to law school instead and the endless minutia of litigation that felt every bit as foreign as the mountain villages of Nepal. And then there was Ella, love of his life, who had been battling fibromyalgia for years, a diagnosis for which Gary partly blamed himself and the extra hours she'd put in as an ESL instructor in order to see them through the lean years of law school. Besides, what little Gary had seen of the world could never live up to the wonders that were tucked away in the crawlspaces of his father's brain.

When Rachel first began showing signs of dementia, Tread took early retirement from the various import/export businesses where he'd been working as a consultant ever since Gary was born, and he and Rachel set off to see as much of China as they could manage, a country that Tread had only visited briefly when he'd been exploring some of the smaller South China Sea nations. They were gone for the better part of a year, and Gary was shocked when they arrived back in Toronto at how badly his mother had deteriorated. Whole chunks of her personality seemed to have been left behind in China.

Rachel's losses profoundly altered everyone's sense of reality. For a while, she was quite delusional and would think that everything she saw on TV had actually happened to her. That was when Tread started avoiding his beloved travel shows. Gary remembered being at his parents' condominium one particular Sunday afternoon, when his mother was fighting Tread's attempts to get her to sip her scalding cream-of-mushroom soup rather than taking painful gulps of it.

"I thought you'd been shot," she said, trickles of soup running down her chin.

Tread spoke through his teeth in a kind of hiss. "She watched police shows on TV last night instead of sleeping," he explained.

"You're supposed to be dead," she said, more definitively.

Tread stared into a flurry of dust motes in the sunny living-room air, his eyes growing smaller. "I want you to take the television set home with you," he said to Gary and Ella, pointing in the direction of the condo's front door.

"There is no home," Rachel interrupted. "I haven't been home in years."

Before Gary or Ella could dream up some frail reassurance, Tread leapt up from the black leather La-Z-Boy. Gary was sure that he was going to stride over to the TV and rip the cords and cables out of the wall. But he just stood there tottering a little and then began telling a story.

"I once met an old man on a path by a river outside of Belfast. It was only afternoon, though the fog gave everything a dusky hue. I didn't know how much farther it was into the city." He cleared his throat and raised his voice. "I asked him to show me where we were on the map I'd bought in Dublin. I held the page close to his face. He wasn't wearing glasses, and his eyes were bloodshot. Finally, he seemed to get a bead on the situation. 'I've been dead too long to know where anything is.' Then he patted me on the back of my hand and said, 'You're dead too, but even the dead's got to carry on.' And then he laughed, and I laughed too. And I carried on, and Belfast eventually rose towering out of the fog, chimneys as far as I could see. Exactly what you'd expect from a city of the dead."

Ella tried to say something about Tread still being very much alive, but Gary just sat there wishing that the story hadn't ended, that it might lead to another one. Rachel's illness couldn't stop Tread any more than the old Irish man had. Let the dead speak for the dead.

Less than a month later, his mother was reduced to nonsense. Gary could hear her in the background when he was talking to Tread on the phone; she sounded like a radio flickering between two stations. Later that same week, the social worker who had been helping the family with the eventuality of a nursing home called to say there was a bed available at their second-choice facility, a sprawling institution that boasted daily creative classes and lockdown wards. He'd expected his father to be resistant and was surprised when Tread walked over to the bedroom closet without saying a word, dragged out a suitcase, and then let Ella start packing Rachel's clothes.

The first few weeks were too confusing for Gary to have a sense of how his father was coping. But he soon realized that Tread was walking several miles a day to the nursing home and then back home again. Ella was worried about his health; it was a hard winter with lots of blustery days. But Gary couldn't hide his pleasure. "He's back on the road again," he said. "It's a good sign." What Gary didn't say out loud was that maybe once his mother had declined to the point that she wouldn't know whether Tread had visited or not, he and his father could take a short walking trip together, perhaps the Cabot Trail or Manitoulin Island. He began dreaming of these trips as the winter nights slid toward spring, Tread always in the lead.

But every time there'd appear to be a bit of clear road up ahead, his mother's condition would create new avalanches. First, she had a heart attack and ended up in Scarborough General for six long weeks. Gary lost track of Tread during those weeks. They saw each other at the hospital, but were usually spelling each other off.

Rachel arrived back at the nursing home just a few days shy of her seventy-fifth birthday. Ella baked a gingerbread cake and made a sign that she had laminated at Staples that read HAPPY 75TH BIRTHDAY TO A WONDERFUL MOTHER AND WIFE. But a bedsore on Rachel's right hip turned into some kind of flesh-eating bacteria, and she was rushed back to the hospital and eventually operated on to have part of the hipbone removed.

In the midst of the final crisis, a bad bout of pneumonia, the brown spaniel, Ballad, was diagnosed with a rare form of blood cancer. When Gary would wake up in the middle of the night and hear Ballad's troubled snore from her doggy bed across the room, he'd sometimes get confused and think that his mother was there in the dark searching for whatever oxygen she could manage to pull into her lungs.

Tread lived on his own in the condominium for a year after Rachel's death. Gary had no idea how much time had passed. His mother's death had divided what was left of life into two realms: the one in which he and Ella grieved the loss of his mother and the ongoing ups and downs of Ballad's illness; and the other, the dark side of the clock, where Tread sat in his condo day after day, waiting for the next bad thing to happen.

But as the following winter began to loosen its grip, Gary started dreaming. First, a road with actual signs promising a destination. Then tiny puffs of sand from someone walking just ahead. One night, he managed to catch up with the traveller and realized it was a much-younger Tread. They walked on together past sign after sign. It was a soothing way to spend the nights. He tried to share this with Tread over the telephone and then one Sunday night in person at Tread's local Swiss Chalet, but got no response at all, not even a frown. It was clear that Tread had given up any sense of the future, that whatever might happen next would have to make the effort to come to him rather than the other way around.

Both Gary and Ella agreed that Tread wouldn't last much longer just sitting in front of the TV set week after week, so they set about arranging the sale of his condo. The plan was to move him up to Queensville with them. They had a small basement apartment where he could retain some independence. And Gary would start working on plans for the two of them to walk together. Hell, even if it was just around the block at first. The world would start moving again if only Tread would take a step toward it. Muse, their surviving spaniel (Ballad succumbed to her cancer a mere two days before Tread moved in), would be a great help. Not even an invalid could bear to say no to a dog desperate to stretch her legs.

It wasn't easy for any of them to adapt to this new situation, but by early summer Tread seemed to have bonded with Muse enough to take over her daily walks, although Muse turned out to be a bit of a disappointment in the distance department, often twisting her end of the leash homeward after one jaunt around the block. Ella began suggesting midafternoon trips to the Holland River, no less than thirty-to-forty minutes away. Tread grumbled over this a little, but Ella made sure to stress that it was she who needed the exercise and that he was doing her a favour.

By mid-July, Gary was ready to participate. He had the first week of August off and rather than try and fit in a short trip for them all, he decided, with Ella's blessing, that he and Tread would walk around Lake Simcoe together. Ella would drive them to their departure point, Kempenfelt Bay in Barrie, and then they'd head off on foot northeast to Orillia, then begin heading south to Brechin, Beaverton, Sutton, and finally Keswick.

Gary announced the trip one night at dinner. Of course, he and Ella had discussed it thoroughly, but this was the first time that Tread had heard anything about the idea. He stopped lifting his fork with a hungry rhythm and turned his head a bit to the right, staring down at the floor where Muse was waiting patiently for crumbs. "Is the dog a part of this?" he asked.

Gary glanced at Ella and saw her upper lip take the shape of a smile. He wasn't sure whether she was tickled by Tread's affection for the dog or amused at what Gary had to admit to himself was a twinge of jealousy. He'd been waiting his whole life to hit the road with his father, to wander for the sake of wandering, and didn't want any distractions, Muse included, to get in the way. "Nope," he finally answered. "Just you and me."

Tread swallowed noticeably even though there didn't appear to be anything in his mouth. He then reached for his glass of cranberry juice, but instead of taking a sip, he laid the cool rim against his forehead and rolled the glass from one side of his skull to the other.

"Are you all right?' Ella asked, sliding her hand across the table, a few inches short of a touch.

"What do you want from me?" Tread responded. At first it seemed that he was addressing Ella, but then he slowly turned to face Gary, who had a forkful of corkscrew pasta just disappearing into his mouth. "You drag me from my home in Toronto, make me leave all memories of my Rachel behind." He flinched when he said *Rachel.* "Then you make me walk your damn dog three times a day." He blushed high on his cheeks then raised his voice. "And now you want me to walk around Lake Simcoe? I'm eighty-two years old." He shook his head twice, the second time harder than the first.

"It's a chance for us to have an adventure," Gary said. "Life isn't over just because Mom died."

"My life is over when I say so."

"So give me something I can remember when you're gone." Gary was surprised at how much this sounded like begging. "I would have given anything to walk across Africa with you."

"You weren't even born," Tread said.

"It doesn't have to be Africa. Lake Simcoe is fine."

"If I'd thought Lake Simcoe would make an interesting trip, I'd have done it years ago." He threw his hands up in the air, which started Muse barking.

Gary tried his best not to sound as hurt as he felt. "It's for me, Dad," he said, hitting the two D's in *Dad* just a touch too hard. "I don't care where we walk; I just want you to walk with me."

Tread looked like he was thinking hard, his eyebrows knit together in a straggly clump. "Then walk me back to Toronto," he said.

Ella cleared her throat before joining in. "Why did you never say that you didn't want to leave Toronto? You signed the papers to sell the condo. We didn't force you to move here with us."

"I moved because you wanted me to. I did it for you." The tips of his ears flushed. "Think of it as a gift from a dying man."

"But you're not dead yet," Gary said, on the verge of shouting. "The journey is still going on whether you like it or not."

"Then walk me to Toronto," Tread repeated.

"You don't have a place in Toronto anymore," Ella said.

"You don't worry about details like that when you travel. You're not trying to get somewhere. That's not the point. You just keep moving until you find the closest thing to home."

"That's me," Gary announced. "I'm the closest thing to home." His voice cracked on the last two words.

"And you're right across the table from me," Tread said. "Three steps and I'd be stepping on your toes."

At this point, Ella suggested dessert, an apple brown Betty with chocolate cookie-dough ice cream. Neither Tread nor Gary accepted the offer, although they both eventually dug into their servings once the dessert plates were placed in front of them. Tread was the first to leave the table, his chair scraping across the wooden floor. Muse leapt to her feet at exactly the same time.

"I never said I wouldn't do my job," he said. "But don't get all gummy and think that I'm taking the dog on some sort of walkabout. She needs to pee, that's the long and short of it." He shuffled out of the kitchen with Muse scrambling behind, her toenails clattering like broken seashells on a beach.

Gary wasn't sure what he felt, or whether he wanted Ella to see that he was feeling anything at all. He got up from the table and helped her carry the plates and cutlery to the counter. Would it be possible to walk Lake Simcoe by himself? He'd run into all sorts of people along the way, maybe even an old man who would remind him of his father. He was grateful to Ella for giving him the space to think. He imagined the conversation he'd have with that old man; they'd share details of their lives like the rivers and towns on a map. Then Gary would go on alone, the blue August lake never leaving his side. He'd arrive home again a changed man. He'd tell everyone the story whether they wanted to hear it or not.

MISTRESS

One could see immediately that Jim Darling was worthy of speculation. He had a sweet face for a man, kind of rosy, but with a roughed-up nose, squashed to the left, that gave him enough manliness to carry off a head of wheat-coloured curls. He loved to laugh, and when he was off on a comic bender, he reminded Jean of a clown doll she'd had as a child. The best way to describe him was Charming with a capital C.

Jim arrived to manage the Texaco after the owner, Russ Robinson, Jean's father, was forced to retire with a bum heart. Jim came from a trailer rental business in Rexdale; he'd been manager for a little more than two years, and his references were extraordinary. Not only good looking, but ambitious, a bit of a prodigy. Plus, he had a two-year-old son, an investment in the future.

Robinson's Texaco was the biggest service station in Toronto and had been featured in both the *Toronto Star* and the *Telegram* several times. It was more than just a place to gas up. After working for a variety of stations for twenty years, Russ had secured this particular Texaco right across the street from St. John's Cemetery, where both of Russ's parents and his baby brother Roger were buried. He knew from the outset that he wanted to create a great atmosphere. Robinson's Texaco became a hangout for the neighbourhood dads. There were seven different snack and drink machines, and a waiting room with soft chairs and music playing quietly in the background. Russ added a small carwash with high-powered jets before the end of the first year. Then he went about involving himself in the businesses in the community, sponsoring a little-league baseball team and an annual golf tournament at the nearby Hunt Club golf course, where he used to caddy as a kid.

Jean joined the team as bookkeeper after she took a few night-school courses. She was a woman who could turn heads; her father sometimes referred to her as an ingénue. There were two other women in the office—Priscilla, who answered the phone, and Sherry, who was in charge of hospitality, making sure that customers got coffee and magazines while they waited—but Jean definitely stood out.

All in all, Robinson's Texaco was much classier than your usual service station. And the gossip it engendered was cleaner than it might have been at other, more uncouth places. The whispers regarding Jim Darling were mostly expected stuff like replacing a taillight on his own car without paying for it or leaving work early one afternoon to take his kid to Sunnyside. But when the rumours started including Jean, they began to take a more serious turn. Words joined forces with other words, and soon it wasn't just lunchroom talk. The buzz got into the community and finally made its way into Russ's living room.

It was Marg, Jean's mother, who was told at the beauty parlour by the woman who washed her hair that Jean and Jim were being included in the same sentences in a number of conversations.

Jean had known this would happen. It wasn't anything that Jim Darling did; he was a perfect gentleman, not only to Jean, but Priscilla and Sherry too. He wasn't a man you flirted with—his charisma went deeper. He talked rather than kibitzed. He looked women in the eyes instead of zooming in on their breasts. Jean really enjoyed listening to him talk about his wife, Audra, what a great mother she was, and how Christopher was the light of his life. It did cross her mind that he made Audra sound more like a governess than a wife, but the fact that his good looks made the whole office warmer and brighter somehow quelled any warning signs. Before too long, she started talking back, telling him about how much she enjoyed night school and how she was thinking of continuing her classes and becoming a chartered accountant; how she'd like to travel, especially to the Florida Keys, where apparently you could look across the water and see the outline of Cuba; and how she had a perfectly decent crush on Pat Boone.

She remembered giggling at this, feeling suddenly childish. It was so out of character that she cut it off with an awkwardness that resulted in a mild case of hiccups. Priscilla was staring at her strangely. And Leo, one of the mechanics, strode into the office in the middle of it all and stopped short with a puzzled look on his face.

This was when the rumours began. Jean could imagine Priscilla cornering Sherry by the pop machine, saying that the hiccupping was a cover-up for something else, or Leo kneeling down where the second mechanic's legs were sticking out from under a Plymouth Valiant and saying, "I just walked into a heat wave, if you know what I mean."

And Jean and Jim kept talking, as did the rest of the staff.

One drowsy August evening, Jean arrived home at the usual time. Her father was in a terrible mood, mumbling to himself, totally ignoring Jean's greeting. She figured the news from his doctor that morning had been bad.

She was shocked when he verbally struck out at her in the hallway outside the dining room. "How could you?" he hissed, and even though Jean tried to feign that she didn't know what he was talking about, dismissing it entirely, she thought of Jim and for the first time realized the illicitness of her feelings for him. Nothing had happened, but she now realized she was just biding her time until something did.

Still nothing happened for a while. Russ hadn't made any ultimatums, but it was nonetheless clear that if this thing, this abomination, turned out to be true, Jim would be out on his ear. Knowing that he could die at any moment had put Russ in the mood for burning bridges. Even just the idea of a wayward daughter was a daughter already lost.

Marg refused to legitimize any of it. "I don't think you're that stupid," she said, and that was that. Jean's brother, Charlie, couldn't have cared less what she did; he wasn't even twenty-one yet but was already well on his way to becoming a drunk. And Beth, the baby, was barely sixteen and couldn't sustain interest in anything in which she wasn't the main protagonist.

Days turned into weeks, and suddenly it was October. Jim was all that Jean thought about: the way the hair on his forehead turned into ringlets when he was sweating, the half-moons of dirt under his fingernails, his smell of grease and burnt metal. She'd watch him sliding across the bays, checking up on the mechanics, greeting customers out in the lot. Whether he was shaking someone's hand or hefting a battery, he had an ease about him like a well-oiled bicycle chain.

Numbers began to bore Jean. Her sole job was to add up daily life to an acceptable sum. She'd sit at her desk wrenching her ankles into knots where no one could see. A few times, she pounded her fist quietly against the adding machine, making rubbish of perfectly good digits. Once she kicked over her trash can, and it clattered and clanged its way across the room. She was sick of hearing Priscilla's high-pitched "Robinson's Texaco" when she answered the shrill telephone's ring.

The only things that kept her sane were the tiny details with which she and Jim made it clear to one another that their relationship existed in a place they had yet to chart, that somewhere amidst the awful routine of longing was a conversation that would eventually make it all possible, erase the mistakes they'd made before meeting one another, and renounce all the gossip for a clear, well-tuned truth.

On Saturday afternoons near closing, Jim would always leave a little something on her desk. He was such a good sneak that she never caught him in the act. A sprig of lavender, a red rose with a clipped stem, a Cadbury Dairy Milk bar, a string of red licorice. The gift never appeared until Priscilla had gone to the bathroom to paint her face, when no one was around.

Most mornings, Jean managed to pull in beside Jim's red-and-white Buick Roadmaster in the parking lot, which allowed them to dally just a little before heading home in different directions at the end of the day. She would always ask about Audra and Christopher and would feel snug inside his answers, especially the ones where Audra sounded merely dutiful. She loved his passion for Christopher, though, and would often bring up something he'd told her about the boy a few weeks ago, point out parallels between Jim and Christopher that she could see brought silver glints to his lake-grey eyes.

One night near the end of the month, she mentioned that it was getting darker a few seconds earlier every night, that the six o'clock sky was already charred like the inside of a Halloween pumpkin.

"It makes me feel like I'm disappearing."

"Like a ghost?" Jean asked, realizing that she loved his body and would be heartbroken if it dissolved.

"No, I'm flesh and blood, all right, but see-through," he said. "Everything shows."

What little light was left was too smudged to see anything clearly. But there was an energy coming from Jim that distinguished him from the darkness. All she'd have to do would be to slip into her car and lean over and unlock the passenger door.

This didn't happen that particular evening, but a few weeks later, each night bringing them closer and closer, until it had begun to feel that the November darkness was swallowing them whole. Jim had whispered, "More" in Jean's ear, and she had murmured back at him, "Yes, yes, yes." Everyone else had left. They went back inside the Texaco, Jean in the lead. The key shook as she struggled to fit it into the lock, until Jim steadied it with his hand. They felt their way through the pitch black office into the small lunchroom, where Jean was relieved to unbutton her Persian lamb coat. She tangled both hands in his curls and tugged until his mouth was squashed on hers. The weight of Jim Darling was such a happy ballast that she heard herself make cooing sounds.

By spring, there had been too many changes to count, let alone understand. Jim handed in his resignation a few weeks after Christmas and started his own business, an automotive parts company at Warden and Lawrence. Jean couldn't bear to be without him eight hours a day, and so she left her job at the Texaco a few weeks later and was already comanaging the new place.

Living in her father's house on Browning was becoming untenable. Once one string was cut, the rest unravelled. Russ went blind at the very mention of Jim's name. Her mother had plenty to say, but all of it was confused and cruel. There was a yellow-bricked apartment building just a block and a bit down Warden. She was able to afford a one-bedroom. The kitchen was cramped and the bathroom only had a shower, but it felt as much Jim's home as hers and was therefore perfect. They walked there together every night after closing and would heat up a canned dinner and wolf it down, leaving plenty of time to fully undress and make love until it was time for Jim to go home.

There was nothing tawdry at play here. It was more a correction than an affair. The suggestion at large was that Jim Darling was using Jean: sex, youth, risk, all those things that middle-aged men need in order to carry on. But Jim wasn't quite forty and, except for his battered nose, was much younger looking. He was a giver, a listener, a player. Less than a month after that first night in the Texaco lunchroom, he had confessed it all to Audra. Sure, she kicked up a fuss in the beginning. But she was a realist; she knew that Jim was in love and that love couldn't be ruled by logic. Holding on to the way she wished life could be would only divide the sorrow into torturous increments. She was the kind of woman who preferred to meet giants and dragons head-on.

They made what Priscilla or Sherry might have called an *arrangement*. Jean, the bookkeeper, thought of it as more of a formula. Jim and Audra, both lapsed Catholics, but Catholics nonetheless, would stay married. He would spend his days at Darling Automotive, his evenings with Jean, his nights back home in time to help put Christopher to bed. He always arrived at Jean's apartment at six in the morning, in great spirits, smelling of soap and shaving cream. He never mentioned his nights, and Jean rarely imagined them.

"Just temporary," he said. "Till Christopher is old enough to understand."

Saturday was always a marvellous day. The business closed at one, and they had the entire afternoon together. They often went grocery shopping as Jean had decided to learn how to cook. Her mother was a first-class baker and wouldn't even let her kids into the kitchen to lick the spoons. Jean wasn't very "domesticated," as Jim joked, but she knew that she could do anything she wanted, that all it took was a combination of focus and persistence. Other outings included windy walks along the boardwalk, drives north of the city, and visits to secondhand bookstores, where Jim liked to hunt down obscure World War One mysteries, a quest that Jean enjoyed being part of, the two of them shoulder to shoulder in the narrow rows, knowing that a treasure might be discovered at any moment.

Saturday night, Jim stayed over. They never went to sleep until after two. Their lovemaking on these nights was greedier than the rest of the week. Sometimes, they would hang back until their bodies ached; others, Jean felt that she was being devoured, that she'd wake up in the morning and find only the barest of traces of who she'd been before Jim gobbled her whole: a few long, brown hairs on her pillow; a silvery stain the shape of a seagull; a wrinkle in the sheets that looked like a valentine; an imprint of two clefts, either buttocks or melons.

He would leave first thing Sunday morning to get home in time for Christopher to rise, and Jean wouldn't see him again until Monday. But she looked forward to sleeping in on Sunday mornings, wrapped up in Jim's smells. She'd usually spend the afternoons trying out different recipes or reading one of the mysteries that Jim had already read, imagining him puzzling over the clues. Sunday dinner was back at Browning, where both she and Charlie took turns being the black sheep. Jim's name was still not allowed to be mentioned, nor the automotive shop, nor her apartment. The pretense was that she just appeared out of nowhere on Sunday evenings and then disappeared into nothingness for the rest of the week. Shame was served with roast beef, fried chicken, ham and beans, whatever Marg had cooked. The dessert was always the star of the evening, though it too felt shameful. How could they be allowing themselves something so indulgent considering the circumstances? Once Marg caught Jean wrapping up a piece of chocolate cake with mandarin orange icing to take home for Jim; Marg made such a ruckus that Jean never tried again.

By the time she got home, she was often on the verge of sobbing. She felt bereft and dirty. How had she managed to fashion such a life for herself? So much of it couldn't be shared with anyone other than Jim. She remembered asking him if he felt like a ghost that night in the parking lot of her father's Texaco. And now it turned out that she was the one with the invisible life. She'd go to bed not caring if she ever woke up again, but then it would suddenly be six in the morning, and Jim would be sliding in beside her under the tightly tucked-in sheets, and she could feel herself being put back together nerve by nerve.

One Sunday afternoon three years later, her sister, Beth, called in tears. Marg had suddenly started talking nonsense over lunch and had devolved into pure drivel by the time Russ reached their family doctor and was told to call an ambulance. Most likely a stroke. How could this be happening? It was her father who'd been opening death's door one creak at a time over the last few years.

"You'd better hightail it to the East General," he said after grabbing the phone from Beth. "But don't you dare bring that Darling man with you."

Marg lived for a few more days, drifting in and out of consciousness, looking deader than dead. Jean had to tiptoe out of the room to sneak a phone call to Jim. When Audra answered, she listened to her say hello three times and then hung up. She tried again just after seven, and Jim answered, offering to join her at the hospital. She explained that it would be better if she handled this on her own, and they agreed to talk again in the morning.

Jim arrived back at the apartment at his usual time the next day. Jean had spent the night at the hospital, but had come home for a shower and a change of clothes. He just wanted to hold her for a while before she hurried back to the hospital, but she almost ripped off the buttons of his shirt. She wished that she could take his penis to the East General with her, hidden at the bottom of her purse.

Russ and all three kids were in the room when Marg died early on Wednesday morning. Charlie was as close to sober as he'd been in years. Jean tried to hold her father's hand, but he shook her off. After the hospital staff took the body away, Jean headed back to the apartment to pack some clothes. She thought it best that she spend a couple of days at Browning. She called Jim, who was just around the corner at Darling Automotive. He wanted to come right over, but Jean was afraid of being overwhelmed again. What if this time Jim wasn't enough to drown out the horror?

The funeral was at Giffen-Mack on the Danforth. The room was packed with family and friends. Marg looked like marzipan in her mahogany coffin. Jean had never felt so alone. She had made Jim promise that he wouldn't show up, but she discovered herself crestfallen when he obeyed. She was going to bury her mother without her lover's arms to collapse into, without the smell of him to drive out the stink of dying flowers and formaldehyde.

A number of times, she seriously considered ending it. After Marg's death, Jean sunk into a depression that made it impossible to stick with even the smallest of decisions—what to eat for dinner or what colour scarf to wear with her forest-green angora sweater—let alone big things like love and the rest of her life. She started writing out her thoughts on Sunday mornings, when she was all alone and could measure Jim's absence with her need to see him again. If there were some way to fold the planet at the corner of Warden and Lawrence so that Darling Automotive went one way and the yellow-bricked apartment went the other, she was sure that she could learn to live with the sadness, proceed with a different future than the one she'd been subsisting on these last five years.

But then Monday morning would come around, and Jim would be standing on the fuzzy rug beside the bed, peeling off his shirt, stepping out of his trousers, joining her under the covers. It was like taking a barely risen sun to bed: he slowly filled her with a light that made everything else inconsequential. He burnt the tip of her tongue; he singed her eyelashes. There wasn't a sensible plan in the world that could outlast this.

There were photos of Christopher in every room of the apartment except for the bathroom. He had just turned nine. Jean could describe every detail of his recent birthday party, held at a riding stable north of Uxbridge, and yet she'd never actually seen him in the flesh. When her father was being particularly mean to her, she'd drag out one of Jim's stories about Christopher and replace Jim's participation with her own. She pretended to be more than a mistress.

What she would have given to have someone to listen to her predicament and not pass judgment, to help her sort her feelings out. Although neither her father nor her siblings had abandoned her, they were constantly making their disapproval known. The truth was that as long as Jim wanted her, she found herself wanting him back. Did Beth feel similarly about her fiancé, Nick, a square, swarthy foreman at a farm-equipment company whose Ukrainian accent made him seem more interesting than he really was? Could she feel him lighting tiny fires in the brittle marrow inside her bones? Did he make her sick with desire?

But even bringing up Jim's name made Beth livid. "He's stealing the best years of your life," she often said. Jean dreaded the day when the best was all used up.

It dawned on her one night, when Jim had left for home, that Audra, his obliging wife of thirteen years, was probably the only person on earth who might understand her. She knew that this was a betrayal of Jim, but she was reeling with so much doubt and confusion that she knew she couldn't be trusted to make the right decision. There was a sourness at the core of her. She had trouble taking a deep breath.

She had no idea how to reach Audra during business hours; all she knew was that she worked in a beauty parlour. And she couldn't call on weekends: Jim was either with Jean or Audra, depending on the day. Her only window of opportunity was the twenty minutes between Jim kissing her goodbye at the door on weeknights and his arrival at his other home. She was afraid that once she started talking, she might not be able to stop. What if Audra was under the same spell as she was? In all likelihood, she couldn't live without Jim either.

On a Tuesday night of no distinction, she simply picked up the phone before the elevator doors had shut completely and dialed the Darling number. Christopher answered. Jean could imagine the flushed look on his face, knowing how much he enjoyed being master of the phone, a rite of passage that would one day seem paltry compared to all the other privileges he'd be discovering. "Hello," he said loud and clear. "Darling family. Can I help you?"

Jean's first words to her potential stepson Christopher were, "Could I please speak to your mother?" She tried to imagine a day when they could laugh about this together. What an inauspicious beginning.

There was a muffled thud as he dropped the receiver into what sounded like a pillow, then the slap-slap-slap of hard-soled slippers drawing near.

"Hallo?" Audra said, sounding nasal.

Jean started off making very little sense, falter upon falter. It crossed her mind for a second that maybe Audra didn't really know about her. "It's me, Jean" was a stupid way to begin. She finally hit her stride when she reached the part about them meeting for lunch on a workday. "I thought we might be able to help one another," she concluded, realizing what a lie it was. What she was hoping for, she realized, was that Audra might be able to show her how not to care.

"Make an appointment," Audra said when Jean finally finished. There was still ten minutes left before Jim pulled into a driveway that Jean had never seen. "It's called The Beauty Mark, on Brimley. You can find the number in the Yellow Pages."

An appointment? Had Audra misunderstood and thought that Jean was someone who wanted her hair done? She usually had a perm, but lately had been growing it out a bit, which, she thought, made her look more like a schoolgirl.

"Make an appointment," Audra repeated, breaking the silence.

"To have my hair done?" Jean asked.

"Whatever," Audra answered, followed by a click.

Jean didn't know whether to laugh or shudder. She could hear her father calling her a tramp. Beth would look aghast. "She'll probably shave your head." Worst of all, Jim might not be able to forgive her. He would know that she didn't trust him with the same unwavering intensity as he trusted her.

Jean didn't even bother looking up The Beauty Mark in the Yellow Pages. What a foolish, dangerous idea. For the next few months, she saw Jim's vulnerability in a whole new light. He reminded her a little of the Labrador retriever her father had brought home when Jean was eleven. Such an obliging creature, so easy to hurt. She couldn't bear to raise her voice even when a situation clearly called for firmness. The only emotion she could sustain was a bottomless tenderness.

She still felt imbalanced in her desire for Jim, how it could empty her head in seconds flat. But her love for him had deepened so that even when he wasn't there, she somehow moved more softly than before, careful so as not to bruise the silence.

Six months had passed since the phone call, when one morning her father had a massive heart attack and was dead mid-fall. He had been alone in the house even though Beth and Nick were living at Browning until they could afford a down payment on their own house. They were both at work, and Charlie was off on a bender. Jean was in the habit of calling him every day at lunchtime, and when she couldn't reach him that particular afternoon, she called Mrs. Priestly next door, who went to check and found him sprawled peacefully on the kitchen floor.

Amidst the planning and mourning, Jean made it clear to both Beth and Charlie that Jim would be attending the funeral. Shame was a thing of the past. Like it or not, he was the love of her life. It felt perfectly natural for him to be by her side. He was cordial to everyone, returning even the crankiest of faces with a warm smile. He was ingratiating without being smarmy. He never let go of her arm during the two nights of visitation and tightened his hold at the funeral itself. If he hadn't been holding her at the graveside, she was sure that she would have slipped into that deep, welcoming darkness.

He didn't spend that Sunday with Audra and Christopher, instead accompanying Jean to dinner on Browning with poor Charlie and Beth and Nick. He and Nick talked cars while Jean and Beth cooked. During dinner, he encouraged them to share memories of their father, including a few of his own from the brief time that he worked for him at the Texaco. There was no question: he was well on his way to becoming a part of the family that night. No more Mr. Married Man.

Surprisingly, he reminded Jean of her father. It shocked her a little to see how alike they were: both big personalities, risk takers. She remembered how as a toddler she'd been crazy for her father, no one else would do. She'd sit by the window at the end of the day and start squealing the minute his car pulled into the drive. She'd be in his arms the minute he crossed the threshold. Nothing was better than to bury her face in his neck and smell that sweet service-station grime.

But now she had Jim to adore, and, more importantly, be adored by, not only at work, but at home. His kisses had adverbs attached to them: *passionately, dreamily, deeply.* He preferred to raise himself up by his elbows when they were making love so that he could watch the intricacies of her pleasure. Or was it so she could watch him? *Powerfully, fervently.* He also liked to watch her eating cereal, the way milk sometimes trickled down her chin. "Everything you do is loveable," was one of his favourite lines. It was the *everything* that spooked her more than the *loveable.* Even when she was in the bathroom, he'd call out to her from the hall, read her snippets from the newspaper or tell her something that he'd forgotten from the day before. Jean could never accuse him of being absent or inattentive. In the movie of her life, he would be the perfect man, except for his wife and kid. Was he the same with them? A dutiful dad, a great husband? Was there someone in between who did the twenty minute drive every night at nine?

Jean was perfecting a little something on her own to counteract the pressure of being *loveable.* The minute he'd leave the apartment, she'd stand in front of the full-length mirror in the bedroom and stare at her body from head to toe. "Mistress," she'd whisper. Then, a little louder, "Scarlet woman," working her way to "tramp" and "slut." She was the only one left who cared enough about her to use those kinds of names. Russ and Marg were both gone, and Jim had won over her brother and sister with an ease that was beyond her capabilities. Even math, which she was good at, took a certain amount of struggle. But as a whore, she was Jim's equal. *Everything she did* ... Effortless. "Whore," she'd say, raising her voice so she could be heard throughout the rest of the empty apartment.

Somehow, constantly crossing the dividing line between good and evil made Jean feel limber. She could be sweet and cushy with Jim, then close the door and curse the day she met him. Her relationship with Beth was good; she instantly fell into the role of perfect aunt the minute little Julie arrived. But she could see clearly that Beth was becoming a bitch with Nick, and she secretly hoped that he'd take a page from Jim and find himself someone who would dote on him and expect nothing in return. She was even able to tolerate Charlie as he fell off the wagon again and again, knowing that he was well on his way to drinking himself to death. "You're a moron," she'd say, but only after hanging up the phone.

She started smoking; she'd always been a social smoker, though a mistress didn't get all that many chances to be seen in public. Jim had wrinkled his brow at first, but soon accepted the bad habit as another of her allures. "You remind me of Lauren Bacall," he said, kissing her even when she had a mouthful of smoke.

The idea of getting fat kept her busy for a few months, but she just didn't have the metabolism. She stopped shaving her armpits until Jim said that he liked the "jungle look." Then, one Sunday, she dyed her hair a rusty shade of red. "Ooh, copper," Jim exclaimed, running all ten fingers through it. Finally, her free will in need of a bigger boost, she ditched her diaphragm at the back of her underwear drawer and six weeks later was pregnant.

Keeping this a secret from everyone, Jim included, was the most exquisite experience she'd ever had. It beat out that first time that Jim made love to her in the Texaco lunchroom. It was better than saying "slut" into her bedroom mirror. She wanted it to last forever. But then one night Jim gripped first her right breast, then her left. "You just keep getting more luscious," he said. It wouldn't be long before that lusciousness started getting out of control.

She knew how Jim would react. Based on over five years of being together, his history of total devotion suggested that he'd be supportive, perhaps even pleased. But it surprised her how sick she was of all that support. Even this wouldn't change a thing. The minute the secret was out, the pleasure would die inside of her. She knew that she'd love the baby, but with more effort than it took to love Jim.

What she longed for was an episode, an accident of some kind, a small but life-altering explosion. She wanted the baby to change everything. And so, the very next day, she found the number for The Beauty Mark in the

Yellow Pages and made an appointment with Audra Darling, using Beth's married name, Andrukh, as a disguise.

She was afraid that night after Jim left, afraid that what she was about to do really might change everything. But there didn't seem to be any middle ground left. She'd gone past the dividing line to a place where anything she did was bound to cause pain.

The Beauty Mark was in a small plaza on Brimley, sandwiched between a convenience store and a dry cleaners. Unassuming, perfect for something illicit to be revealed. Jean parked in front of a dental office a few doors from the hairdressers; there were teeth the size of Jean's hands dangling from white ribbons in the window front.

When she pushed on the door to The Beauty Mark, it stuck, causing her to push so hard that when it finally gave, she was propelled into the shop like a clumsy ballerina, a set of bells ringing madly above her. All that was missing were bugles.

The room was divided into three pod-like spaces joined by a long mirror that repeated everything, making the place seem bigger and more colourful than it actually was. A row of hairdryers lined the opposite wall, plus a small waiting area with a round, low table strewn with fashion magazines. At the back, Jean could see a couple of sinks.

A white-haired woman in black Capris and a baggy blouse that shimmered like gold foil was removing rollers from a younger woman's hair; the younger woman was saying "ouch" every time a strand of hair got caught in the grip of a roller. At the second station, another woman was sitting in a chair with one leg stretched across the other; she appeared to be napping. Down by the sinks, another, older woman was cleaning up.

Jean was fascinated by the white-haired woman's hairstyle. It seemed to start out as a bouffant, but then tapered into a braid at the back. Taking a second look, the woman didn't look old enough to have such peerless white hair. Was this Audra? Jean had never seen a picture and had asked for a description so long ago that all she remembered was Jim saying that she'd been a stunner in her day.

"Can I help you?" the white-haired woman asked. She gave Jean a great big smile. Her teeth were a greyer shade of white.

"I have an appointment," she said, feeling a bit woozy. What if Audra knew what she looked like? Surely, she would have been more curious than

Jean, being the wronged wife. Somehow Jean had always imagined Audra to be less appealing than herself.

"Hey, sleepyhead," the white-haired woman said, banging her heel on the wooden floor three times. "Your ten thirty is here."

Her eyes fluttered open, and she looked into the mirror. It was obvious by the way she curled her bottom lip and sighed that she didn't particularly like what she saw in Jean.

"I'm Audra," she called rather casually. "Just a sec," she added, her voice deeper than Jean recalled it from the phone. She slipped out of the chair and gave herself a bit of a glare in the mirror. She had gleaming strawberry-blond hair parted down the middle and flipped into waves at her shoulders. Jean made everything blurry by squinting her eyes. She couldn't bear to take in any more details for the moment.

The chair felt final; anything might happen. She might emerge from this with chunks of her hair ripped out, her scalp bloodied. One of those trimmers could make a real mess in the wrong hands. But it was too late to back out now. She couldn't walk out on Audra any more than she could leave Jim.

She slipped on a patch of cut hair on the floor, and Audra clutched her by the elbow, her fingers cold and rather bony. Once Jean was in the chair, she was surprised by her face in the mirror: a patchwork of blushes. And her hair looked dry and unappreciated.

Audra asked her what she wanted: "Colour? Cut?" When Jean said that she wasn't sure, Audra started offering a string of possibilities. Jean finally confessed that she'd like something with float to it, something softer.

"I can do that," Audra said, "I can definitely do that."

Jean's thoughts hadn't gone as far as how to handle the intimacy of Audra up to her wrists in her hair. She could feel Audra's breath on the back of her neck. At any moment, she might slit Jean's throat. How to tell this woman that she was pregnant with her husband's baby, a sibling for Christopher, who was now officially an adolescent?

"What's your name?" Audra asked her.

Jean felt scrambled with panic. What name had she chosen? Hadn't Audra written it down in the salon's appointment book? But when she lifted her head and looked in the mirror, she could see that Audra sincerely didn't remember.

"Beth," she said, her sister's name tripping off her tongue.

"From Elizabeth, or just plain Beth?" she asked.

"Just plain Beth."

The blur continued. Audra sent her down to the sink area, and the older woman, who identified herself as what sounded like Bianca, proceeded to massage her scalp with various floral and citrus scents that made her dizzy. Despite her nervousness, she relaxed into it and was sent back to Audra's chair feeling lightheaded and painfully vulnerable.

It was from this state of inward calm that Jean braved her first complete look at Audra. Her hair was perhaps too perfect; it could even have been a wig, and her chin was unsettlingly sharp. If she'd been a marble statue, it would have been obvious that the sculptor had gotten carried away and scraped her within an inch of having no chin at all. But her eyes were beautiful, that shade of green that just screams early spring. And her cheekbones made up for the chin; they took her face and gave it a lift. She looked her age, but striking, with just a hint of somewhere foreign that no one knew that much about, like Lichtenstein or Moldovia.

She couldn't really see her body as it was hidden behind the high-backed chair, but she'd thought of her as being on the petite side when she'd first seen her napping. Still a desirable woman, Jean thought. *Why?* she asked herself. Then, *Why not?*

Audra moved gracefully and gave the silence an open-endedness. Jean could see how easy it would have been for Jim to fall in love with her. The lips above her pointy chin were very full, with a pinkish tone like the skin of a just-picked peach. The thought of Jim being kissed by those lips made her feel strangely close to Audra. She imagined her pulse would be slow and steady.

As if sensing the closeness that Jean was awash in, Audra tried again to initiate a conversation. "Do you live around here?" she asked.

"Not that far. Warden and Lawrence," she said, feeling faint at giving up such a major detail of her life. She might have said *I live around the corner from where your husband works.*

But Audra didn't look the least bit startled. "Married?" she asked.

"No," Jean dared another truth, fighting off the impulse to say *mistress* or *slut.*

"Not the ball-and-chain type?" Audra asked. "A working girl?"

"I'm a bookkeeper," she answered. "Almost a chartered accountant." She felt like she was going deeper and deeper into a forest and would never be able to find her way out again.

"Good for you," she said, giving Jean a pat on the shoulder.

Jean could feel the silence start to settle in again. She hurried to stop it from taking over completely and heard herself say, "What about you?"

"Ball-and-chain," she said, grinning. "One kid, one Siamese cat, one mother-in-law."

Jean fumbled to remember whether Jim had ever mentioned a cat. It wasn't the kind of detail that Jean would have even registered, not being a cat person. But a mother-in-law? She knew that Jim's mother was still living, but she thought she resided in Winnipeg, in her own apartment, near Jim's only sister, Teresa.

"I'm also taking classes in fancy hair design," she continued. "Who knows, maybe I'll be a stylist for the rich and famous one of these days. Move to Florida."

"Leave behind the ball-and-chain?" Jean imagined Jim staying over every night. They would have to talk this over.

"Nah," she said. "Florida would be good for him. He's a terrible workaholic, so I might have to tie him up and steal him away."

"What if he wants to stay?" Jean asked, wondering whether she was pushing too hard.

Audra gave her a clueless look. "Jim and I have a plan," she explained. "Once our son has flown the coop."

Jean felt her throat closing. "I'm pregnant," she let slip. *Mistress. Mother.*

That seemed to bring back the silence. Jean could see that Audra was struggling with this information.

"Lots of good people are choosing not to do the legal thing these days," she finally said. "Love is more than just a piece of paper."

Before she could think of a reply that might bring the conversation back to risky ground, Audra was unclasping the cape and folding it in two, careful not to get any hairs on Jean's blouse. "Ta-dah," she said. "Hope you like it."

Jean looked hard at herself in the mirror. She saw a softer, perhaps even bouncier version of herself. But beneath the hair, she could still see the old self that Jim could never get enough of. Taking her eyes off herself, she found Audra still standing behind her, waiting to be praised, Jean thought. Portrait of a woman who'd been lying to herself for so long now that she believed that one day soon she'd make it as far as Florida, hair *artiste* to the stars.

Audra had moved over to the cash register. It was clear that Jean's announcement had shaken her. She might have been a bit befuddled at the moment, but when she was home and let the details wash over her, it would hit her that this strange customer was Jim's mistress; that a child was about to be born who would change the direction of everything.

Jean tipped her generously with what was technically her own husband's money.

As Jean opened the door to Darling Automotive, it struck her for the first time how strange it was that Audra had never visited the business. Wouldn't most wives have wanted to check out where their husbands spent so much time? Maybe the world of The Beauty Mark was on a different planet than Darling Automotive. Maybe Jean had just driven from one galaxy to another. That would explain a lot of things.

Tony, the stock manager, was flipping through a Buick catalogue at the front counter. "Nice hair," he said as she slipped past to the main office.

Jim was hunched over his desk with his reading glasses perched on the edge of his nose like a Dickens character. With his head bent over, his curls were extravagant. On the drive here, Jean had decided to ask him about his mother. Was it possible that she was now living with Audra and Jim and not-so-little-anymore Christopher? She wasn't sure why this made her feel so desolate. *A husband, a child, and a mother-in-law.* Even a Siamese cat. She felt such a pressure beneath her left breast that she wondered whether her heart was expanding.

Jim and his curls. He hadn't seen her yet, so she was free to just drink him in. His hands that she loved so much: smaller than most men's, chapped around the knuckles, lightly freckled. Hands that could conjure happiness. Hands that had held her grief without dropping it. Hands that the baby, their baby, would inherit, whether or not Jim left every night at nine and disappeared entirely on Sundays.

A part of her was seething with resentment. Another part wanted to leap over his desk, send him flying, cover as much of him with her ten fingers as she could manage, wolf him down with kisses.

"Hey," she said, leaning against the door frame.

"Hey," he responded, drawing the word out, making it feel liquid. "Where were you?"

"Notice anything different?" she asked, not sure whether to shake her head or stick out her belly.

"Just that you're more gorgeous than the last time I looked." He winked, he actually winked. Where could she ever find another man who winked after a half a dozen years?

"That sounds like the right answer to me." She couldn't help but laugh.

"Over here," he said, wheeling his chair back and patting his lap.

She considered teasing him, playing hard to get. It even crossed her mind to turn around and walk back past the counter and out into the parking lot, drive to The Beauty Mark, and tell Audra that she couldn't help herself; maybe if they helped one another, they could figure out a way to stop loving this man. But she really didn't want to do either of those things. She walked straight to him, collapsed herself into his arms, her feet dangling off the floor.

"Oh, babe," he sighed.

She made herself as heavy as possible, but his legs remained steady, not so much as a quiver. One day, sooner than later, she'd take his hand from her breasts and place it on her stomach just in time to feel a kick. A surprise gift, for no reason other than she loved him that much.

He lowered his mouth to hers and scorched her with a kiss. And then he ran his fingers through her hair, the way Audra had dragged a comb through the wet strands. Jean shivered at the thought of the ghost of Audra's energy still prickling her scalp. Did Jim feel it too? She imagined herself calling Jim's mother *Mother Darling* and Christopher *Chris*. If the baby was a girl, she and Audra would probably settle on something royal like Victoria or Anne. And a boy would definitely be James Jr., Jim for short.

PERSONAL VALUES

René Francois Ghislain Magritte was born a Scorpio like Ryan Dennis Meredith, just a day apart, though seventy-two years in between. There were other parallels: both of their fathers had been tailors, or rather Ryan's had designed uniforms for security and janitorial jobs; one mother a suicide by drowning, the other never quite the same after a too-deep dive into the Otonabee River, her head glancing off a rock; wives, Georgette and Georgia, variations on the masculine "George."

There were other minor synchronicities. For example, René bought a bowler hat, much like the one Magritte had painted, in a secondhand store in Providence, Maine. He wasn't thinking about Magritte when he bought it; in fact, the only thing on his mind was the bald spot at the back of his skull, big as a tea-cup saucer. But the minute he placed it on his head and felt its perfect circle, he immediately thought, "Magritte!" And then there was the matter of their shared favourite colour: blue. And the eeriness of reading somewhere that Magritte had died on August 15, a Leo death, the very day, years apart, of course, that Ryan's black lab, Pepper, ran away. Pepper had been a work of art, and her absence was like the black pupil floating in that Magritte painting of an eyeful of sky.

No doubt their differences outweighed these incidentals. Ryan wasn't an artist, for one thing. Or Belgian. But Magritte's breezy surrealism had a way of capturing the world inside his head. The floating men in black overcoats matched how meager he felt on the subway each morning as he made his way to the Royal Bank's mortgage department on Bay Street. And that painting of a man staring into the back of his own head in a mirror had the same loneliness to it as the bachelor apartment on Sherbourne that he'd moved into when Georgia had had enough. Even the painting of the fish couple sitting on a rock by the sea, the bottom half of their bodies human, matched the way those coffee dates with women he met on eHarmony made him feel.

One Friday night, he managed to persuade one of these women, a copyeditor named Denise with thick black bangs and strangely chapped hands, to stop by his apartment on their way to dinner. She said nothing about the pull-out couch sitting there in bed mode, the sheet askew across the top. She simply walked over to it, sat down on the edge, and then waited for him to add his weight, make the springs sag even lower. When their clinch (what else could he call it?) was over, Ryan offered her a glass of red wine in a green glass, and she placed it on the carpet. When he came back from the bathroom, the wine glass seemed to loom there on the cheap rug, more vivid than Denise in all her solidity. He ended up leaving it there even after she'd gone (feeding off each other had somehow wrecked their appetite for a public dinner), but it wasn't until the morning, when he woke to his bare window filled with indulgent white clouds, that he realized something Magritte-like was going on.

He slipped out of the crooked sheets and crawled across the carpet. He felt a tiny pain on his right buttock and remembered Denise's fingernails. He found his book of Magritte reproductions leaning against the empty bookshelf and started flipping pages. The wine glass was the very centre of a painting called *Personal Values*: a room with a bed, a glass, a giant comb and shaving brush, a bar of orange soap, a huge pink match with a yellow sulfur tip, and a wooden wardrobe with double doors, part-mirror, part-window. It was a vastly more interesting room than his own refrigerator box of an apartment.

On Monday morning, hanging from a hand grip on the subway, he looked at himself in the dark, rattling window and for a moment saw someone he didn't recognize. There was a bulkiness about this stranger, as if he had several canvases tucked inside his coat. And the top of his head was cut off by the window's frame. An image like this might have unsettled him back when he was still with Georgia. This was something she would have been likely to point out. He would have responded by trying to pose, hunker down until the whole of him filled the window. "Now you look like a blob," she might have said.

Later that day, washing his hands after taking a long, dreamy piss, he saw that his arms were cut off in the mirror, that he could only see himself from the elbows up. When he raised his head a little, it looked like light was sliding down both temples, a bowler hat cut into two pieces and set aflame.

When he stood in front of his apartment door that evening, fumbling with his clump of keys, many of which were for the house where Georgia still lived, Ryan mistook one of his own fingers for a key, reaching for it with his other hand, shocked by the feel of his flesh and bone. He remembered crouching on the shore with his sister Wendy as his father leapt into the cold Otonabee to try to transform the empty circle that his mother had become back into a woman in a bright blue bathing suit. It had been Magritte-like, although the surrealist's mother had been fished out dead and had been wearing both a dress and a coat that had probably floated up around her like a dark parachute.

The first thing he noticed when he finally got the door open was that the pile of sweaters on top of the wardrobe looked like a huge shaving brush. And something on the badly made bed was very comb-like, teeth and all. It turned out to be a pillow made jagged by shadows. Ryan couldn't remember shoving it vertically into the corner of the wall, but perhaps that had been achieved by Denise as she dug her hips into the mattress. All he could remember of her at this point was the fingernail scratch on his ass.

The next night, a dismal February Tuesday, what little there was of a sunset pooled in front of the wardrobe like a round orange bar of soap. A pair of his underpants lay beside the bed, the dingy white shaded pink by the burgundy tones of the rug. Between these two illusions, the green glass remained where Denise had placed it.

For the rest of the week, he was sliced or chopped by every reflective surface he happened upon. In the icicles that dangled over the subway entrance a few blocks from his apartment, he was the size and shape of an elongated teardrop. In passing cars, he was a streak, here and gone in one glance. When he turned on his computer screen at the office, there was a wide circle of shimmer that in a matter of seconds burst into a Magritte sky daubed with clouds.

By the time Friday rolled around, he felt completely amiss. He'd walked toward his office, feeling his skull vibrate. He had to stop at the glass door with his name engraved on it and grip the brass door handle with his fist until the building stopped moving.

That evening he had agreed to meet another eHarmony woman at the same pub where he'd met Denise the Friday before. Her name was Gail, and she was supposed to be wearing a scarf with the Eiffel Tower on it around her neck. He stiffened when he caught sight of Denise standing with her back pressed against the bar, staring into space. They ignored each other long enough for Ryan to relax and note that everyone in the place looked lonely, even those who were throwing their heads back and laughing like giant gulls. He could vaguely remember a painting by Magritte where a gull just hung in the sky. Or was it a dove? Or some type of angel?

Magritte died in 1967, three years before Ryan was born. Every so often, Ryan checked the math on this, wondering whether time and dimension might change the older he got. But no, three years was still three years, even in this humid bar. He thought he could smell Denise's sweat across the room.

She'd been just sitting there for ages. He was on the verge of concluding that Eiffel Tower Gail wasn't going to show.

Slowly, over the course of many scotches, he and Denise found themselves elbow to elbow. "Hmm," he said, and she twisted the top of her body to look at him, specifically his mouth and chin. By the time the rest of her body had followed, he was helping her into her coat, a long, black, woolen beast that swallowed her whole.

They entered the cold Toronto streets together. When they came to the subway, they left clouds of their breath behind as they descended. They sat side by side without touching. Ryan started telling her about Magritte's painting of a birdcage and the moon-like white egg that perched inside. Apparently, it had been Georgette's favourite. Georgia had had a different reaction though: a captive egg was even worse than a captive bird. "What do you think?" he asked Denise, who was too preoccupied with staring down at her red fingernails to respond.

Not a word on the walk from the Sherbourne subway stop to his apartment. He unlocked the door with what felt like one of his own fingers and cried out at the sight of the green wine glass that seemed to have tripled in size since that morning. Denise didn't seem to notice, in fact she walked right over to it, where she disappeared for several minutes. He found her again on the bed, glassily naked, both hands clenched between her legs. Ryan quickly undressed. He stepped over a beam of moonlight that lay plastered on the rug. He entered the bed at a tumble.

As he felt himself sinking into Denise's flesh, he wondered how Magritte might have painted them had they posed for him in his Brussels studio. Their skin would have been white (bunny white, crushed-pillow white) and tucked into their bones with perfect symmetry. Most likely, their heads would have been missing.

The closer he tried to get to Denise, the more resistance he felt. There were too many arms between them and the redness of her cunt. Too many fingers. It felt like he was rubbing against a comb, the teeth leaving trails of scratches across both his back and front. His cock was a match searching for something to strike itself against. He said, "Ow" and then said it again.

He finally left his body and floated up to the top of the wardrobe. Whoosh! From his perch, Denise appeared to be breaking herself against one of his knees. Slowly, this spectre part of him, spectator extraordinaire, softened. He ran his palms over his own neck and realized that both the feeling and the felt were satiny. He came then the way a cloud might come: round and airy and torn.

Sometime in the night, he returned to bed and bruised himself against Denise's hipbone. She hoisted the green glass to her lips and that was that, another disappearing act. Ryan was left to ponder how women were able to hide themselves in the most curious objects: Georgia and her locks, Georgette and her egg, his own mother and a rock in the middle of a river.

When he was completely alone again, he dreamt that when his head detached itself from his body, it rose a few inches and then hung there, midair, refusing to actually leave him. He was already living in the gap, a space as real as the air between the comb's teeth, the empty hall of the wine glass, the sky beyond the flagrant clouds, the unlit match.

THE RED-FRAMED GLASSES

Clark never actually took a drink in high school. Pretended, yes, what looked like a sip from a buddy's sonic screwdriver or a swig from a passed-around bottle of red wine that would later be used in a game of spin the bottle. But he never swallowed. He'd been raised to believe that alcohol was inherently evil, that the old-fashioned name for it, *spirits*, suggested something out of his control, like a haunted house.

Uncle Don, absent yet eternally soused, was the example of all examples in his moral education. He was a common drunk who would turn up a couple of times a year asking for money in exchange for promises that might as well have been written in invisible ink. His hair would be straggling over his collar, and he'd often have an infected cut or two on his face or hands. "That's what drink does to you," Clark's mother would broadcast once Uncle Don had been dispatched with a twenty and a bag full of ripe fruit. He lived on the streets, which caused Clark to picture him walking day and night, his shoe soles as thin as those pancakes Clark later learned were called crepes.

To Clark's mother, alcohol was worse than tattoos or piercings. He'd rather be caught with a hula girl swaying on his bicep than with a beer bottle sweating between his fingers. Clark's father was a teetotaler by proxy, having married into it. But his own conscience allowed him a nip of rum in the eggnog with Uncle Doug and Aunt Faye at Christmas and a modest glass of · champagne on New Year's Eve. Clark noted these lapses every year, although his mother never mentioned them. She simply poured apple cider for herself and Clark, a drink that always left a bit of sludge at the bottom of his glass.

It was the sloppiness of inebriation that disgusted Clark's mother, the chance that things no one wanted said might be shouted across the room in a voice that wasn't even yours, a breakdown of boundaries that led to vomiting and unconsciousness, two things his mother found highly repugnant. She would point out drunks on the Bloor subway line when she took Clark downtown for new shoes. "Drunk," she'd say, pointing across the aisle with just a slight nod of her nose. And then, arriving at their destination, hurrying up the stairs to the brighter world of the streets, she'd take a big breath of smog and shudder. "Imagine, passed out in front of everyone."

Freshman year university, living on his own for the first time, Clark quickly began having trouble avoiding alcohol. The second night of frosh week, his roommate, Mario, part-Spanish, part-Polish, ordered him a margarita at a Mexican restaurant just off campus. Clark had washed away an entire rim's worth of salt before he realized that the chortles slowly rising up his esophagus had nothing to do with the conversation. "Something's the matter," he slurred in Mario's remarkably round ear. Mario swatted him away, then rolled his eyes in disbelief. "No one gets pissed on one margarita," Mario said, quoting from some non-existent rulebook, letting Clark know that there was a hierarchy to drunkenness.

Within weeks, he was drinking more nights than not. One beer and he'd hear himself giggle. Two and he was offering opinions on subjects he hadn't even considered before, such as immigration or whether Muslim and Christian fundamentalists were the same thing. By the time he tipped the third bottle upside down without so much as a single drop coming out, he'd find himself swearing like a Quentin Tarantino character. Saying *fuck* and *cunt* out loud gave him a rush that felt close to courage. It was when he began to lose count, when four fumbled to five or six, that he'd end up divulging something awkwardly intimate—that he could pick his nose with his toes, for example, or that he was still a virgin at nineteen.

Not all drinkers are alike. Some of his acquaintances achieved a level of charm that was almost magical. They'd eventually blow it, one gulp too many, but for a short time everything they said filled Clark with admiration. Then there were those who grew more dangerous with every swallow, as if they were drinking Molotov cocktails, their anger flaming out at whomever happened to be standing in their way. There was nothing pathetic about these drinkers; they had a purity to their drunkenness that was terrifying but beautiful. Finally, there were the quiet ones, the ones who used alcohol to find a warm, peaceful spot to sink into like a tide pool.

What a shame that he wasn't one of the chosen—the gifted, the psychopathic, the secretive. Instead, he was everything his mother hated. Most nights ended with him gripping the edges of the sink and tossing at least three-quarters of the tally down the drain. It wasn't a Saturday night if his unmade bed didn't smell of vomit.

During the week, Clark's classes sobered him with how little he was learning. He was either stupid or a poor listener or had already damaged so many cells that his memory was soggy. He tried his best, making up a slew of mnemonics that ultimately overwhelmed the things he had invented them for in the first place. He spent the fall scraping by, alarmed to be encountering this underachieving part of himself.

Around the end of November, having received a C- for an essay he'd written on hyperbole in romantic poetry, he drank for the sole purpose of reaching that blank place in record time. Along the way, he managed to get into an argument with one of the mean drunks. It started out with Clark exclaiming that he loved poetry, all its pomp and flourish. The other guy had apparently been tortured by a course he'd taken on John Donne and so countered with a hatred for all metaphors. "You're barely a pronoun," Clark shouted. "What the fuck do you know about poetry?" he asked, slugging back another mouthful of instant opinion.

The fight continued between swigs. Clark remembered a blond girl wearing bright red-framed glasses hollering in his direction, "Poets rock!" Then he had a vague memory of the guy knocking over a table and lunging in Clark's direction. After that, there was nothing but a dark lapse into a state where his only awareness was of faint background sounds.

He woke up in what might have been a different decade and opened one gummy eyelid. He didn't recognize a single thing in what was surely someone's bedroom. A white chest of drawers with colourful bits of fabric sticking out of every crack was directly across from the bed. A ceiling fan above him flapped at the air like a lazy helicopter. On a tousled red, black, and white yarn rug just below the edge of the mattress, a pair of mauve panties lay looking like they'd floated there from the ceiling.

Slowly, Clark raised himself on both elbows. He was still wearing the khaki t-shirt he'd put on the last morning he could remember, but nothing below the waist. His cock looked like a snail that had misplaced its shell. Further down, his toes could have come from ten different feet.

His elbows gave way under him, and his head hit the pillow with a whoosh. Nothing particular seemed to be hurting, so maybe the madman who had been about to squash him in the name of poetry haters everywhere had been too drunk to actually strike him. There was a small stuffed monkey taped to one of the ceiling fan's blades, riding around and around the room with a look as close to sorrow as a stuffed toy could get. Where the hell was he? He turned to investigate the rest of the bed. Someone else had definitely been there—the sheets were thoroughly rumpled. On a small white table between bed and wall sat a pair of red-framed glasses. Did both the glasses and the panties belong to the blond who'd shouted her support of poetry just before he'd blacked out last night? Had he lost his virginity?

He couldn't bear the thought of looking into the eyes of the girl, who, with or without her glasses, would probably be able to see deep inside him now. Trying to tune into the rest of his surroundings, he could decipher the hard splash of a shower coming from a door at the far end of the bedroom.

It took him less than a minute to throw on what clothes of his he could find. He wasn't sure whether he'd actually worn any underwear the day before, but felt such a dislike for the one sock he couldn't find that he left the other sock behind like a long, grey snake skin. His bare feet felt fragile in his black Oxfords. He tiptoed into a living room he'd never seen before with his shirt still completely unbuttoned. The outside door led to an apartment hallway. He didn't register what floor he was on, pressing G for ground and then closing his eyes until the elevator bumped to a stop. Fleeing the neighbourhood, he didn't glance up at a single street sign. By the time he happened upon the Sherbourne subway, he'd made such a confusion of turns that he'd never be able to retrace his steps.

Of course, he couldn't go out to the bars anymore after this, no matter how hard Mario rode him. The situation isolated him until he couldn't even attend his last week of classes. He stayed in his room for four days straight before heading home for the Christmas holidays. Surely other young men had lost their virginity in similar ways. It wasn't even that big a deal when he seriously considered the mechanics of it. Regardless of whether the receiver was a vagina or his own fist, the act was just repeated friction. As long as he didn't drink, there'd be a more memorable second time somewhere down the line.

But then he pictured the blond in the bar that night, how she wore those red glasses so proudly. She had drawn him into her circle of self-importance, believing, for one night at least, that he was the voice of modern poetry. For all he knew, sex was something she'd bestowed on him with great compassion and courage. He imagined telling her that he loved her and then watching her eyes swimming in tears as he entered her the way a raindrop enters a river. Had shyness overwhelmed his pleasure? Did he cry out a little when he came and had she breathed that cry into her own lungs, a mingling of spirits?

There had never been an inkling of sexual energy between his parents, yet his mother would often stand just outside the open bathroom door when his father was sitting on the toilet, telling him about her day. The closeness of this sometimes made him feel doomed to be alone. How could he ever find a girl he could take a shit in front of while making small talk? For all he knew, sex with the chunky girl might have been dreadful. Had she locked the bathroom door while she showered? Had she hoped that he'd be gone when she came out cleansed of all his fingerprints?

Clark had lost more than his virginity that drunken night: he'd lost the entire narrative leading up to it. This very moment, behind her red-framed glasses, the girl might be mulling over the details of what was her story as well, the whole beginning, from how they hooked up in the bar to the moment just before she'd slipped her mauve panties down to her ankles (or had he been the one to do the slipping?), shook them off one foot at a time, and spread her thighs wide apart. Was there any dialogue in this story? She was the keeper of the details, peripheral things like how he might have nibbled on the cartilage of her ear as he was sliding back and forth or the tiny shiver that stopped him moving when her thumb strayed into the crack of his ass and gently put pressure on his anus. Had she whispered, "Asshole" or just giggled at her own boldness?

Everything that might have been was downgraded to fiction. There was no closure when he couldn't remember whether he'd taken her hand and placed it on his penis, guiding her into a rhythm like ironing the sleeves of a shirt—or had she needed no coaxing, reaching for him before he'd even undone his zipper, rubbing so hard against the rough denim of his jeans that it made his balls throb. And what about his own storyline? Had he licked her vagina? Did not remembering erase the fact that it had really happened? There was always the chance that they hadn't done anything, just passed out on the unmade bed. Maybe he couldn't get hard. Or maybe he'd ejaculated on one of her thighs, failing to go the distance.

When his mother picked him up at the Ottawa train station, he had to bite his bottom lip hard in order not to blubber. She mistook his puckered face for a grimace and hugged him a second time. "Mothers are put on this earth to embarrass their sons in public places," she said.

Over the next few days, Clark noticed that she didn't lecture him as much as she had in the months leading up to his leaving for university in Toronto. He wondered whether she sensed that he'd learned some hard lessons on his own or whether a certain stage of her mothering had passed. It must be difficult, Clark thought, to think of your children as adults, to know that they're out there making all sorts of major mistakes, going so far in some cases as to do permanent damage.

His father pretty much ignored him, as if he'd given up parenting entirely. Their only connection was a shared love for the 1951 movie version of *A Christmas Carol* starring Alastair Sim. They loved watching Scrooge being pried open and tortured by his own conscience. It made them feel good to be reminded that they were their own worst enemies. Other years they'd watch it together two or three times, but this year all that rattling of chains reminded Clark of the blond girl who knew something about him that would make both his parents hang their heads in shame. He left his father to the TV set and slumped off to bed.

On the night before Christmas Eve, his good friend Evan was having a party with the old high-school crowd. Since Clark hadn't started drinking until after moving to Toronto, no one from the past would give his sobriety a second thought.

Despite Evan's parents being away in Montreal, their house had a motherly/fatherly vibe to it. All the decorations looked like they'd just been dusted; the gifts under the pine tree were expertly wrapped. The crystal bowl of spiked punch on the dining-room table still had most of its cups hooked onto the rim. The punch itself was a deep cranberry red, and no one wanted to be the first to splash any of it on the white tablecloth.

It took a few hours for the sheen of the evening to start developing a few fractures. Empty beer bottles were discarded in clumps on the floor between large pieces of furniture. Three-quarters of the punch had been poured into cups and all the melted ice cubes had changed the colour to a soggy pink. Fiona Apple was playing on the Bose, doing an angry vibrato thing that came close to a wail.

Clark was tired of catching up with everyone and was leaning against the only empty wall in the dining room. Every university tale sounded the same: the daunting size of their classes, the hours-long lectures that were often impossible to keep listening to and think about at the same time. A few mentioned alcohol, how they were drinking way more than they used to, a couple of them even alluded to blackouts. Clark tried probing a bit, but a blackout didn't really have much in the way of detail. No one mentioned anything about regret other than getting a lower mark than expected or waking up with a killer hangover.

By midnight, the music had been turned down to a mumble. A few people had paired off and were snuffling at one another like horses; one pair was stretched out under the tree, hardly moving. Clark had forgotten how to fit in and was just about to let the wall stand up on its own again when a girl he didn't know all that well, Gilly Kingsley, sauntered by, stumbling over her own stocking feet. He reached out and steadied her. She leaned herself against him, so he kept his hand on her right elbow.

"Are you okay?" he asked.

She raised her eyes from the greyish silver of the carpet and gave him a dizzy, the-world-is-spinning kind of look. It was like she'd lost the knack for looking at and was being forced to look *through* everything instead. "My shoes," she said, slipping one foot on top of the other and falling sideways into Clark's arms.

They remained entangled until he was able to spin out from the wall and let her lean against it. It wasn't enough to keep her vertical though, and she slowly slid until Clark couldn't support her anymore, and she landed on the floor with her hands clutching his ankles. He tried to step free of her, but she brought him down as well. He ended up sort of plopped in her lap. "Sorry," he said.

By the way she leaned over him with her neck bent and her mouth open, he thought for a second that she was going to throw up in his face. But she ended up plastering her teeth and gums against his lips. Her tongue felt so huge at the top of his throat that he thought he was going to gag. Their positions changed as they slithered free of the wall, rolling under the dining-room table. Clark bumped his head on the table's round column base and wasn't able to easily disengage when he felt Gilly, several inches below him now, fumbling at his groin with both her fingers and her mouth.

"Stop," he rasped.

Gilly lifted her face and stared up at Clark with a little girl's exaggerated frown. "But I wanna," she slurred, disappearing back into the shadows, tugging at the zipper of Clark's jeans. He raised his hips trying to get away without banging his head again, but that only gave Gilly more access to his lap.

The deeper she went, the more trapped he felt. He finally gave up on protecting his head and started thrashing with both his shoulders and his legs. Something about this struggle was familiar. Had he fought like this to escape the blond girl with the red-framed glasses? Had she pinned him down in some similar fashion? He tried to picture what might have happened and was alarmed when, for a few fleeting seconds, he saw the blond girl beneath him, pushing against his chest with all her strength, sobbing into his ear. He could hear the word *stop* being pleaded over and over.

"Oh my God," he said out loud, seeing the terror in the blond girl's eyes without her red-framed glasses getting in the way. He recalled the sound of the shower coming from the closed bathroom door. Now he pictured the girl curled up in a corner of the tub, water pounding down on her, failing to wash anything away. He felt sick to his stomach, details swerving in and out of focus.

He'd lost track of Gilly Kingsley. By shifting his weight, he could feel the heft of her head on his thigh; she definitely wasn't groping at him anymore. Boosting himself up on his elbows, he twisted one leg then the other, the back of Gilly's skull dropping to the carpet with barely a sound. She was out cold, her features strangely askew, and was snoring the tiny snore of a cartoon mouse.

Stretching his legs out from under the table, he squirmed the rest of the way until he was completely visible to the room again. A couple of his former classmates were walking by on their way to the kitchen and had to step over him. "Did you get lucky, bro?" one of them asked.

Clark tried to explain what was going on, but they were too busy snickering to listen. He turned around and ducked his torso back under the table, gathering Gilly's shoulders in one arm and scooping the other beneath her knees. He pulled out from under the table again. Lifting from his thigh muscles, he picked Gilly up and carried her into the living room, lowering the two of them into a plum-coloured love seat. He gently wiped a thick stream of drool from the seam of her lips down to her chin. Did good acts have the power to erase bad ones? Even if he were only imagining the worst, it could have happened. It could very well have happened. All he knew for sure was that he'd stay put like this until Gilly was sober enough to wake up. "Nothing happened," he'd say, wondering who she'd think he was when she finally opened her eyes.

UNTITLED

It was a humid April afternoon at the Whitney when she happened upon a particular Rothko *Untitled*. Her hair was damp and disobedient; trying to pat down the sides left a thin film on her palms of what earlier that morning had been hairspray, but now felt sticky like not-quite-dry paint.

She found herself underwhelmed by a Rauschenberg and then a Haring. An Alice Neel portrait of a woman the colour of a white crayon left her numb. It was a mistake to seek out art on such an unruly day. Life was the lens through which transcendence struggled. If she were miserable, even secretly miserable, the canvases would soak up her misery and return it to her in disturbing new ways. By the time she reached the horizontal colour palette of the Rothko, she was so toxic she could have poisoned a Turner sunrise.

What little she knew of Rothko was dreary: his emigration from Russia when he was just a boy; the death of his father soon after; the periods of depression, blotting what had otherwise been an illustrious career. And finally his suicide in 1970. She had visited the Rothkos at the Tate Modern a few years back and had been driven from the gallery by an overwhelming claustrophobia. She'd seen photos of the Rothko Chapel in Houston that had made her think of tombstones being rolled into place.

There had been no art in her childhood. Her father, a salesman with a cruel streak, had frowned on creativity, hers and everyone else's. Her mother had once mentioned that she'd briefly entertained the notion of becoming a glass blower, to which her father had snorted out loud.

Rebellion at various crucial ages had been acts of survival. At fourteen, she wore makeup that conjured bruises and black eyes. At sixteen, she dyed her hair blond and wore it much shorter on the left side than the right. At eighteen, she brought home a boyfriend named Scoot who always stood with both hands tucked into the front of his pants, a stance that made the serpent tattoos on the backs of his hands stand out more than if his arms simply dangled.

A stint in the design department of a city newspaper (after two years at art college) was followed by what was supposed to be a temporary position at a small advertising agency, dreaming up soothing caricatures of various versions of consumer happiness: bath products, Italian sausages, wristwatches. After a year of this, she was promoted to account manager. It wasn't until she'd been doing the job for another year that she was struck by the irony of having ended up in sales like her father.

Her artistic life was consigned to the occasional independent film, a relish for the twangy heartbreak music of Lucinda Williams, Gillian Welch, and Patty Griffith, and art galleries on business trips when she really should be back at the you-can't-tell-them-apart hotels boning up on pitches and presentations.

It was the thick streak of midnight blue headlining the painting that gave her an initial shiver that day at the Whitney. It had the presence of something like fear, like endlessness. The woolly green stripe at the bottom of the canvas was what grass would look like if it were made of polyester: sensible grass that she could easily convince anyone to buy.

The yellow in the middle was egg-yolk buttercream or mashed squash drizzled with maple syrup. It was the shade of an apricot that had been grown on the sun. It was sex while still half-asleep, one hand trailing in a wake of waves. It was a crayon tucked between a five-year-old genius's fingers.

Untitled was more intense than anything she could have imagined on her own. It was an accumulation of all that had gone missing over the last few years. She longed to enter the painting, boost herself into the green swathe, reach for the blue, her bones melting the way sugar did when placed directly on the tongue. Her right hand ached to touch the painting. She could imagine the bumpy dryness of the canvas like an old woman's skin, the old woman she would one day become. But she held back, aware of the security guard keeping an eye on her from the far corner of the room: a broad-shouldered fellow with an Adam's apple too big to be swallowed.

It had been years since she'd felt anything close to passion. When she was eleven or twelve, she went through a serious crush on Jesus that made it difficult to sleep. Church had nothing to do with it. It was the fact that a man, not just any man, *the* man, supposedly understood her inside out. Christ seemed less complicated than her father. She knew that no matter how many times she let Him down, He'd just keep loving her.

But the relationship didn't last. He started repeating Himself and refusing to even consider the other side of an argument. He was already inside her body, so sex was out. Real men offered a bit of titillation, at least.

She left the Whitney feeling glum. Her throat was dry. She wished she could cry a little, lubricate her breathing passages. Standing outside the gallery, she noticed that the yellow cabs for which the city was famous weren't anywhere close to the sensuality of Rothko yellow. They were pale canaries instead of flames, breeze rather than wind.

The next day began with a meeting at the Chrysler Building, the gaunt boardroom table weighed down with platters of perfectly ripened fruit and pastel coffee cups. Lunch materialized at the stroke of noon as shapely bits of bread and garnish. Talk and more talk. She and her colleagues were selling Ontario, not the actual rock and root province, but an idea of it, a holiday contraption of verdant poses and storybook skies. When she was finally free, close to four, the streets of Manhattan looked like they'd spent the day indoors. She hailed a cab and said "Rothko" to the driver instead of "Whitney."

A new security guard, a chalky black man who wore his wire-framed glasses at the tip of his nose, was standing near *Untitled* but was watching a pair of teenaged boys mesmerized by the Neel nude. Her right hand darted across the distance, and her fingertips brushed against the painting. She then lifted her hand to her nose and sniffed: beneath the bitter smell of cold coffee, she caught a whiff of oils, as if she and the yellow had exchanged molecules.

If anyone had noticed her, they would have registered nothing more than a well-dressed woman strolling back through the lobby, flowing out onto Gansevoort Street with complete confidence that everything she needed was just ahead of her. She kept up that pace as she made her way over to the High Line. She stopped at the first park bench she came to and sat down, smoothing her grey silk skirt over her knee caps.

She felt the wooden slats of the bench beneath her hips. She was in control of the world now and could make colour lie or tell the truth, whichever she pleased. Her fingers lay in her lap like quills or bristles. She stretched them ever so slowly, blood rushing back into her knuckles. She turned them over: there, on the tip of her index finger, was a yellow smudge that continued to spread until her entire hand turned yellow.

By the time she'd arrived back at the hotel to pick up her bags, the yellow had extended up to her wrist. The muscles beneath her flesh were hardening. She went into the bathroom and scrubbed at herself until she was raw. It wasn't the hand of an advertising executive anymore; it would have to be stuffed deep into her pocket in order to sneak it onto the flight home. She could already feel heat prickling in her left hand. And when she glanced down at her feet, she had a brief vision of artificial grass.

It wasn't the first time that a foolish act had transformed her. Sex with Scoot in the beginning had made her whole body feel like a huge vagina. She'd been forced to lock herself in her room until she could feel the pulsing folds abating. And the day that her father died, her tears ran black despite the fact that she wasn't wearing any mascara.

There was no option other than to outlast the irrational (or was it pure recklessness?), patiently wait for her regular paleness to return. This wasn't a two-way street. The Rothko canvas back at the Whitney wasn't being leached of its golden yellow. The dab of her DNA was already disintegrating. She was the one in danger of losing herself.

She boarded the plane as soon as business class was announced. She tried to picture Toronto, wondering whether the April colours would be less vivid than the ones she was leaving behind in Manhattan. But when she closed her eyes, all she could see on the insides of her eyelids was a rose-tinted darkness. It was such a beguiling shade that she didn't open her eyes again for the entire flight.

HALF
A MAN

Charlie almost ruined their wedding day with his insistence on being involved with every little detail, from the flowers in Nessa's bouquet to the caterer's menu. He knew he was being obnoxious, but couldn't help himself. His mother had taught him well to always be the one in control. After the nth revision of the vows, Nessa detonated one night when they were getting ready for bed. "What's wrong with you? They're just words. We can vow to always play Scrabble on Sunday afternoons or to sing one Bob Dylan song a day. Hell," she said, clearly exasperated, "are you sure you wouldn't rather marry your mother?"

Charlie struggled with a clever comeback. At times of anxiety or change, his own voice winnowed away to next to nothing, and he heard his mother's words marching from his mouth. "Save me, for Christ's sake," he said, his face cracking into a feeble grin.

The last two days before the ceremony were a little easier. Charlie did his best to control himself rather than the situation. Still, there were a few things he couldn't let go. Even though it was clear to him the silver tie that Nessa had bought to match his black velvet jacket was very classy, it didn't change the fact that his mother had made him wear ties every Sunday of his childhood regardless of the fact that he felt like he was choking every time he moved his head. In the end, though, since standing up for his right to breathe was actually an example of Charlie going against his mother's wishes, Nessa even suggested he leave the top two buttons of his white shirt undone.

On the morning of their wedding day, watching Charlie in his white underpants doing his ritual crunches and push-ups, Nessa admitted that she loved him beyond any good sense. "In a way, I'm the one marrying your mother," she said, slapping her hands down on the edge of the bed. "I don't care," she sighed loudly. "I'd marry you even if your mother was Genghis Khan."

Charlie's grin broke new ground. "I love you too, limitlessly," he said, drawing out the adverb like taffy, "which is why we don't need any of that love, honour, and obey stuff."

"But we agreed that those things are timeless," Nessa said.

"But there's a negative vibe to them." He knew this wasn't enough; he'd have to do a lot more work in order to convince her.

"I'll make you a deal," she said, eyes piercing. "We keep one for me. How about 'in sickness and in health'?"

"What about just 'health'?" he asked. Begging in his underpants didn't give him much advantage.

He got a stitch in his side at the look of *sickness* on the page. The hard hack of the *ck*, how it rhymed with *dick* and *prick*. It reminded him of his father's death two years prior. He and Charlie's mother had been divorced for years, but she still ended up at his deathbed beside his second wife, a Filipino woman at least a decade younger. "I don't want to think about illness on my wedding day," he said.

"You took away my orchid corsage and my hors d'oeuvres. You're not taking my 'sickness.'"

A few hours later, Charlie, standing in front of the minister, could feel his mother's eyes boring holes into the back of his neck. The moment they were pronounced man and wife (the actual words were *man and woman*), Queen's "You're My Best Friend" exploded through the chapel's speakers, drowning out any words his mother had planned to say.

Since Charlie's best buddy, Grey, was taking pictures of the bride and groom in the small park across the street, they were the last ones to arrive at the small reception hall. The guests had already helped themselves to the modest buffet. Charlie's mother had insisted.

Nessa was biting her bottom lip so hard that Charlie expected a trickle of blood to run down her chin. "The pickled beets are gone," Nessa stated, just loud enough for Charlie to hear.

Even after his first stroke, Charlie still considered Nessa and himself a lucky couple. They'd lived through both their mothers' slow deaths and their own four miscarriages. Charlie had a bout with prostate cancer before he was even forty, but the tumour was tiny and hadn't spread. And Nessa only suffered a slight left-leg limp after a fall while cleaning out the eavestroughs. Not long after that, she got a dream job in the graphic arts department at *House & Garden*, and Charlie's first book of poetry was nominated for the Governor General's Award. Their three-bedroom split level with a third of an acre of woods was definitely a gift from the gods. The only thing that had truly threatened their togetherness was Charlie's stupid affair, which neither he nor Nessa ever talked about.

Early retirement was the best choice they ever made. Charlie left his job teaching English at Birchmount Park Collegiate, just a ten-minute drive from their house. He was only fifty-five and was having a ball learning how to break all his previous routines. Two years later, at fifty-seven, Nessa followed suit.

His first stroke, three years later, was hardly worth the bother of writing a poem about. *Ischemic* and *embolic* were apparently the words a patient wanted to hear. A small clot, most likely from one of his legs, had slipped free and popped up into his grey matter. He felt weird for close to an hour, as if he'd been sucked dry by a vampire. The worst of it was that he couldn't remember the name of anything, not *hospital* or *doctor* or even *Nessa* or *wife*. But after a shot of a drug called tPA, he could feel himself returning to his body, and after a good night's sleep, he was completely normal again.

The second one hit him harder a year later, leaving him paralyzed on his right side. For the first few days, he could talk in a slurry kind of way, but on the third his ability to form words just went away. It felt like his tongue had been zapped from its anchor, the lingual frenulum.

"How's this for luck?" Nessa said. She was wearing her tan suede jacket with dark blue denim jeans, and he would have given anything to tell her that she still looked young and beautiful.

He couldn't walk for the first few months, but he worked hard at physio and was finally able to stumble across a flat surface. He couldn't pee standing up anymore. His right arm just hung at his side. Having to learn how to use his left hand was much harder than he would have thought. Utensils flew across the kitchen table. He'd fumble with the TV remote. He couldn't button his own shirts let alone undress Nessa.

It was when he had software installed on his laptop that allowed him to speak again that he began to really lose hope. His computer voice was tinny and robotic, completely devoid of emotion of any kind. Whether he was asking for the salt or cursing God, it was the same monotonous drone. He hated the voice and often wouldn't speak for days.

Nessa didn't like to leave him alone, so his lifelong friend Grey would often come to stroke-sit, as Grey called it. They'd usually watch TV, which caused Grey to give a long, rambling commentary on anything that stirred his interest. It drove Charlie batty.

"Do you have to talk non-stop?" the awful computer voice asked, not a hint of the disdain that he meant to be there.

Grey just snickered, then started up again. In profile he resembled Humpty Dumpty.

"Shut the flock up," Charlie said. Apparently the program refused to swear.

Things only got worse at bedtime, when he was stripped of his computer and couldn't communicate at all, couldn't turn over on his side, had no way to reach for Nessa, who was curled into a shell shape on the other side of the bed. His only chance to connect with her was when she leaned over to kiss him goodnight. He'd sometimes manage to swipe his left hand across her breasts, but the gesture resembled a slap more than a caress.

One morning, he refused to take his blood thinners. "I don't want to continue," he announced.

Nessa's entire face flushed bright red, and she grabbed him by the chin and shoved the pills into his mouth, clamping his jaws shut while the medication dissolved into a sour mush.

This reminded him of his mother, who had often force-fed him from the tiny pile of peas on his plate. He'd tried to spit once when she released him, but all he could produce was a string of green drool.

The more Charlie thought about it, the more he realized that what he called luck was really a combination of his pig-headedness and Nessa's take-charge attitude. No wonder they were often described by others as a team, a force to be reckoned with.

One of their best pre-stroke experiences had been the month they drove around Spain. It was July and extremely hot. The olive groves shimmered in the afternoons like the mirages Charlie had loved to read about when he was a kid. There were orange and lemon orchards a short walk from the village of Chite, where they'd rented a house. All they had to do was reach up and pick the fruit from an overhanging branch. The oranges were warm, just born.

To an outside observer, it might seem that they were one of those couples who bickered all the time, who couldn't agree on anything. But that wasn't the case at all. They shared most of the same passions: art, literature, ecology, socialism, foreign films. There was nothing that drove them apart.

Nessa was a bit more argumentative, but Charlie had his opinions too. Nessa wasn't into music as much as Charlie was, but she'd listen to practically anything. He was a secondhand record store sort of guy. If she lived alone, music would just be background, but with Charlie the soundtrack of each day was an eclectic mix, from Etta James to Lyle Lovett.

One day, they were listening to the Lucinda Williams live album, driving to Córdoba, a few hours of highway from Chite. The outside temperature gauge read fifty degrees Celsius. The highway felt like it had been stripped to bone. They missed the first exit because Nessa couldn't find it on the map and therefore decided it didn't exist. They succumbed to their usual cranky banter until the second exit appeared, which Charlie took with a squealing of tires.

A few kilometres further, Nessa insisted on a left turn, which immèdiately began to narrow. They had rented a Chevy van and were soon driving so close to the buildings on either side that they could have each easily reached out their windows and touched stone. Nessa panicked for real this time and ordered Charlie to back up. But they'd already wound their way so deeply into the old part of the city that their only choice was to slowly inch forward.

Charlie insisted on staying the course. Nessa did what Nessa did best: reconnoitered. If someone had been in the back seat, he or she would have mistaken the raised voices and accusations for a real showdown, but deep down inside, they were having fun. By the time they came to a roundabout that led them to a wider road, they were cheering one another.

But now there was only half a person for Nessa to manage. A clumsy, uncooperative half. And all that Charlie had left to insist upon was that he didn't want to continue living this way. Perhaps the discord kept Charlie alive. Who would Nessa take control of if Charlie was gone? It didn't feel like a game anymore. This wasn't Spain. It was barely Scarborough. But how could he explain that in his robot voice?

The only time that Charlie had seen Nessa truly lose her cool was after the third miscarriage. The first had happened on a workday, but because she'd stayed until midnight the night before trying to meet a deadline for the spring issue, she was taking the morning off. It struck quickly, a sudden attack of cramps, then she could feel herself bleeding. By the time Charlie got home from work, she seemed more worried about his disappointment than her own feelings. She said that she'd had an inkling that something was going to go wrong. Lots of first pregnancies result in miscarriages, she'd said. Next month, she was ready to start again.

The second time, they were getting ready for bed, discussing Stanley Kubrick's *The Shining*; they were on the verge of understanding the ending when Charlie noticed a dark wet spot on Nessa's nightgown. She hadn't felt a thing.

She cried that time, two tears on each cheek. And afterwards she admitted to a day or two of negative thinking, but she wasn't one to wallow. It took about a week for her to say, "Third time lucky."

But the third time was unbearable. She woke up one Saturday morning and had sharp pains in her abdomen. She had just passed the three-month point. An hour later, she was wailing. Charlie bundled her up and drove her to the hospital, where she lost the baby in the emergency room.

For months, she let Charlie make meals and do the laundry. He got her out of bed every morning, persuading her to bathe and dress. She wasn't able to go back to work for over a month, and when she was ready, Charlie drove her there and picked her up at the end of the day for the first few months.

When she told Charlie that she was pregnant for the fourth time, he was afraid that she might never recover if this one ended in tragedy. But she was so ready for the worst to happen that when it did, at work this time, she actually felt relieved .

"That's enough," she said, and returned to making everything else just the way she liked it.

No sooner had Charlie and Nessa given up on having children than Charlie found out that he had prostate cancer. The radiation treatment made him sterile. When he was told that this would be a side effect of the treatment, he wanted to reach across the file-strewn desk and slap the oncologist, a swarthy middle-aged man with a dyed black moustache. But Nessa was asking so many good questions that he focused on her until the urge passed.

But something went awry in their relationship after this. Nessa's inner strength began to grate on Charlie. Some days, her determination to get on with life felt to him like simple bossiness. He let himself stumble into a brief affair with a new English teacher in his department named Anastasia Goldberg. With her long neck and soft lines, she reminded him of a vase. Her passion was poetry. Charlie had recently published his book *The Dreaming Willow* and was putty in the hands of a compliment. He hadn't planned on anything happening, but one day they were in the photocopy room together, and she asked whether she could teach one of his poems. He said that he'd be honoured. Next thing he knew his lips were buried in her neck, his dick solid in the palm of her hand.

It wasn't a long relationship, less than two months. And there were no proclamations of love. Charlie would have thought that a fling born of poetry would be mushier, more intense, but it was such an untethered experience that it couldn't survive the first snag.

One night, after he'd followed Stasia in his car from the school parking lot to her condo complex, driving underground to the visitor parking, he thought of a line from Dante's *Inferno*: "In the middle of the journey of our life I found myself within a dark woods where the straight way was lost." He was making a terrible mistake. He shivered at how easily his car fit into the slot. Stasia was waiting for him at the elevators. Although they rose to the ninth floor, they were deep in the core of the building, not a hint of sky.

"You'll never leave your wife for me," she'd said after they'd made love and he was perched politely on the edge of the bed.

"No, of course not," he said far more quickly than he'd expected. Why would he leave Nessa? She was more beautiful than Stasia, with her spectacular breasts and dazzling green eyes. Stasia had a starved look about her, and the swing of her white-blond hair exposed her large ears every time she tilted her head.

"Then why are you here?" Stasia asked, staring him down with her wolf-blue eyes.

He was surprised at how cold he sounded when he finally responded. "Because this means nothing," he was able to say without her so much as blinking, "and nothing feels good."

Leaning down to where Stasia's head was boosted on a folded-over pillow, he licked a wide swathe across her lips. Then he just waited. Her breasts were so still that they might have belonged to a dead woman. He couldn't stop himself from longing for Nessa's breasts.

The next night, getting ready for bed, he made a mistake and called Nessa Stasia. "Hey, Stasia, did you remember to record *Jeopardy!?*" he asked. He was all the way to *Jeopardy!* before he could put on the brakes. He looked up to see Nessa watching him in the dresser mirror. And then the moment passed.

She'd heard him praise Anastasia: great new teacher, good egg, pretty woman. Mentioning her name seemed to reduce his guilt. If he could toss her into ordinary conversation, then he knew he hadn't gone too far. He was so used to Nessa being the guiding force in their lives, he wasn't sure how to keep secrets from her without both of them sinking into a terrible state of feeling totally alone.

The next time he tested the waters and shared a little anecdote about Anastasia, he used the diminutive of her name consciously. "Stasia had a kid in her poetry unit try to pass off Dylan's 'Like a Rolling Stone' as his own writing."

"Don't call her Stasia," Nessa interrupted. "It's too familiar." He could tell that she was angry by how her gaze refused to meet his eyes, landing just above his eyebrows.

"Sure, whatever you say." He could feel a blush flooding his face.

"Cut it out, Charlie," she said. "You're making an ass of yourself."

It made him feel queasy and stupid not to know whether Nessa knew the entire story or whether she just thought Charlie was on the verge. Did she even think Charlie was capable of that level of deception and betrayal? The man she'd married was a control freak, not a cruel piece of work.

The next morning, he dashed into Anastasia's class between periods. He knew he was being cowardly, not giving her time to even think about what he was saying. "Best we stop the hanky panky," he said in his most efficient manner.

Before he could add a touch of regret, she responded, "Exactly what I was going to say. Good show, Charlie. I was dreading tears."

He didn't know whether she was concealing any sadness. The grade elevens were arriving with their wrinkled copies of *Life of Pi* and their utter disinterest in what went on between two teachers. Later that day, Charlie would drive past the door to Anastasia's underground parking twice. He would punch in the numbers of her cellphone, but hang up before it even rang. There were two nights of awful dreams and a short, violent sob in the shower on the third morning. Nessa was tender with him, as if she knew that he was in more pain than either Anastasia or herself. The affair had been crazy, destructive, and not worth the bother.

Charlie later referred to that year as his midlife crisis, which included taking on a grade-nine special-needs class, going rock climbing with Grey and a couple of other buddies, and taking banjo lessons. There were no more stories about Anastasia, of course. Nessa called him Charles for a while, until it became clear to both of them how much they missed the intimacy that *Charlie* created. Everything slowly went back to normal, and to the awareness of how good normal was.

Nessa had little tolerance for self-pity. She often bragged that she couldn't hold a grudge, that it took more energy to cling to negativity than it did to come up with a solution.

"We're flying the coop on Saturday," she said one morning as she helped Charlie maneuver spoonfuls of oatmeal with his left hand. "We're going to Florida," she announced, "and Grey and Christie are coming too."

This was serious stuff. Nessa wasn't fond of Christie. She thought that liking her was a betrayal of Grey's first wife, Carla, who had died of breast cancer a decade ago. Taking a trip together meant that Nessa was serious about being happy again.

He tried to refuse, to hold back all cooperation, but a man in a wheelchair doesn't have much say in the matter of where he might end up. Before he knew it, he was being wheeled through the Pearson terminal and then lifted into a seat on the airplane, riding the turbulence, leaving winter and its suicidal thoughts behind.

Indian Rock Beach was just outside of Largo, a twenty-minute drive from St. Petersburg. They shared a unit on the first floor with a patio overlooking the Gulf of Mexico. They flipped coins over who would get the front bedroom and Nessa and Charlie won. The sound of waves dogged Charlie night and day, hurting the inside of his head.

The first night, as the sun was slipping down into the horizon, painting the entire beach orange, Grey picked Charlie up in his arms and walked him down into the pool until they were both fully submerged. If Grey were to let go of him, Charlie would drown. Trust of this size was too big for words.

Later, he lay in bed with the back of his head still damp. Nessa lay beside him breathing lightly. He would have liked to talk a little, but his laptop was on the dresser. He let himself entertain a small fantasy of being healed. Grey's arms had dipped him into the pool so delicately, his left side had shivered.

The week became routine, as everything ultimately did. The only thing he liked about Florida was the palatial bathroom in their condo, all done up in pink and grey tiles with a shower stall the size of a walk-in closet. With the help of his walker, he was able to spin a little in front of the floodlit mirror.

He hated the mornings on the beach, sand wedged between his fingers and toes. Grey would deposit him on a plastic chaise longue, which would stick to the hairs on his body and make him itch. The three of them kept him under a canopy of shade while they frolicked in the surf. Nessa was throwing herself into the physicality of it all and seemed to have found a new best friend in Christie, who looked wan and ragged in her blue bikini. Despite being twenty years older, Nessa, in a black one-piece with ruffles around the crotch, looked far more substantial, flesh instead of paper.

Grey had a gut the size of a football, but no one on the beach seemed to mind. The back of his baggy swimsuit showed a bit of ass crack, but again, no one even gave it a second look. No one was judged in Florida. Maybe it was the glare, maybe the drunkenness of imbibing so much salt water and adrenaline. After the three of them had played themselves out, Grey would come and fetch Charlie, carry him into waist-high water, and let him paddle with his good hand. Charlie knew that he looked like an idiot, but never caught anyone actually glancing in his direction.

Midweek, he began to feel normal. As if he'd long ago forgotten what it felt like to be more than half a man and had learned not to feel shame or sadness about it. Some people carted huge secrets with them everywhere they went, from terminal illnesses to the kind of guilt that left them feeling shucked. Charlie was who Charlie was. He wanted to whisper this into Nessa's ear, to thank her for sharing his despair and helping break it down into its lesser components.

Their last evening, they drove to a place called The Kapok Tree that served seafood so fresh it was like the waves themselves were delivering dinner to their table. Christie had a heaping stack of mussels swimming in butter, while Grey had the swordfish, a daunting plateful. Nessa settled for hot-pink crab cakes the size of catcher's mitts. Charlie chose the lobster ravioli in cream sauce. Because it was an ordeal to eat—the bad side of his mouth spilling what he managed to stuff into the good side like a wonky assembly line—he still had loads of food left by the time he was totally exhausted. Nessa arranged for it to be put in a Styrofoam container. She sat it up on the dashboard while strapping Charlie into the passenger seat. Then Grey gunned the engine, pitching forward clumsily, and sent the lobster ravioli flying straight onto Charlie. It hit him mid-chest, and the lid popped open, the food drenching his lap.

They gave Charlie a shower back in the condo, Grey supporting him while Nessa scrubbed his nooks and crannies. He wished he could die right there in the huge pink and grey shower. Shame could kill, he knew it. Later, in bed, Nessa tried to talk to him, to make him laugh a little, calling him her Lobster Man. But Charlie wouldn't budge from his misery. He decided to find the right opportunity to die.

On their way to the airport, they had to stop at a car wash that offered both exterior and interior washes. The car reeked. It was a smell that flew back to Toronto with them and managed to survive the dry, cold air, following them all the way home. It was a smell that Charlie would never forget. It even outranked the bleach and urine stench of nursing homes.

They were well on their way to Quebec City for their honeymoon when Charlie couldn't bear himself a moment longer. "I've been a twerp," he said as they searched for a spot to have lunch in Trois-Rivières. "Why didn't you just kick me in the balls and be done with it?"

"That was yesterday. Stop living in the past," Nessa bossed. "We've got much more important things to think about."

They rarely agreed on anything when it came to little things like restaurants, paint colours, or TV shows. But this was part of the thrill. It felt great to fight for what you wanted.

"Your choice," Nessa said. "My wedding gift to you."

"Damn," Charlie muttered. They ended up driving around the town four, five times before he chose a dolled-up diner where he had French onion soup and Nessa ordered chicken salad.

That night, tucked in their Quebec City hotel room, Nessa got very sick, most likely the chicken. Charlie did his best, holding her hair back while she heaved. She sometimes tried to push him away, though there were moments when she asked him to just hold her. He hummed John Denver songs, "Sunshine," "Take Me Home Country Roads," and "Annie's Song," until she'd had enough.

"You're an incredible husband," she whispered. "A weird incredible husband." She paused for a moment as if she might start to gag again. "Aren't you glad that I made you vow 'in sickness and in health'?"

"Didn't we take that out?"

"I sneaked it back in again."

"I had my fingers crossed," Charlie said, smiling.

Who fell asleep first would remain a point of contention for the rest of the honeymoon, but Charlie was definitely the first one to wake up and see the Quebec City sunlight splattered around the room. It was old sunshine with a French sparkle to it. He just knew that Nessa would love it too. But he let her sleep until midafternoon. He was secretly glad she was ill. How else could he have become an incredible husband so quickly?

Charlie swore to himself after the trip to Florida that he wasn't ever going to smile again. He was dedicating the rest of his life to being miserable. There wasn't a specific plan yet, but he fully intended to die as soon as possible. But then one day he watched Nessa singing along with Leonard Cohen's *Tower of Song* as she made one of her famous meal-in-one salads, and he glimpsed the pain it would cause her. What had she ever done but loved him, even when it meant looking the other way?

He noticed that she was keeping closer tabs on him. Even Grey seemed worried when he came to stroke-sit. One day, Christie tagged along. When

Grey was in the bathroom, she leaned in really close and asked him whether he was going to kill himself anytime soon. He thought for a second what he might say that wouldn't be either a threat or a cop-out, but ended up giggling the instant he opened his mouth.

It felt good to have people worried about him. A half a man didn't automatically mean that just the bad half remained; maybe he was all good, maybe the best of him was carrying on.

When Nessa was in the bathtub one morning, he decided to surprise her by making her tea and toast. He climbed out of the wheelchair and attached himself to his walker. If he leaned his dead side against the walker, he found that he was able to reach with his good hand. He squashed the bread badly getting it into the toaster, but he did it. Unfortunately, he wasn't so lucky with the kettle. His wrist brushed against the element and the sleeve of his shirt started to smoke. He managed to pull his arm away, but had nothing to snuff out the sparks. Finally, he tipped over the kettle, extinguishing the fire, but almost scalding his good leg. He then tried to back away from the stove and slipped in the puddle of hot water, going down with a series of thuds.

Nessa appeared in a bright yellow bath towel and looked stricken when she saw Charlie sprawled in the middle of the kitchen floor. She saw the overturned kettle and the red-hot element and must have thought that he was trying to set himself on fire.

"My God, Charlie," she gasped. Her cheeks were so pale, they looked like mushrooms.

Since his computer was in the living room, he couldn't explain it to her. He lifted his left hand and pointed desperately at the toaster.

"Were you that hungry?" she asked. "Couldn't you have waited until I was out of the bath?"

"No, no," Charlie tried to scream. He pointed at her, thrusting his finger.

"Did I do something?" she asked. "Is it my fault?"

He lifted himself up on his left side, dragging his legs behind him.

"Oh, dear God," Nessa said, kneeling down and grabbing him by the feet, bringing him to a stop.

They tousled a little. The dead weight of his paralyzed side was too much for Nessa. He made some distance. She just stood there, gaping at him like something completely beyond her control.

He made it partway to the couch, his sweater and trousers covered in wisps of dust. A scrap of orange peel was stuck to his chin. The couch was within sight. He had never loved its south-of-France blue and white stripes more. He could see the edge of his computer on the coffee table.

"Please," Nessa said from close behind him. "Calm down."

Another set of laborious squirms and he was there, but without the energy to hoist himself up on the couch. Somehow he twisted himself around (the Human Pretzel!) and, almost upending the entire coffee table, tossed his good arm over the edge and rose up to his knees. "Holy shit," he would have said if he could. Nessa was staring at him with a look that suggested persistence had just crossed the line into Crazy Land.

He stretched his fingers a few times, simulating a spider's crawl. He was within seconds of getting his voice back, of making sense again. "Oh key," the voice that was him said. "Break fist." A robot gone rogue.

Nessa's face went overcast, and she threatened to call an ambulance. "You've had another stroke," she said, smoothing the front of the yellow bath towel as if beginning to make herself presentable to strangers.

Charlie blew it again. "Bake fast," he said.

Nessa's stare narrowed. "Breakfast?"

"Breakfast," he confirmed in his tin voice, his fake self, the half a man who remained. "I was making you breakfast."

She stared hard at him as if he'd said something miraculous.

"I'm a ninny," he apologized. "Hard to surprise and ask for help at same time."

Colour swelled back into her face, floodgates open. "You weren't trying to kill yourself?" she asked.

"With toast?" he said, which made Nessa giggle. He let his jaw drop, hoping she might see the gesture as a stroke-blasted version of a laugh.

Then she was crying, down on her knees, bundling Charlie into a hug. So this was sickness, he thought. This was what a vow looked like after thirty years of knowing it was there but thinking it might never have to be used. It was like a backup generator in case the power went out.

"We'd better clean you up," Nessa said, returning to her love for tidiness and order. "You look like a lint brush."

Not for long, Charlie thought. Soon he'd be spiffy again. Nessa always did what she said.

ACKNOWLEDGEMENTS

Many thanks to the literary magazines where some of these stories first appeared. "Grey Metal Desk" was first published in *Event*. "The World Cup" in *The Fiddlehead*. "Tread" and "Personal Values" in *The Antigonish Review*. "Untitled" in *Prism International*. "The Hired Hand" in *Existere*. "Half a Man" in *The Dalhousie Review*.

None of these stories are one-man shows.

A galaxy of gratefulness to the brilliant and beautiful Karen Dempster, who often does the heavy lifting in these stories. She sees through my tendency to entertain and reminds me constantly that to deepen is to come closer to the truth.

Three cheers for my editor, Alayna Munce. Her combination of encouragement and devotion to excellence gave each of these journeys a much needed boost.

I'm also thankful to Jim Nason, emperor of Tightrope Books, for the example he sets by being such an artist himself, and to his staff, Deanna Janovski, Heather Wood, and David Jang, who made every step along the way a pleasure.

Much appreciation to Brian Vanderlip, who spent part of his vacation two summers ago on quality control; his cautions were always on the mark, his praise something to treasure.

Hugs to Sharon Wilston, Carol Gall, and Hyacinthe Miller for taking on the responsibility of being first readers of the very first story. This collection might have come to a grinding halt were it not for their challenges.

And to Mike Madill, who has taught me a thing or two these last few years about friendship and courage.

Finally, kudos to my writing groups and friends for often lending me bits and pieces of their characters, from warts to wings. Your lives inspire me on a daily basis.

ABOUT THE AUTHOR

Barry Dempster, twice nominated for the Governor-General's Award, is the author of sixteen poetry collections, two novels, and two previous books of stories. His poetry collection *The Burning Alphabet* won the Chalmers Award for Poetry in 2005. In 2014, he was nominated for the Trillium Award for his novel *The Outside World*.